A joke

If I'd Killed Him When I Met Him...

Sharyn McCrumb

If I'd Killed Him When I Met Him...

WHEELER
PUBLISHING, INC.
ROCKLAND, MA

★ AN AMERICAN COMPANY ★

Published in Large Print by arrangement with Ballantine Books, a division
of Random House, Inc., in the United States and Canada

Wheeler Large Print Book Series.

Set in 16 pt Plantin.

Library of Congress Cataloging-in-Publication Data

McCrumb, Sharyn, 1948–
    If I'd killed him when I met him / Sharyn McCrumb.
        p. (large print) cm.(Wheeler large print book series)
    ISBN 1-56895-472-7 (softcover)
    1. Large type books. 2. MacPherson, Elizabeth (Fictitious character)—
Fiction. 3. Forensic anthropology—Virginia—fiction. 4. Virginia—Fiction.
I. Title. II. Series
[PS3563.C3527I36]
813'.54—dc21
                                                            97-24406
                                                                CIP

To
Deborah Adams,

with thanks for the title, which she
overheard from a battered woman:
"If I'd killed him when I met him,
I'd be out of prison now."

Pray do not, therefore, be inducted to suppose that I ever write merely to amuse, or without an object.

—Charles Dickens

If I'd Killed Him
When I Met Him...

When the Himalayan peasant meets the
  he-bear in his pride,
He shouts to scare the monster, who will
  often turn aside.
But the she-bear thus accosted rends the
  peasant tooth and nail
For the female of the species is more deadly
  than the male.
                              —RUDYARD KIPLING

PROLOGUE

On the first morning of her husband's lingering death, Lucy Todhunter came down to breakfast alone. She explained to the houseguests—Mr. Norville from the railroad and her North Carolina cousins, the Compsons—that her husband was not feeling well, and that she would take some nourishment up to him on a tray.

"He's such an old bear when he's sick," she said, with a little laugh, as she sat down to a bowl of porridge and cream. "I can't think how he made it through the inconvenience of the war." This unfortunate reference to Philip Todhunter's military infamy (i.e., serving in the Union Army during the Late Unpleasantness) brought furrowed frowns to the faces of the Compson cousins. Lucy blushed and said, "I do beg y'all's pardon. My mind is on my husband, not my manners."

Still, her appetite and the gaiety of her table

1

talk suggested that she was not unduly concerned about Philip Todhunter's illness. Lucy's long hair was artfully arranged into a chignon, with not a single hairpin showing, and her cheeks were smooth with rice powder.

She wore a morning dress of faded green silk, carefully darned here and there on the long skirt, but still serviceable. Lucy's attire favorably impressed Cousin Mary Hadley Compson of Maysville, North Carolina, who was later to say grudgingly: "Even though Lucy married a carpetbagging Yankee so soon after the war, she didn't put on airs with their new money." Of course, the imported Spanish mahogany dining-room table with seven extra leaves and a dozen matching chairs upholstered in crimson Moroccan leather might be considered showy. The drawing room, shining with a green satin suite and matching portieres, boasted a semigrand pianoforte in walnut by Collard & Collard of England that had cost a pretty penny. But that was keeping up appearances. A prominent man of business needed such a showpiece. There would be no illusions in local society about whose pride was on display. *Mr.* Todhunter was householder, and any *Mrs.* Todhunter he cared to install, merely housekeeper.

Lucy Todhunter was generally conceded to be a sensible woman, even by those who had reason to dislike her. Her Todhunter in-laws disliked her very much, indeed. When Philip, formerly a major in the Union cavalry, returned to Virginia two years after the war to start a textile business with cheap land and even cheaper labor, his relatives approved, boasting of Philip's reputation as a shrewd and unsentimental man of business. When ten months later, Major Todhunter married a honey-haired Southern beauty less than half his age, and proceeded to furnish a new home near Danville with furniture imported from England, they declared that Philip had gone native, and that the torrid Southern weather had unhinged his judgment.

Lucy went on smiling, and adding cordial postscripts to his letters back to Maine, inviting her *dear* new kinfolk to come and visit them. (If nothing else, the excursion would have set them straight about the climate of piedmont Virginia, but the offer was not accepted.)

Lucy had been orphaned by the war, but she came of good family and could claim even a North Carolina governor a few branches down in the family tree. An only child, she had inherited the graceful house of her childhood and the many acres that surrounded it, but very little money. At fifteen the orphaned Lucy had gone to live with her godparents in Danville, and with vague affection for the pretty but reticent child, they had given her a home and completed her genteel upbringing. At seventeen she knew how to manage a house, how to play the pianoforte to accompany her own singing, and how to comport herself gracefully in good society, even if her acquaintance with formal education had been slight by Todhunter family standards.

She had met Philip through mutual friends on one of his visits to Danville. A few months later, he chose that river city in which to establish his new business, perhaps influenced by the presence of the young and lovely Miss Lucy Avery. By the simple expedient of joining the correct church and making substantial contributions to it, Todhunter had persuaded the local gentry to overlook his unfortunate past connection with the Union Army. Ensconced among the "right" people, he had pursued his acquaintance with young Lucy Avery at formal dinners and garden walks.

Her godparents had been taken aback when eighteen-year-old Lucy announced her engagement to the stern and charmless Major Todhunter, but they told themselves (and those who tactfully inquired) that the war was, after all, over, and that one had to give poor orphaned Lucy credit for realizing that *someone* would have to support her. They reasoned that being forced to choose between congeniality and prosperity, Lucy had taken the wiser course. Whether or not this prudence brought her happiness in her eighteen months of marriage was a source of considerable speculation in Danville society, but no one really knew.

Lucy had been taken ill a few months after the wedding, and so ill again six months later that she had been sent to the Montgomery White Sulphur Springs resort in the shadow of the mountains just east of Christiansburg, Virginia. Fears that the young bride had come down with consumption were curtailed in hushed whispers by her godmother: Lucy had lost a baby, each time in the second month of pregnancy. She emerged from each illness more frail and slender than ever, but she kept her beauty, and her spirit was not broken. There were also rumors that Philip

Todhunter was a harsh and exacting husband, but no word of complaint was ever
heard from his wife. Lucy Avery had never been
given to confiding in her acquaintances.

"Too bad that Philip is feeling seedy,"
Richard Norville remarked, helping himself
to eggs and fried kidneys. "I hope it wasn't the
lateness of the hour that indisposed him. We
were quite a time with our brandy before the
fire, refighting the war, you know." He smiled
at his fellow guests, whose composed expres-
sions did not reveal what they thought of
boastful drunkards who gloated over their
victories. The Compsons glanced at each
other, and went back to their porridge without a word. The more they saw and heard of
Lucy's husband and his friend, the shorter their
intended stay became.

"But how are *you*, Lucy dear?" asked Mary
Compson. It seemed to her that after two
miscarriages in a year, Lucy ought to be the
one to take to her bed.

"Oh, I can't complain," said Lucy with a wan
smile.

Norville, who had failed to interpret this
coded feminine message, said, "Haven't caught
the grippe from your husband, I hope."

"Philip's digestion has been plaguing him
lately, that's all," said Lucy with her sweeest
smile. "It's all that rich food he *will* have
Cook prepare. He's paying for it now, though.
I haven't been able to get him to eat a thing
since Sunday. I don't suppose that it helped
him any to indulge in brandy at all hours
with you, Mr. Norville." Lucy smiled to take
the sting out of her reproach. "I shall take up

5

a tray to poor Philip directly. A bit of beef tea and one of Cook's wonderful beignets may tempt him to eat. Have you all tried them? They're simply lovely." She picked up one of the square pastries and bit into it, dislodging a small puff of powdered sugar, which floated downward and settled on her bodice. Lucy blushed. "Well, laws, they are a bit untidy, but so delicious. Philip generally has one for his breakfast, you know. He acquired the taste when he was stationed with the army in New Orleans. Perhaps I can persuade him to try one now."

Her guests each took a pastry from the silver plate. Lucy picked up the pitcher of unsweetened grape juice and poured each guest another glassful. Then she drank hers down and set the plate of beignets on a large silver serving tray beside the bowl of beef tea, saying, "I shan't be a moment, my dears. Do go right on eating."

Richard Norville was on his feet in an instant. "Let you carry that heavy thing, ma'am?" He beamed at his shapely young hostess. "Not while I know it." So saying, he snatched up the footed silver tray and nodded for her to show him the way, which she did, with much simpering about his gallantry.

They went up the stairs, stopping outside the closed door of Philip Todhunter's bedroom. Lucy tapped softly and called out that dear, kind Mr. Norville had graciously carried up Philip's breakfast tray, and that he proposed to pay his respects to his ailing friend.

"Let him come in then," growled a voice from the other side of the door. "I'm not contagious."

As cheerfully as ever, Lucy eased open the door, bustled over to her husband's bedside, and bestowed a wifely peck on the cheek of the invalid, who scowled at her. "Is that my juice?"

"Yes, dear," she replied. "But do try to eat something as well, won't you?"

"Stop clucking over me," said Philip Todhunter, waving away the beef tea. "You know I can't touch that muck, Lucy." He reached for a sugared beignet from the pile on the plate. He was a dark-eyed man, lean of feature, with a sallow, waxy complexion beneath a graying beard. He had never been handsome, but prosperity had given him a certain air of distinction, now lacking in the querulous invalid before them.

Richard Norville began to regret his gallant gesture. "See here, Todhunter," he said in the gruff voice that signifies embarrassment, "I can go if you're not up to receiving visitors, but hadn't we better have the doctor round to look at you?"

"I can manage without one, thank you," said Todhunter, holding up his pastry in a mock salute. "I haven't eaten in a day and a half. Starve a fever, they say. Better than the quack remedies you get from the medicos."

"Is it the grippe, do you think, Todhunter? Or worse?" Norville edged away from the bed.

"I feel like the little Spartan boy who put the fox in his tunic," said Todhunter. "Even now it gnaws through my vitals seeking egress. And there is a numbness in my limbs, worsened by this cursed cold."

Norville raised his eyebrows. The weather

7

was quite mild, in fact, and there was a coal fire in the grate; but he did not care to argue with a man who was suffering. "Well, I hope you throw it off soon," he said.

Dutifully, Lucy sat down in the chair beside the invalid's bed and patted his hand. "Do let me know if you would care for anything else," she murmured. "I worry so." Absently, she broke off a bit of her husband's pastry and nibbled on it.

Her husband finished the rest of it and sank back against the pillows with a sigh. "I feel like Death's orderly," he remarked to Norville, wiping his sugared mouth against the back of his hand. "But perhaps a bit of nourishment will do me. It always does, doesn't it, Lucy dear?"

She nodded, looking distressed. "Philip—"

"That will do, Lucy. Norville and I have business to discuss." He leered up at her. "Isn't she lovely, Norville?"

"The flower of Virginia womanhood," said the railroad executive with borrowed gallantry. He had heard the phrase used by a Southerner at a party once, and he'd committed it to memory. Apparently, these people expected you to say things like that.

Lucy smiled uncertainly. "Is there anything else I can get for you, Philip?"

"No," he said without looking up. "Norville, did you bring the papers?"

"You will drink your beef tea, won't you, dear? It will give you strength."

"Damn the beef tea!" shouted Todhunter, slamming his fist against the tray and spilling the contents of the bowl. Tray, bowl, and pastries tumbled to the carpet. "Can't you see you're not wanted... ?" His words trailed off into a howl of pain as he doubled over in the bed, clutching his abdomen.

Norville watched his friend in silence for a moment, and then turned to the pale young wife. She had poured herself some grape juice in Philip Todhunter's crystal tumbler, and she was sipping it in an abstracted way, her hands trembling as she lifted it to drink. "Mrs. Todhunter," said Norville, "whatever your husband may say to the contrary, his illness is grave. Either you summon a physician, or I will."

MacPherson & Hill
Attorneys-at-Law

Danville, Virginia

(Pardon the stolen stationery. Elizabeth.)

Dearest Cameron:

I'm back in Virginia, instead of in Scotland, because the remnants of my family still seem to need the presence of a sane person, and since we aren't related to such a being, I am having to impersonate one. It's probably good therapy for me anyhow. There's a very earnest psychiatrist named Freya (no wonder she went to med school: intellectual parents) who insists that no matter what my feelings are, I do not need solitude right now. She uses words like *brooding* and *self-pity* and *clinical depression*. I have pills to take, but they might as well be Reese's Pieces,

9

because they certainly aren't cheering me up any. But I take them anyhow, in case they happen to be working, which means I'd be even worse without them. At least I have things to keep me occupied here.

Besides, there's a limit to the amount of time one can stand on the shore at Cramond, staring out at the dark water of the firth.

Freya says it's all right for me to write to you. Therapeutic, she called it, in that smug little way of hers. It must be wonderful to be a shrink. I can't think why I became a forensic anthropologist. Anytime you disagree with Freya, she just smirks and says that you are "in denial," and therefore she gets to be right *all the time*. It's maddening—which drums up more business for her, I suppose. Why do the rural good old boys bother to stage cockfights when they could put two psychiatrists in a pit and watch a real bloodbath?

I'm going to try to stick to what's going on here, instead of writing analytical and/or maudlin letters about Us. I don't need to belabor points about missing you, or being paralyzed with worry, because if everything turns out all right, these letters will look ridiculous, and if it doesn't, I couldn't bear to have a record of my sorrow. So I will make this a running journal of family life as I observe it.

The first observation, of course, is that there's damned little family life to observe. I feel more like a war correspondent. Mother and Daddy are still in the process of divorcing, despite the best efforts of Bill and me to reconcile them. Now they aren't even speaking to each other! We are obviously no great shakes as mediators, my brother Bill and I. If the UN sent us to the Middle East as peace-keepers, we could probably pull off Armageddon in a matter of days.

Bill is still eking out an existence in his Danville law practice with his partner A. P. Hill (who resembles her namesake, the Confederate general, except that she's much more stern and commanding). I don't know that I like her all that much, but I admire her for being such a force to be reckoned with. If *I* were five-foot-three-inches and blonde, I'd have gone for perky and cute, but A.P. somehow manages to be terrifyingly competent.

Since I haven't had the peace of mind to go out looking for a job in my field, Bill and A.P. have sort of hired me (although I have more money than both of them put together) to be an "investigator" for their law firm, at an hourly wage that is laughable, especially considering that I have a Ph.D. But they mean to be kind, I know. They want to keep me busy. But so far there hasn't been any call for an investigator's talents (even assuming I had any). All their clients have either taken the plea bargain or agreed to work through their divorces without resorting to storm-trooper tactics.

That word again. Divorce.

At least you and I were spared that.

Sometimes I think that there is a great war going on between men and women. There is so much dislike and distrust in the air. Prenuptial agreements; kamikaze divorces; law-suits over emotional matters: how very unro-mantic. The monasteries should be packing them in. Not that I care, personally, because at present I am a noncombatant. I am, as I said before, a war correspondent, writing sad communiqués to someone behind enemy lines.

I have no quarrel with you, dear Cameron. Except that you were selfish enough and stupid enough to go sailing away into the wild North Sea on that stupid, antiquated *little* boat. And so, goodbye for now, my dear. I must close.

If I knew where you were, I'd mail this.

Love,
Elizabeth

How do you like your snow white pillows,
And how do you like your sheets?
And how do you like the fair young maid
Who lies in your arms asleep?
                    —*"LITTLE MARGARET"*
          (Traditional folk ballad)

CHAPTER 1

The fact that Eleanor Royden was putting on lipstick at 4:45 was not unusual; the fact that it was 4:45 in the *morning*, however, made it an unprecedented departure from her usual routine. Eleanor was not known as an early riser, although, since the divorce, she'd had to get a clerical job, which meant that she had to show up at the real-estate office at 8:30 looking presentable. But she didn't get up at 4:45 to do it. On a good day, she managed to rise (if not shine) at 7:45. But today was Sunday— no real-estate office to go to, and usually Eleanor slept in, letting the drapes stay drawn and the Sunday paper turn brown in the delivery tube until midafternoon. She used to read the society column, but none of those people spoke to her anymore anyway, since Jeb had kept the house and the country-club membership; so she no longer bothered to keep up with them.

She blotted the Berry Stain lipstick with a square of toilet paper and looked at herself in the medicine-cabinet mirror. Not bad for

13

fifty-one, she thought. She had long ago lightened her mousy-brown hair to blonde, and now that it was surely gray under all that L'Oréal, the hair coloring gave her carefully bobbed hair the shimmer of moonlight. Cucumber slices placed under her eyes for fifteen minutes each night had gone a long way toward reducing the baggy look of half-a-century-old skin, but a face-lift would have been easier and more effective. In the right light she might pass for thirty-nine, she thought, as long as she remembered to keep her eyes wide open, arching her eyebrows for a face-lift via muscle control.

She let her features relax into a series of crow's-feet and laugh lines, and the dozen years came seeping back, etching a great weariness on her face. She might look better if she hadn't been up all night. But what did it matter if you could look thirty-nine, when *she*—the Bitch—was *twenty-nine*, not by artifice, but by the simple expedient of having been born during the presidency of Lyndon Johnson?

It wasn't fair. Jeb certainly didn't look thirty-nine. He had more white hair than a skunk—not the only thing the two creatures had in common. Eleanor smiled, etching wrinkles back into her face, which made her solemn again. Jeb was fifty-one. He did not jog. He did not starve himself. He did not take any steps to keep from getting run over by Time's Winged Chariot. And that simpering teenage bride of his didn't mind in the least. It was okay if *men* got old. She would see about that.

It wasn't fair for him to have it all. He got to grow old gracefully, and still be loved, despite his age. He got to make a lot of money, and keep it all, even though she had given up a perfectly good bookkeeping job to marry him all those years ago. Even though she had cleaned his house to his fanatical standard of cleanliness; cooked delicious, well-balanced meals from his short list of acceptable foods; and played the thankless role of stage manager to his star turn in their upwardly mobile, career-oriented social life. He got all the applause: she got to do the housework *backstage*.

And now the play had closed. And good old Jeb was starring in a new production: same old show, but this time with a young and pretty leading lady to share the spotlight.

Eleanor never said *that woman's* name aloud; she hardly ever thought it. Someday she might try to summon up the first name to find it had escaped her completely. Their last names were the same. That was the problem. Two Mrs. Roydens: the hag of marriage past, and the whore of marriage present.

Eleanor called her replacement the Bitch or the Bimbo. Sometimes in public Eleanor had called her La Chaplin, which her women friends understood to be a code term, referring to the silent film star's greatest role: the Little Tramp.

At luncheons with her old friends, in the early days of the divorce proceedings, they had made a game of thinking up things to call the creature. To keep on saying the Whore would have been monotonous, and above all, one must not be tedious. Of course one had to put on a brave face, and affect amusement at Jeb's stu-

15

pid weakness and lust. ("Of course he had a pet name for his penis, dear. He wouldn't want to be ordered about by a *stranger*.") Eleanor christened the future Mrs. Royden *the Gap*—not a reference to her fashion sense; *the One-Trick Pony*—not a musical reference; and, because the creature had been a landscape architect, *the Lay of the Land*.

Eleanor was the hit of the luncheon crowd with her wicked wedding parodies of Jeb's second nuptials. "The organist ought to play 'Send in the Clowns,'" Eleanor suggested. Her tablemates shrieked delightedly and countered with suggestions of their own: "Heat Wave," "Almost Like Being in Love," and "Call Me Irresponsible."

She could get her wedding attire from Frederick's of Hollywood, one of them suggested. "We could give him a certificate for prostate surgery!" whooped another. They spilled their cappuccino laughing at each other's suggestions for additions to the traditional wedding vows. Eleanor Royden had kept everyone entertained for months. But underneath all the hilarity, Eleanor wasn't laughing: she was using the only weapon she possessed to keep from going mad while she lost everything. And every hilarious luncheon had ended in an ominous silence, as the foursome contemplated the fact that no matter how much they ridiculed the problem, it wasn't going away. And one of them might be next.

Now Eleanor no longer bothered to pretend to be bravely amused, because nobody cared. The idle, well-to-do friends in Jeb Royden's set had drifted away to new amusements (or

16

to troubles of their own). At any rate, they stopped including Eleanor in their get-togethers. For a while she didn't notice, because her new job was time-consuming, and in the evenings she would come home too tired to cook, much less to socialize.

But lately Eleanor had been taking stock of what she had left to sustain her as she grew old, and the answer was: not much. The sprawling house in Chambord Oaks had been remodeled by that creature. Eleanor wished she had taken pictures of the rooms, so tastefully decorated in stripped pine woodwork and country French furnishings. She had spent many hours poring over fabric books and paging through North Carolina furniture catalogues to achieve just the right look, and then it had all been sold, and replaced with (in Eleanor's imaginings) tubular steel chairs and erotic neon sculptures. Eleanor's new apartment was furnished in discounted floor samples from the local furniture store and luxuriant green plants, trailing vines onto the carpet. She had sold the Mercedes and bought herself a sensible little Dodge, more in keeping with her new, muted lifestyle. And she now had paperback novels instead of friends, because you didn't have to entertain fictional characters or buy them dinners.

Eleanor Royden was quite alone, with her aching feet and her Budget Gourmet evenings, while Jeb's life sailed on like the ship of state. And that was not fair. She had sat up all night pondering the inequities in life—the fact that men got more than one chance to live happily ever after—and she decided that it just wasn't right, this cosmic double standard.

17

At 4:58 A.M., her makeup neatly applied and her old London Fog belted across a gray wool dinner dress, Eleanor selected a sturdy but unmatching red Capezio handbag, large enough to hold her car keys, a flashlight, two lace handkerchiefs, and a Taurus PT92AFF fifteen-shot 9mm semiautomatic. People who wanted to start a new life ought to have to completely vacate their present one first—and hope that reincarnation was an option. Besides, it was about time that people started taking that phrase *until death do us part* more seriously.

Bill MacPherson was having morning coffee with his law partner A. P. Hill. Actually, neither of them drank coffee—she started the day with a pot of unsweetened Earl Grey tea and he drank hot chocolate made by squirting chocolate syrup into a pint of milk and heating it in the office microwave—but they called their morning ritual *coffee* because they felt that it sounded sophisticated. When you practice law in a sparsely furnished office the size of a broom closet in a shabby building with wanted-poster tenants, you need all the elegance you can muster. When Bill complained that the office lacked class, A. P. Hill had offered to put a photograph of her cousin Stinky, Virginia's attorney general, on the wall of the waiting room, but when the aforementioned eminence was asked to inscribe said photograph, Stinky declined and bought the novice law partners a microwave as an office-warming present, on the condition that they *not* put his picture anywhere on the premises.

If it had been in Bill MacPherson's nature to be suspicious of anyone, he might have surmised that A. P. Hill had planned the photo gambit to turn out exactly that way.

"So is there any new business?" asked Bill, stirring his hot chocolate with a yellow pencil. Bill was not good at what he called the "aluminum-siding side of a law practice"—that is, drumming up business.

"Someone named Morgan is coming to see us at ten," said A.P. "Edith has written *re: marriage* beside the name in the appointment book. Did she mention it to you?"

Bill shook his head. "Not a word. A prenuptial agreement, do you suppose?"

"Maybe. Or an annulment. Whatever it is, it's all yours, Bill. I don't do family law."

"So you keep telling me. Fortunately for the practice, I do. In fact, I could specialize in the family law of my own family and stay busy indefinitely."

"Or you could have commitment papers drawn up in form-letter style. Fill in the blanks." A. P. Hill smiled sweetly. She had met most of Bill's family.

Bill helped himself to the last stale doughnut. "Speaking of family, have we got anything for my sister to investigate yet?"

"She's a forensic anthropologist. You think the coroner's office will ask us for second opinions?"

"She can do regular investigative work, too," said Bill. "She's very capable—just a little depressed right now."

"I know," said A. P. Hill. "It's completely

19

understandable. I just hope that investigating seamy divorces and whatnot for you doesn't make her more depressed."

"Oh, I think other people's troubles are easier to bear, don't you?"

"Sure. That's why I'm a lawyer." She was pouring herself a second cup of tea when the phone rang.

"Edith still isn't here," said Bill. "I'd better get it. You always swear in Latin and hang up when they mistake you for a secretary."

He lunged across the desk and snatched up the phone. "MacPherson and Hill."

Bill's partner made a face at him. She had wanted to call the firm "Hill and MacPherson," and he had countered facetiously with Hill and Bill, a suggestion later withdrawn when Edith pointed out that they might be mistaken for a more exalted legal team from Arkansas. They settled on MacPherson and Hill when Bill won the coin toss.

He listened for a moment. "Yes, there is a woman attorney named Amy in the firm. Are we what? Say the last name again, please." Then a pause while he listened again. Finally he said, "No, I think we can promise that we are not friends of that gentleman. What? Well, whatever. I mean, we didn't know him. Would you like to speak to A. P. Hill?"

Bill handed over the phone and took his mug to the tiny office refrigerator to begin a second cup of cocoa. When he returned, the telephone was back on the hook, and A. P. Hill was staring into space. "Aside from the fact that she called you Amy, is anything wrong?"

She nodded. "I think so. That was Eleanor

20

Royden, calling from jail in Roanoke. She's just given herself up for the murder of her ex-husband and his new wife."

"Great!" said Bill. "Well, not for the happy couple, of course-but you love murder cases; so it looks like your lucky day."

"Don't be too sure," said A. P. Hill, reaching for her purse. "Do you know who Eleanor Royden's ex-husband was?"

"I'm going out on a limb here," said Bill. "A Mr. Royden, perhaps?"

"No. *The* Mr. Royden. Jeb. The famous trial lawyer in Roanoke. He was known for showmanship and for getting multimillion-dollar damage awards for his clients, and there was talk of him running for the Senate."

"Roanoke is ankle-deep in lawyers. Why did she call you?"

"Her explanation wasn't particularly flattering. She said she'd heard of my suit against the National Park Service on behalf of female reenactors, and said she liked my willingness to take on the male establishment. Also she knows Cousin Stinky."

"Oh, the attorney general recommended you?"

"Just the opposite. She says she met him at a party once, and she got the impression from him that we were legal lepers, and that's exactly why she wants us to defend her."

"Why?"

"Because we're outsiders. When she goes on trial for the murders, everybody from the judge to the bailiff will be one of her ex-husband's cronies. She thinks I'm the only one she can trust not to throw the case. I said I'd drive up there today and talk to her. Can you manage here?"

"Family law? Sure. Piece of cake."

"Tell that to the lawyers for the Menendez brothers," said A. P. Hill.

An hour later Bill, in his navy-blue jacket and spotted power tie, was practicing looking professional and reassuring while he waited for Edith to usher in Mrs. Morgan. When she appeared in the doorway looking dumpy and dowdy in a shabby cloth coat, Bill felt a pang of dread. She was fifty-something, with unkempt graying hair and a sorrowful pudding face. Her brown eyes were already brimming with tears. *Not another discarded wife,* Bill thought with alarm. *It's like looking through the chain links in the back of the dogcatcher's truck.* He hoped that the bright young women in his generation wouldn't end up like that—fading and sad, while their husbands went on to a second youth. He tried to picture a fiftyish A. P. Hill in such straits, but his imagination was not equal to the task. In twenty-five years A. P. Hill would probably be a tiny, testy federal judge with a stainless-steel heart. His new client sniffled ominously. Bill shoved the box of tissues to the edge of the desk and asked her to sit down.

"My name is Donna Jean Morgan," said the woman, dabbing at her eyes with a tissue. "My sister said I had to come talk to you, but I want to tell you right up front that I don't believe in divorce."

Bill sighed. "I don't believe in being overdrawn at the bank, Mrs. Morgan, but it happens to me occasionally all the same."

"It's against my religion," she said.

"Being overdr—"

"Divorce."

"Why don't you tell me about it?"

She opened her plastic handbag and drew out a family photo. Set against the blue haze of a shopping-mall 14.99 portrait special (two 8x10s; four 5x7s; twenty wallet size), Bill saw a solemn family group. There was Donna Jean Morgan, looking like a nervous mud hen in an unflattering brown dress, with tendrils of graying hair escaping from a clumsily pinned bun. Beside her sat a large florid man of about fifty, tanned and beefy, in a light blue jacket and an open-necked shirt. He smiled at the camera with boxy horse teeth and crinkled eyes, with a smugness that income and education could not account for. Bill wondered about the source of that pride. Was the man an aging athlete, still vain about his days as a high-school halfback, or was he a country singer on the local beer-joint circuit?

"Nice-looking fellow," said Bill, thinking that the weather-beaten face looked familiar somehow. Then he got it: this man could have been the real-life model for Fred Flintstone.

"Yes, he's a handsome one," said Donna Jean Morgan, dabbing her eyes again. "Always has been, and it's a cross I've had to bear these twenty-seven years. He's my husband, Chevry."

Bill looked at the third face in the portrait. Standing behind the middle-aged couple stood a grinning teenage girl with a heart-

23

shaped face and a tangle of shoulder-length brown curls. She was wearing a navy-blue dress with a square white sailor collar and a red tie. Bill wondered where she got her looks. "What a nice smile," he said. "Your daughter is very pretty," he said with more sincerity. "You must be very proud of her."

"I hate the bitch," said Donna Jean. "That there is Chevry's second wife."

Bill blinked at the sudden vehemence from his client. "Mrs. Morgan, you're divorced? I thought you said—"

"I said I didn't believe in divorce on account of our religion. Neither does Chevry. We're still married. But a month ago, he ups and brings home this other wife. And now he's trying to give her my car. Can he do that?"

A. P. Hill had a purse full of tissues, but she wasn't going to need them. Before she left to interview her prospective client, she had emptied the box in her office, thinking that any middle-aged woman who had just shot her former husband was sure to be a basket case. A.P. pictured herself trying to elicit the facts of the case syllable by syllable, between shrieks and bouts of wild sobbing.

Eleanor Royden was not like that at all.

When A. P. Hill entered the interview room, Eleanor Royden was reading the Extra section of the *Roanoke Times & World News*. She was chuckling as she peered over the top of the page at the visitor. "I was reading my horoscope," she announced. "It says: 'Show family and friends who you really are. Clean out your life and meet some interesting new people.' Well,

24

I've taken care of that, haven't I?" She looked appraisingly at the young attorney. "*You* look interesting. Actually, you look about sixteen, but you must be a good lawyer. You've certainly annoyed enough of the big boys."

A. P. Hill permitted herself a smile as she sat down. "I call them silverbacks," she said. "In primate studies that's what they call the large male gorillas who try to dominate the rest of the troop."

"How very apt," said Eleanor, nodding approval. "Are gorillas monogamous, do you think?"

"I can't imagine it's a big deal to them." A. P. Hill looked at her client, wondering if the woman was insane or in shock. She appeared to be neither. She was as frank and cheerful as someone chatting during a coffee break.

A. P. Hill's experience with murderers was minuscule, but she had never heard of one wanting to chat about natural history instead of about legal strategies. A. P. Hill decided that the poor woman was in denial. She *looked* all right. Her silvery-blonde hair had seen a beauty parlor recently, and her gray wool dress seemed oddly formal against the fake paneling of the conference room of the county jail. Eleanor Royden resembled someone who had come from a bridge game at the country club, not from a room with a bunk, a lidless toilet, and electronically operated steel bars. A.P. began to toy with the idea of an insanity defense.

"Why don't you tell me what happened, Mrs. Royden," she said.

"It's a long story. But the last chapter was

pretty action-packed." She folded the newspaper carefully and set it down on the table. "Who do you think would play me in the movie? I'm partial to Susan Lucci, but then I haven't given it much thought. Sally Field, perhaps. I've always liked her. She does Southern really well."

Time to play hardball, thought A. P. Hill. Leaning forward, stern-faced, she said, "How about Susan Hayward in *I Want to Live*, Mrs. Royden?"

Eleanor shook her head. "Much too earthy. Oh, I see. Gallows humor. Was your comment intended to remind me of the gravity of the situation? All right. I suppose it was too much to hope that you'd have a sense of humor as well as satisfactory legal credentials."

"Tell-me-about-this-case," said A. P. Hill through clenched teeth.

"Oh, all right. Oh, listen, can you get me some Rancé soap? Do you know they use green *powdered* stuff in here. Can you believe it? I'd rather scrub my face on a Brillo pad!"

"The case, Mrs. Royden."

"Oh, call me Eleanor. *Mrs. Royden* got to be an unpleasant epithet in the last couple of years." She rested her head on her upturned palms and gave A. P. Hill a dazzling smile. "You don't smoke, I suppose? I quit years ago, but I feel that this is a special occasion."

"I don't smoke," said A. P. Hill, momentarily distracted. "I have breath mints."

Eleanor shook her head. "Not the same, Ms.-well, what shall I call you? Amy?"

"Not if you want me to take the case. Just make it A.P. I answer to that." She looked at her watch. "I also charge by the hour. Now, are you going to get down to business, or am I going back to Danville?"

Eleanor Royden made a face at her. "Party pooper," she said. "I've just killed my husband and his unspeakable child bride. Can't you let me enjoy it?"

"Mrs. Royden, did you talk that way to the police when you turned yourself in? Because if you did, it's going to take two magicians and a hypnotist to get you out of here."

The accused nodded approvingly. "That was mildly funny," she said. "If you ever stop taking yourself so seriously, you'll be all right. Now, what did you ask?"

"Did you say anything incriminating to the arresting officers?" A. P. Hill sighed. "Surely you exercised your right to remain silent until you had an attorney present?"

"I think I was pretty subdued then. It was about seven A.M., which helped, because I am *not* a morning person." She paused for breath and eyed the younger woman. "I expect you are."

"Yes. That's about the time I finish jogging. Now I really need to hear your side of the story, Mrs. Royden, because you're about to get charged with murder in a state that has a death penalty. You'd better stop joking and concentrate on the fact that you could lose your *life*."

Eleanor Royden shrugged. "I already have."

CHAPTER 2

Lucy Todhunter paused for one stricken moment, staring at the spilled beef tea that was slowly staining the linen sheets—and at the writhing man in the bed. Then she turned and ran from the room.

Richard Norville grasped his friend by the shoulders. "Todhunter, what is the matter with you? I haven't seen anything like this since the war." He thought of the gut-shot youths he had seen right there in Virginia, and his face grew gray. "We'll have the doctor around to you soon," he said.

Philip Todhunter's only reply was a guttural cry and more thrashing among sweat-soaked sheets.

"What was that?" asked Norville, straining to catch the word. He thought he heard the word *basin*, but when he moved the china bowl closer to the bed, Todhunter only shook his head and howled, clutching at his abdomen with both hands. Trying not to glance at his wretched friend, Norville picked up the towel from atop the oak washstand. "Perhaps you'd like to bathe your forehead," Norville muttered, eyeing the door with longing. "The doctor should be along presently."

This time the gabbled cry was—distinctly— "Don't leave me!"

Norville sat down again, trying not to fidget. Absently, for want of anything else to do, he picked up a copy of *The Lady of the Lake,* leafed through the pages, and began to read aloud: " 'Soldier, rest! thy warfare o'er, Dream of fighting fields no more—' "

For three quarters of an hour Richard Norville read aloud Sir Walter Scott, while the sick man alternately drowsed and screamed. Then the retching began. Twice he filled the basin with the blood-streaked evidence of his distress.

It was nearly noon when Lucy Todhunter returned, ushering in Dr. Richard Humphreys. They entered during one of Philip's somnolent periods, and he lay motionless with his back to them while Norville fidgeted in his eagerness to be relieved of duty.

"How is he?" asked Lucy, giving the invalid a tender glance.

Norville indicated the basin, spilling over onto a now stained carpet—evidence of the recent illness. "I have never known a man so stricken to live," he said. "His suffering is piteous."

The doctor edged past them and bent over the patient. "How long has he been like this?"

"The pains and vomiting began just this morning," said Lucy. "But for a day or two he has been seedy."

Humphreys held his fingers against Philip Todhunter's wrist. "Seedy!" he said in a voice tinged with sarcasm. "What has he eaten, Mrs. Todhunter?"

"Only a little pastry. I brought beef tea, but—"

"Last night, then. Was there seafood in the house? Mushrooms? Did anything taste as if it had spoiled?"

"Nothing," said Lucy Todhunter. "But Philip did not dine with us. He has refused his meals since Sunday. He said he could not bear the sight of food."

The black-bearded doctor scowled at her and leaned down to feel the patient's forehead. "Clammy," he remarked to no one in particular. "So he has eaten nothing these two days, madam?" She nodded. "Then what has he taken?"

"But I told you," she said, giving him a bewildered look. "Only some water now and again, and his beignet a little while ago. I brought him beef tea, but he spilled it without taking any."

"Madam, I ask you again. What has your husband *taken*? If he had dined on a bit of questionable beef or the odd mushroom, I should put this down to gastric upset. But since he has not done so, I must regard this as a case of poisoning. Make no mistake about it." He turned to Richard Norville. "Sir, I shall need some of the basin's contents collected in a small container for analysis. And bring me the breakfast pastries as well."

Norville, happy to be given an honorable excuse to flee, hurried from the room in search of a jar. Lucy Todhunter joined the doctor at her husband's bedside. "Philip," she called out. "Oh, my dear, can you hear me?"

Todhunter groaned, but his eyes remained closed.

"He will be all right, won't he?" she whispered to the doctor.

Philip Todhunter opened his eyes, and groaned. A shudder of pain convulsed him, and when it was over, he lay back against the pillow, panting, and cold sweat beaded on his brow.

Dr. Humphreys leaned close to his patient's ear. "Todhunter," he said, speaking slowly and distinctly. "You must tell me what you have taken, or you will surely die."

Todhunter stared up with unseeing eyes, and one trembling hand flailed at nothing. "Lucy!" he cried. "Why did you do it?"

Bill MacPherson was still holding the photograph of the frowsy middle-aged couple and the smiling teenage girl. Funny how one bit of information can completely change what you see. Suddenly the dull but pleasant family group had changed into a leering tabloid peep show. Bill had often heard the phrase *the mind boggled;* this was the first time his had actually done so. In fact, it was boggling like mad.

"Your husband brought home this girl—this kid in the picture—and said she was his *wife*?"

Donna Morgan dabbed at the corners of her eyes with a crumpled tissue. "Yes."

"Did you know her?" Bill looked back at the photo, half expecting to see a cringing kidnap victim with pleading eyes, but the grinning girl looked as saucy as before. He might even venture to say *smug*.

"Knew who she was. From church. Her name is Tanya Faith Reinhardt. Well, she goes by Tanya Faith Morgan now, and I-I guess I ought to—"

"How old is she?" asked Bill, forestalling another cloudburst.

"Sixteen."

Bill glanced at the doorway. Surely this was a prank at his expense. Surely any second now Edith and A. P. Hill were going to leap out grinning, and shout, "Gotcha!" But the damp silence went on and on. Bill sighed and made a note on his legal pad: *sixteen*. "What do her parents think of this?"

"Oh, they won't stand in the way of the Lord's will. They're stronger in the faith than I am. Though I do pray for the strength to accept this with a loving heart."

Bill nodded. That was reassuring. Most of the women of his acquaintance would have prayed for the strength to lift a newly sharpened double-bladed ax. He was glad that violence was not an issue here, but he still couldn't figure out how polygamy had arrived in Danville without his noticing. "The Lord's will?" he said. "I still don't follow you."

"Chevry is a minister. He has a little white-frame church out in the country past Pumpkin Creek. There's no steeple or anything. It used to be a Baptist church, but that closed years ago, so the congregation got it cheap. We fixed it up ourselves. The men made benches for pews, and Chevry laid the carpet."

"Protestant?" asked Bill, for want of saying that Chevry seemed to lay a lot of things.

"Well, we're not connected to any worldwide denominations. We're just simple country people-"

From the planet Twilo, thought Bill, but he nodded sagely for her to continue.

"Not too well-off. Chevry preaches at night, but he has a day job laying carpet for the big discount carpet place here in Danville."

32

Bill swallowed a quip about prayer rugs. She's probably not kidding, he kept reminding himself. "I see. And when did your husband receive his—um—revelation?"

"It's been three weeks now. He said the Lord spoke to him while he was in his truck driving up Highway 86. First he told Tanya Faith about it, and after she accepted him, they went and told her parents."

"Who went ballistic?"

"I believe Dewey Reinhardt took it hard at first, but Chevry said it was a test of faith, like Abraham being called to sacrifice Isaac and that they hadn't ought to question it."

"Wait," said Bill, glancing around for the office Bible. "Hold it right there. Unless there has been a major rewrite since I went to Bible school, Abraham *didn't* end up killing Isaac. When God saw that the old man was willing to go through with it, He allowed him to sacrifice a sheep instead." He shuddered. "I don't suppose your husband—"

"Oh, no," said Donna Morgan. "He went ahead and consummated it all right. You should see them together. She's all over him."

"But they actually got married?" Bill tried to remember the legal age limit for marriage in Virginia. Of course, with parental consent, sixteen was probably old enough. Except for the spot of bother about bigamy.

"Well... it wasn't a formal wedding, but he says they did solemnize their heavenly vows."

"With a state marriage license? Justice of the peace?" Bill was scribbling furiously now.

"Neither one. Chevry said they didn't need

33

to fool with paperwork for a divine union."

I'll bet it was. Aloud and willing his lips not to twitch, Bill said: "They did this in your husband's church? Before witnesses?" He wrote *common law* and a question mark.

"No, they didn't have a church ceremony," said the first Mrs. Morgan, her voice quavering again. "They just knelt in the back of Chevry's carpet truck and promised to be man and wife."

Bill pictured himself repeating his client's story to A. P. Hill. He could sell tickets to *that*. To say that A. P. Hill would not be amused was a foolhardy understatement. She was practically the poster child for the humorously challenged anyhow; this little tale of lust and lunacy would enrage her beyond the power of tranquilizer darts. If there was anything Amy Powell Hill hated more than chauvinistic men, it was the women who let them get away with it. "They make it harder for *me* to get taken seriously," she would rage.

He looked at his notes, thick with underlinings and exclamation points. "All right, Mrs. Morgan," he said. "Let me see if I've got this straight. Your husband, a part-time minister, claims to have received a directive from God, instructing him to marry a sixteen-year-old girl named Tanya. Her parents agreed to it. They plighted their troth in the back of a carpet truck, and then he brought her home to live with him and with you, his legal wife. Is that correct?"

"Yes."

Bill sat back and silently counted to ten. Mrs. Morgan did not burst out laughing. No video

34

cameras appeared in the doorway. No one giggled in the outer office. She really wasn't kidding. Bill sighed. And she was his problem. Sooner or later he would accept the reality of the situation, and then no doubt he would be just as appalled as A. P. Hill. Just now, though, he was trying not to be overwhelmed by the absurdity of it.

"A couple of things come to mind here, Mrs. Morgan," he said, doodling a row of vertical bars on his legal pad. "Statutory rape is a possibility, or a quaint old law that Virginia still has about seduction. We can even look into the exact wording of the statute on bigamy. We may be able to get him on his own admission of polygamy. I'd say the odds are favorable on Chevry doing jail time. That, of course, will strengthen your position in divorce proceedings."

"But I don't want a divorce," said Donna Morgan.

Bill blinked. "You don't?"

"I told you that it's against our religion."

"Yes, ma'am, but harems—I mean, multiple marriages—are against the laws of the Commonwealth of Virginia. I don't even have to look it up to be sure. The government feels quite strongly about it."

"And I didn't come here to get Chevry put in prison."

"Mrs. Morgan, I'm a lawyer, not a marriage counselor. What *do* you want?"

"I just wondered if there are any rules about wives having to be treated alike. Maybe some kind of contract spelling out our rights? I mean, I believe the Lord willed this and all, but I don't think He'd want me to take a backseat to Tanya Faith, do you?"

When Bill could trust himself to speak, he said, "I'm sure that the Lord is entirely in sympathy with you, Mrs. Morgan. Why don't you let me do some checking on the legal ramifications of this? I'll get back to you."

Mrs. Morgan gave him a misty smile. "That sounds fine," she said. "And could you talk to Chevry, too?"

"Believe me," said Bill. "I am most anxious to do so."

A. P. Hill's client interview wasn't going any better than her partner's. Eleanor Royden was chatting with cheerful lack of remorse that would have gotten her a life sentence for jaywalking. As she talked she paced the concrete floor, looking at nothing in particular, but her delivery was as polished as a stand-up comic's. She's in denial, thought A. P. Hill.

"How long have I known *the deceased*?" Eleanor Royden toyed with a lock of faded blonde hair and looked thoughtful. "That phrase will take some getting used to. I feel as if I'd just sunk the *Bismarck*. Oh, I've known Jeb since before *your* diapers ever polluted a landfill. I met him when I was a freshman in college."

"So you went to school together?"

"No indeed. I wish I had a cigarette. No, we weren't at the same school. Jeb was at North Carolina State University, very macho and self-important in prelaw, and I was bouffant hair and a string of cultured pearls at Meredith,

36

which is a Baptist women's college. I think the State boys saw Meredith as a kind of stocked trout pond." She shrugged. "And maybe we looked on them as potentially wealthy patrons. I majored in art. Not even art education so that I might have been able to get a teaching job. Just *art*. And I can't draw worth a damn. It was just a fashionable way to pass the time while I primped and partied, and looked for a breadwinner." She bent down and peered at the young lawyer. "Can you relate to any of this, Sunshine?"

"No." A. P. Hill gave an involuntary shudder. "I'd sooner join the marines."

"Yes, I believe you would," said Eleanor, resuming her pacing. "But you are of a different generation, you know. In my day, that is what proper young ladies did. They were supposed to be half of a career. The dinner party and housekeeping part. We were raised to think that those things mattered."

"I see."

"Oh, I had a bookkeeping job for a bit, working for a friend of my father, but everybody called that *working for dress money*. It meant they didn't have to pay me much. And I suppose I was glad enough to quit and become Mrs. Jeb Royden, do-mes-tic engineer."

"So you did not work outside the home," said A. P. Hill, making notes. "You devoted yourself to your husband's career and well-being."

Eleanor Royden hit the conference table with her fist. "And I did a good job, too, damn it! I can cater a cocktail party on forty minutes' notice. I had our Christmas cards done every year by November twenty-ninth. Our house

37

is spotless, and in all these years I never once asked Jeb Royden to pick up a sock, or wash a dish, or take out the trash. I never let him see me in curlers. And I can still fit into my college ball gowns! I did everything *right*!"

A. P. Hill sighed. "And he divorced you anyhow."

"Yes! Was that fair?"

"Mrs. Royden, I'm afraid that justice doesn't have much to do with human relationships."

"It does now." Eleanor pantomimed a pistol shot with her thumb and forefinger.

"You have to stop doing this," said A. P. Hill with a note of desperation in her voice. "The legal system takes a very dim view of people who gloat."

"You don't know what I've been through these past two years."

"So tell me. What happened to your marriage?"

"Jeb turned fifty. Don't men get strange when they hit middle age? I think it's testosterone poisoning. Do you suppose anyone is working on a cure? We could organize a telethon." She struck a pose. " 'Poor Baldy is doomed to a life of bimbos and NordicTrack, unless you help....' "

A. P. Hill sighed impatiently. "I realize that this humor is a defense mechanism, Mrs. Royden, and that you are probably experiencing a delayed shock, but I need to hear the facts. Do you feel up to talking about the divorce?"

"Why not? I've dined out on it for two years now. What do you want to know?"

"Well... what were the circumstances leading up to your separation?"

"My husband the legal piranha defended the bimbo landscaper against some unhappy clients, and he won the case, and out of gratitude or opportunism—opinions vary—she tapped his maple tree, to use a colorful plant metaphor."

"Hmmm," said A. P. Hill. "Can you tell me something a little more concrete about the second Mrs. Royden?"

"Well, she died young." Eleanor Royden's cackle of laughter ended in a smoker's cough. She patted her chest and continued. "Oh, there wasn't much to her that I could see—except youth. A valuable, but perishable commodity. She was young and pretty, with a mind like an Etch-A-Sketch toy. She had a good figure, though. It pleased Jeb's vanity to see the lust on other men's faces when he walked into a room with her. Men would nudge him and say, 'You sly dog!' That's puzzling, isn't it?"

"How so?" asked A. P. Hill.

"It's like being praised for buying a Mercedes. I mean, if you won one or even stole one, there might be some distinction in it, but any fool with a fat wallet can obtain one, so what constitutes the triumph? So if a fat, ugly, *poor* middle-aged bore managed to snare a young beauty, then maybe it would be a coup, but, hey, with Jeb's money, he could have rented sweet young things by the hour, so why the to-do that one of them let herself be taken by him on a long-term lease?"

"You ought to recruit for convents, Mrs. Royden," said A. P. Hill. "You make marriage seem like a disease."

Eleanor smiled. "Yes, but it's generally

fatal to women only. In my small way, I hope to have changed that."

"Will you stop!" A. P. Hill shook her head. "This is not how people facing a murder charge ought to talk. You should be contrite, tearful. You should be terribly sorry that you were overcome by emotion. You should be grieving for your loss."

"Oh, honey, I did all that when we went through the divorce. All I did this morning was finalize the decree."

"But why did you shoot them? Lots of women end up being divorced after years of marriage, and they don't resort to violence. Why didn't you just say, 'Screw the bastard,' and get on with your life? That's what a jury will want to know."

Eleanor Royden smiled bitterly. "Why? Because my husband considered divorce trials a blood sport."

MacPherson & Hill
Attorneys-at-Law

Danville, Virginia

(I would get my own printed, but I'm not sure what it ought to say. No job; apparently no husband, no life. A real identity crisis. How about: WATCH THIS SPACE? Elizabeth.)

Dear Cameron:

This is probably a letter that I would stick in a drawer even if I *did* know where to reach you, because the last thing my self-esteem needs is for me to publicize more evidence of my family's eccentricity. I'd be afraid that someone, somewhere, would be saving it all up for my commitment hearing. (Hmmm. I suppose the same could be said for writing letters to *you*.... People keep telling me I have to come to terms with your... um... absence, and get-on-with-my-life. I guess I would if I had one.)

I could talk about this new family development with Dr. Freya, but she would pretend not to know why I was upset, which would only make it worse. She loves to be politically correct, and seems to prefer it to common sense every time. And Bill always seems on the verge of crisis, so I can't add to his burdens. Cousin Geoffrey, who actually can be sympathetic, though he tries not to have it known, would be no help, either. So I might as well pretend that I'm telling you. If you can't be honest—and politically incorrect—in unmailed letters, when *can* you tell the truth?

So here goes.

I had lunch with Mother today so that she wouldn't feel too alone, what with us kids grown and Dad in his second childhood with his Girl Banker. We all thought she was bearing up wonderfully well after the divorce. She seems busy, and cheerful—not at all bitter about Dad's defection after nearly three decades of marriage. (I did wonder if all this serenity had been prescribed in tablet form by the family doctor, and if so, whether she could get *me* some of the same, but no, she is not medicated. Mother is just naturally a calm and forgiving person. A recessive trait, apparently.)

We went to the Long River Chinese

41

Restaurant out at the shopping mall, because Daddy never cared for Chinese food. Mother seems to think that Oriental food isn't fattening. As she says, Asian people are so little and delicate. In the interests of diplomacy, I do not say a word about sumo wrestlers.

Mother wanted to know how Bill was, and how I was, and if there was any word about your boat. It must be hard to get out of maternal gear after all these years of putting everyone else first.

"Let's talk about you," I said, because nothing is ever new with Bill, and if I tried to talk about you, I'd have started to cry right there over the kung pao chicken, which would have completely defeated the purpose of the luncheon, which was to Cheer Up the Aging Parent. "How have you been?"

"Quite well, thank you," she said with a little smile. "I'm starting to meet new people. Now that I'm not tied down in the evenings by a comatose man in front of a television, I can get out more and socialize."

"That's wonderful," I said, thinking to myself how brave she was to put up such a good front. "You're playing a lot of bridge, I guess?"

"Oh, no. I've taken up photography. Casey and I are doing a multimedia show about women in transition. Would you like to model for me? I could use a few more portrait shots."

"Oh, sure, whenever," I murmured. "But I didn't know you were into photography."

"I used to be very interested in portrait studies," she said, toying with her shrimp lo mein. "I took it up again because Casey saw some of my work and said it was a shame to let my talent go to waste."

"Casey?" I said, keeping my voice light. "This isn't the fellow you went white-water rafting with, is it?"

Mother looked pleased. Her favorite sport lately has been shocking the children, meaning Bill and me. Big brother and I have tried to remain calm and behave like adults while our fiftyish mother went hurtling about on a killer river with a blond undergraduate named Troy. I have *sweaters* older than Troy. But with frozen smiles and careful attention to controlled breathing exercises, we managed not to get worked up over Mother's little pregeriatric rebellion. It helped not to picture having a stepfather with an earring and light-up L.A. Gears. Now, sure enough, it appeared that Troy was history. Or at least he had been supplanted by Casey. Please, I thought to my fairy godmother, who has come to resemble Joan Rivers in my imaginings, don't let him be the paperboy.

"So," I said. "This is news. Tell me about Casey."

Mother looked amused. "You'll probably be relieved to hear that Casey is nothing like Troy. Much older, for one thing."

"Really? Be still my heart. A senior, perhaps?"

"No, Elizabeth. Casey is an assistant professor in the English Department. In fact, we are about the same age. In fact, we have a great deal in common: bridge, a fondness for the big-band sound, and Frank Capra movies. It's very pleasant."

Pleasant, indeed, I thought. In fact, too good to be true. "I don't suppose Dr. Casey is married, by any chance?" I said. I thought we might as well deal with the problems at once,

when Dr. Bell appeared, puffing from the exertion of the stairs. Elderly Royes Bell, who had seen hell on earth as a surgeon in the Army of Northern Virginia amputating limbs without morphia and watching soldiers die of fever for want of pennies' worth of medicine, was a jovial man who kept his nightmares to himself. He was as round and solid as his name implied and he was revered by the townspeople, who had absolute faith in his expertise.

He shuffled over to the bed and put a hand on his colleague's shoulder. "What do we have here, Humphreys?"

Richard Humphreys glanced at Lucy Todhunter lingering in the doorway. "Mrs. Todhunter, I wonder if we might have some coffee brought up for Dr. Bell and myself." When she had gone, he said in a low voice, "This gastric attack is sudden and severe, but by all accounts he patient has eaten next to nothing. I may as well tell you at the outset that I broached the subject of poison with Mrs. Todhunter straight out. She denied it."

"Well, she would," said Bell with a grim smile. "Better get your facts first. Have you collected samples for testing?"

"Yes."

"Then I suggest that we do what we can for this poor man—and leave the accusations until we know something. Have you questioned the patient?"

Humphreys nodded. "As best I could in his condition. I told him that he was on the point of death and that I must know what to treat him for. Whereupon, he looked at Mrs.

Todhunter, and said, 'Lucy, why did you do it!' He has not spoken coherently since."

Royes Bell pulled up a brocaded satin chair and lowered his bulk into it. He grasped Todhunter's wrist and felt for a pulse. "So he thinks that his good lady poisoned him, does he?"

Dr. Humphreys hesitated. "He seemed *urgent*, but not angry. It isn't the tone of voice that I should have used to a murderous spouse. Perhaps he was delirious, after all."

Bell completed his examination of the patient. "Well, if the lady did poison him, Humphreys, I hope she wasn't stingy with the dosage. I think the best we can wish this poor devil is that it be over quickly for him."

Philip Todhunter lingered three more days, his stupor punctuated with retching and pain-racked delirium. Finally, at dawn on the fifth day of his illness, he slipped into a last, quiet sleep from which he never awakened. Lucy Todhunter was not present at the bedside when her husband passed away. Worn-out from nearly a week of ministering to the dying man, she had retired to her bedroom shortly after midnight for her first real sleep in days.

The doctors had taken turns keeping watch over Todhunter, although there had been little that they could do in the way of treatment. On the second day Humphreys had administered injections of brandy, since Todhunter was too weak to take it orally. This seemed to make the sick man rest easier, but it did not counteract his decline. He took no nourishment. At her cousin's insistence, Lucy and the housekeeper applied mustard plasters to Philip's chest—to no avail. For want of any other remedy, Humphreys administered *nux vomica*, a preparation of white arsenic and carbonate of potash, used in treating dyspepsia. This, too, had no effect. Death finally came when Todhunter's body was too weakened by pain and vomiting to withstand further rigors. His heart simply gave out.

Dr. Royes Bell was in attendance at the time. His first thought was to summon Lucy Todhunter to her husband's bedside, but as he reached for the doorknob another idea occurred to him. He turned away from the door and began quietly searching the room, easing out dresser drawers and examining each item. Ten minutes later he had checked every possible hiding place in the bedroom, even under the mattress, but he had found nothing. He decided to awaken Lucy Todhunter and beckon her to pay her last respects to the deceased. While she was gone he would have a look in her room.

Dr. Bell knew what he was looking for. When the sample taken from Todhunter was analyzed, he knew that it would show traces of arsenic in his system. Meanwhile, before he summoned the authorities, Bell hoped to find more evidence.

When Donna Morgan left, having exhausted the contents of the tissue box on Bill's desk, Bill sat for a while contemplating the complexities of his new case. Then he went into the outer office to talk to Edith, the firm's cut-rate legal secretary, fresh from the business college.

"Interesting case," he remarked, trying to sound casual about it.

"Don't tell me *she* wants a divorce," said Edith, looking up from her typing. She settled her reading glasses on the top of her head and peered up at him. "That woman doesn't look like she could support herself for more than ten minutes. What'd she do, win the lottery?"

Bill shook his head. "She doesn't want a divorce. At least, not personally. She'd just like her husband to give up his other wife."

Edith sighed. "You just attract them, don't you?" she said. "They come out of the woodwork to be represented by you. Cranks, weirdos, refugees from the enchanted kingdom. I don't know how you missed representing the Bobbitts. Are you going to tell me how this woman happens to find herself in the one and only harem in Virginia?"

"I'm not sure *harem* is the correct term," said Bill, frowning. "Her husband is a backwoods fundamentalist. Apparently, he interprets the Bible in his own original way."

"Yeah, I heard that saying about the devil citing Scripture for his purpose."

"This fellow is a country preacher named Chevry Morgan. He has a little church some-where in the western part of the county. Ever heard of him?"

"No, but I expect I will. The tabloids and the talk shows will be fighting over him in no time. How come he isn't in jail, though? Or isn't bigamy illegal anymore?"

"Technically, he's not committing bigamy. He didn't get a marriage license for wife number two, who is, by the way, sixteen years old."

Edith considered it. "Kind of makes *your* father seem downright respectable, doesn't it?"

Bill blushed. His father had filed for divorce the previous year, prompted by an infatuation with a twenty-something woman banker named Caroline. This evidence of midlife frivolity had been acutely embarrassing to the grown-up MacPherson offspring, but Edith was right: compared with Chevry Morgan's creative lechery, Doug MacPherson was a saint. "Maybe I'll mention that to Mother," said Bill. "She seems to be getting back her sense of humor."

"You'd better not mention it to A. P. Hill," said Edith. "We'd never hear the end of this new affront to womanhood. She'd want this joker put *under* the jail."

"Why would those poor women put up with it?" asked Bill. "I have enough trouble getting someone to go to a movie with me, and this guy—Would *you* settle for half a husband, Edith?" He added hastily: "And leave Mel Gibson out of this!"

"Seriously?" said Edith. "I can see a feather-brained teenager being flattered at the attention, and looking at it as a one-way ticket to being grown-up. And I can see an aging housewife with no education, trapped in whatever situation her husband cares to put her in. The question is: What are you supposed to do about it? Turn him in?"

"I promised Mrs. Morgan that I'd talk to him first. She doesn't seem to want him put in jail, but she isn't happy with the little threesome at home. Maybe I could acquaint Mr. Morgan with a few of the penalties for sexual mis-

50

conduct. I guess I'd better do some homework on the subject."

Edith smirked. "Would you like me to call and set up an appointment with Secretariat?"

"Not yet," said Bill. "Would you like to take a look at this guy?"

"Are you selling tickets?"

"No. I thought I might go to church tonight."

It was fortunate that Bill MacPherson's budget for office decor did not run to hand-hooked oriental rugs. At the rate A. P. Hill was pacing his floor, she would have worn them out in a matter of hours. "It's weird, I tell you!" she said, for perhaps the fifth time, punctuating the statement with a two-handed gesture of despair: palms up, fingers outstretched. "They have denied my client bail. Can you believe it? In a domestic case!"

Her law partner watched her with interest, feet up on his desk and a can of root beer poised ready to drink, except that he had to keep nodding in agreement to all her rhetorical questions. "Well," he ventured at last, "she did kill two people, you know. A conservative would call that mass murder."

"Domestic!" said A.P., waving away the issue.

"Uh—so was Bluebeard," Bill pointed out. "And What's-his-name in England, the one who kept drowning his wives in the bathtub."

"George Joseph Smith," said A. P. Hill, whose grade-point average in law school had owed much to her memory. "But he preyed on women for their fortunes. Eleanor Royden committed a crime of passion."

"I don't know how passionate one can be at six o'clock in the morning when the other party is peacefully asleep," mused Bill. "To my mind the real reason the court is taking such a dim view of Mrs. Royden is the fact that she blew away a lawyer. Not a precedent they want to encourage."

"Ha! Yes!" said A. P. Hill, smacking her fist into her palm. "Craven attorneys. And I'll bet a few of those old stoats have ex-wives somewhere in the background, too! They figure they'll be next. After all, it wouldn't do to give the ladies any ideas, would it?"

Bill considered the matter. "Well, since this is the state that hosted the Lorena Bobbitt trial, the Roanoke courts may feel that women have far too many thoughts on the subject of vengeance as it is."

"Don't get me started on Lorena Bobbitt," said his partner. Indeed, that famous Manassas trial had been so thoroughly scrutinized and vicariously debated in the offices of MacPherson and Hill, that Edith, their legal secretary, had imposed a twenty-five-cent fine on anyone using the word *Bobbitt* on the premises. Henceforth, in deference to A. P. Hill's Civil War ancestor, they referred to the case as the *third* battle of Manassas.

Quarters were duly deposited in the spare coffee mug, and the discussion continued.

"You should have seen their faces when I went in and said that I was defending her. You'd have thought that I had asked them for kitten recipes the way they stared at me in horrified fascination. And then they started telling me what a swell guy good old Jeb had been."

"He probably was, if you didn't happen to be married to him," said Bill.

A. P. Hill stopped pacing and glared in his direction. "That's right. Stick up for him. Typical male trait: close the ranks. Crimes against women do not count."

"Not at all," Bill replied. "I did not know the man. All I'm saying is, if his only crime was to get a divorce and remarry, then it looks like Eleanor is a poor sport, to say the least, and there aren't many courts who consider her justified in executing the happy couple."

"But you haven't heard anything yet, Bill! This poor woman went through two years of hell. Imagine being married to a razor-sharp, reptilian attorney who equates legal cases with chess games."

"Yes, yes, I am imagining it," said Bill, grinning. "And a lovely bride you'd make, too, Amy dear."

She made a face at him. "No, seriously. You devote twenty years of your life to being the perfect little wife, a small grace note to his magnificence, and then one day he replaces you with a newer model. And instead of pensioning you off as decency and fairness—if not sentiment—require, he decides to turn the divorce into a legal Super Bowl."

"And she has to be the Buffalo Bills, I suppose?"

"No. She's the guy whose ticket was stolen and who didn't even get to see the game.

Nobody in town would take her divorce case. Two different guys from other counties signed on, and then mysteriously quit. She couldn't get a change of venue to some other

53

town, because everyone who had a say in the matter was a friend of Good Old Jeb. He used every trick in the book to hide his assets. He had all their furniture and household goods moved out of their house and put into storage, pending the settlement."

"Furniture? What for?"

"Because she didn't have any money to replace it! He just went out and bought all new stuff. Poor Eleanor couldn't afford to do that. He even took the Waterford crystal and the silverware that had been left to Eleanor by her grandmother, and when she tried to go to the storage place to get it back, Jeb Royden had her arrested for trespassing."

Bill shook his head. "It doesn't ring true," he said. "Mother and Dad weren't like that. Why would Royden be so vindictive toward his own wife?"

"I asked her that!" said Powell Hill triumphantly. "She said that Jeb was so used to getting his own way that he couldn't believe she was putting up a fuss about the divorce. He thought she should just submit meekly to whatever decision he made—and take whatever he chose to give her. When she made a fuss about it, he turned nasty. Then he decided to use all his legal skills to punish her. I have to document all the details of this for the defense. It's a very depressing case."

"I don't know," said Bill. "It makes *me* feel better."

"Why?"

"It gives me a new perspective on my parents' situation. Now I realize how much worse things could have been."

"Don't relax yet," said Powell Hill. "The Roydens' divorce went through more than a year ago, but she only shot him yesterday. Your mother may still be simmering."

The small white frame church sat back from the road like a humpbacked Brahma bull, glowering at the world through eyes of crimson glass. The building was old, and it had once been a fine, but simple country church. Through the years jackleg carpenters had remodeled it to add plumbing and electricity, and to cover the weathered exterior with aluminum siding and the cracking plaster walls with cheap paneling, and the result was a serviceable structure without a scrap of grace. The old cemetery that formed a semicircle around the structure had a certain somber beauty, but otherwise the building and its surroundings, hemmed in by scrub pines and weedy locust trees fringing a gravel parking lot, completed the picture of an edifice that only God could love.

Bill MacPherson edged his shabby blue Tempo between a couple of battered pickup trucks. A single streetlight glowed above the parking lot, illuminating the dents in the aging vehicles and silhouetting the gun racks in the truck cabs. "I don't think we look too out of place," he said, looking approvingly at the faded Fords and Chevys lined up in front of them.

"No," said Edith, slamming her door. "This clunker of yours can match rust spots with the best of them."

"I drive this car as a safety precaution," said Bill. "It deters thieves."

"You couldn't pay one to steal it, if that's what you mean," Edith replied. "But it is useful for undercover work. If anyone suspected that this car belonged to an attorney, applications to law schools would plummet." She eyed him critically. "I'm not so sure about your clothes, though."

"What's wrong with them?" asked Bill, straightening his burgundy silk tie. "This is what I always wear to church. Navy blazer, khaki pants, blue oxford-cloth shirt. A suit would be more formal, I know, but it's only a Tuesday-night service. Don't I look all right?"

"Call it a hunch." Edith, who was in a shapeless polyester dress, shrugged. "But I think you're going to look like a peacock in a bird-bath."

"Maybe I should have brought my raincoat," said Bill, loosening his tie and glancing nervously at the closed church door illuminated by a single yellow bug light. "We'll sit in the back row and try to stay inconspicuous."

"Just watch me," said Edith, heading for the door. "I grew up in a little church like this one. Don't genuflect. Don't kneel. Don't put your MasterCard in the collection plate. And if somebody starts passing around a little wooden box with a metal latch, don't take it."

"Why not?" asked Bill. "What would they have in a little wooden box?"

Edith opened the door and slipped inside. "Rattle-snakes," she whispered. She slid into a wooden pew to the right of the door, pulling Bill's sleeve to rouse him from the stupor that seemed to have struck him as he con-templated her last remark. "Come on, Bill. I

56

was kidding about the snakes," she said in his ear. "Probably."

As Bill edged toward the pew he stepped on a black cylindrical shape coiled at his feet, and his mouth opened to let out a scream that would have rattled the stained glass, but before he could get his diaphragm to work, his brain realized that he was in fact standing on the cord to the ministerial microphone, which was attached to the sound system in the back corner. The mike itself, a cigar-shaped hand-held instrument, was perched on a plastic stand atop a homemade pine lectern at the front of the sanctuary.

The small sanctuary was so jammed with bodies that it was difficult to make out the look of the room, but when Bill's eyes adjusted to the dim light, he saw that a wagonwheel chandelier illumined the altar area, casting a sickly yellow glow on the lectern, but shedding very little brightness elsewhere. The walls were lined with a dark pressed-wood paneling (sold at building-supply stores for about five dollars a square mile) that seemed to absorb light, and the ceiling was low, adding to the catacomb effect of the room.

"Where's Mrs. Morgan?" whispered Edith, elbowing Bill in the ribs.

"Which one?" he hissed back.

"Well, *exactly*!" said Edith. "I'll bet most of this congregation is here for the *begats* instead of the *amens*."

There was a shuffling of feet and a murmur of voices, and then a slender, middle-aged woman in a crimson robe made her way up the aisle and sat down at the upright piano to the right of the lectern. She pounded out a few bars of "Come to the Church in the Wildwood" to announce the start of the service, and the congregation struggled to its feet.

"All rise," muttered Edith. "The honorable rooster is about to crow."

"Behave!" Bill whispered back. "This crowd might believe in stoning unbelievers." No one was paying any attention to them, though, because the Reverend Chevry Morgan had chosen that moment to make his grand entrance. A side door at the front of the room opened, and Chevry Morgan sauntered in, wearing an unmistakable smirk of satisfaction. Trailing behind him were two women. The dowdy, middle-aged one stared at the floor, and the ferret-faced teenager tossed her head and smiled at the crowd like a beauty-pageant contestant.

Bill craned his neck to get a better look at the man he thought of as the defendant. Even with his shiny pompadour hair, Chevry Morgan did not make it to six feet in height, but he was big-boned and burly, with a ruddy complexion and a toothy grin. He was wearing an old tweed sport jacket over a teal-blue work shirt and khaki pants. He had on a bolo tie. Bill decided that his own coat and tie probably qualified him to be a bishop in this laid-back crowd.

Morgan walked to the podium, threw back his head so that his dark hair whipped back from his face, and hoisted the microphone into the air as if he was displaying a trophy. "Hallelujah!" he shouted.

"Hallelujah!" the crowd roared back.

Bill was still watching the two Mrs. Morgans.

58

They stood together for a moment on the left side of the podium; then the minister set the microphone back on its plastic stand and motioned for them to join him. As they stood on either side of him he took their hands and held them up, shouting "Hallelujah!" above a chorus of applause and whistles from the audience.

Edith began flipping through a hymnal. "Looking for airsickness bags," she murmured in answer to Bill's look of inquiry.

Bill turned his attention back to the family tableau at the altar. Donna Morgan looked mortified to be the center of such raucous attention. She kept her eyes fixed on the carpeted floor and tried to smile, wincing a little when her husband dropped her hand and wrapped his arm around her for a bear hug. Tanya Faith Morgan seemed much more at ease. She grinned out at the applauding darkness and stood up on tiptoes to give her husband a peck on the cheek. She was a scrawny sixteen-year-old, trying hard to appear grown-up with a sophisticated hairdo, a white sheath dress, and two-inch heels, but she certainly didn't look like someone who had been sold into bondage. Bill wondered which of the people in the audience were her parents and how they really felt about the matter.

After a few more moments of applause, the congregation sat down, and Bill could see Donna and Tanya Faith making their way to front-row seats. Apparently, they sat together at the services. Now Chevry Morgan had the stage to himself, obviously the way he wanted it.

He stepped up to the podium and gripped it with both hands. His wide-legged stance reminded Bill of a rock star. "Good evenin', believers!" he roared at the crowd.

Most of them hailed back. Bill took out his pen and a small notepad to take notes on Morgan's sermon.

"Are you strong in the faith, tonight?"

A louder roar answered him.

"It's not easy, you know," he said, picking up the microphone as if he were about to break into song. "It's not easy being a believer, when what you know is right differs from the opinion of the majority."

There were murmurs of assent from the congregation.

"People don't believe that we can speak with the tongues of angels when the spirit moves us. Don't believe that I had a revelation from the Almighty."

Bill heard Edith mutter, "Amen!"

"But I did," said Chevry Morgan, raising his voice to preaching pitch. "The Lord told me that man wasn't any different from the rest of His creatures. He said, 'Chevry, look at the rooster. There's one rooster strutting around that barnyard, being husband to a couple dozen hens. And there's one stallion presiding over an entire herd of mares, is there not?' "

Edith snatched Bill's pen, and wrote *Animal Husbandry?* on his notepad. Bill tried to look stern so that they would not both collapse into helpless laughter. They were a definite minority, though. The rest of the audience was murmuring encouragement to the florid man, who had loosened his tie in preparation for a real harangue.

"So the Lord told me that man was meant to live like the rest of His creations."

Edith wrote: *Outdoors? Eating raw meat?*

"—He told me to take another wife, to show my faith in His teachings." He strode away from the lectern to point dramatically at Tanya Faith. "Behold the woman!" He shouted. "A gift from God!"

Tanya Faith stood up and waved solemnly to the congregation. Chevry Morgan motioned for her to sit back down.

Speaking of thinking you are God's gift... Edith scribbled hurriedly.

The minister bowed his head, and the room filled with an electric silence. Finally he raised his head, eyes closed, and intoned, "There are those who would persecute me for my faith, believers." His eyes blazed open, and he began to pace back and forth in front of the lectern, still clutching the microphone. "There are those who would mock my divine revelation. They call me names and laugh at my belief. They try to shake the faith of my wife Donna, and to make her think that the Lord's chosen way is wrong. They want to lock me away in a jail cell for what I believe. In *America*, neighbors! Religious persecution!"

There were murmurs of protest from the crowd. Somebody shouted, "Keep the faith!"

What if you're a devout ax murderer, and the Lord told you to do it? Edith wrote on Bill's notepad.

Bill wrote back: *Praise the Lord and Pass the Ammunition.*

Danville, Virginia

All right... I'm calm now. I can continue writing this letter as a mature, objective adult, who is adjusting gracefully to the fact that her dowdy and probably senile old mother has just decided in the twilight of her life that she is a lesbian! My first dizzy thought was that she had her terms muddled, and that she was actually going in for amateur theatrics *(you know: a thespian)*, or that she had moved in with someone from Lesbia, Mississippi, or something. If you were reading this, Cameron, you would be snickering at me, or telling me how naïve I am, but, really, consider the situation. Here is poor old Mother, who got married as a teenager (back during the Crimean War or so) and has stayed married just *forever*, being a den mother, station-wagon mom, and all the rest of it; and then Daddy gets all lusty and peculiar with his midlife crisis and divorces her, and suddenly she decides that she prefers *women*?

I mean, *now*? After fifty-something years? It just *dawned* on her? And, let me tell you, there were no signs of it prior to this, I can assure you. Why, I've seen that woman watch old Steve McQueen movies with such a look of rapt adoration on her face that she'd hardly even *blink* while he was on the screen. We're talking serious magnetism here. And now she'd have me believe that it was Natalie Wood she preferred all along? I think not. I said as much to her in the Chinese restaurant while

I finished pulverizing my fortune cookie.

Mother smiled sweetly. She admitted that she still thought Steve McQueen was adorable in an aesthetic sort of way—you know, the way one can admire irises or gazelles for their natural beauty, without wanting to get intimate with one. She explained that she was a *political* lesbian.

"Which is?"

"It is a philosophical stance," she explained to me, sounding as if she were reading an invisible cue card. "Women have been oppressed for centuries by the patriarchal male. Woman-centered religions were dismissed as witch-craft. Female equality was denied by law. There has been systematic repression and exploitation of women by the male authority figures throughout the ages, so that to participate in a heterosexual relationship is to sleep with the enemy."

"Political lesbianism," she finished triumphantly, "is a conscious decision to renounce the male oppressor as a sacrifice to the struggle for liberation of our gender." If I had heard that from one of my college friends, I probably would have applauded her dedication to a political ideal. To hear this, though, from someone who used to fox-trot with Dad when *The Lawrence Welk Show* came on, was a bit unsettling, to say the least.

I said that I thought sexual orientation was something you decided on at an early age, *not* as an afterthought when one is a divorcée in her fifties. I ventured to express this opinion to the flaming radical herself, and she said that political decisions were governed by reason, not by glandular impulses. Doesn't that statement take the shine off all those old Cary Grant movies? Ugh. She went on to say that she had never realized what a lovely relationship one could have with other women. Such a lifestyle simply hadn't been an option in her early years.

Then she gave me an ironic smile and said, "Besides, dear, once a woman is past fifty, she might as well be a lesbian. *He* certainly doesn't want you anymore."

"Who?" I said.

She shrugged. "Men. Any of them."

Isn't that a cheery little aphorism to pass along from mother to daughter? She probably wouldn't have said it if you had been—you know—*still around*, but even in my present solitary state, it wasn't the sort of womanly wisdom I wanted to hear from my aged parent. Whatever happened to gray-haired grandmothers who talk baby-talk to cats? Now, apparently, they're all out having sex lives that make us look like seventh graders. Here I am, still in my twenties, sleeping alone, going to bed at ten, flossing, and alphabetizing my spice rack, while my mother is living a TV movie of the week with some mysterious femme fatale named Casey.

Dr. Freya is going to be no help at all with this. She'll just look at me over her horn-rim glasses and ask me why I am so upset—and perhaps I am repressing similar feelings, *nicht wahr?* To which I will reply, "Not unless Kiefer Sutherland is one hell of an actress." But, of course, she won't be convinced. Apparently, once you get into psychoanalysis, every opinion you have about anything is considered a symptom of something.

So I had to work it out for myself. I finally decided that what's bothering me is that I thought I knew my mother. Now it seems I didn't. Parents aren't supposed to have interesting lives. They're supposed to be dull and conservative and vaguely worried about us, while *we* go out into the world being outrageous and daring. They are not supposed to change. They're our safety net, in case the world out there knocks us for a loop. Then we have some place to retreat to. But where can I go? Dad is busy being Casanova-the-Hamster with Caroline; Mother is Danville's answer to Isadora Duncan; and you are... lost at sea. (There. I said it. But it doesn't mean I believe that it's forever. After all, Penelope waited twenty years for Ulysses, and it turned out she was right. By that logic, I still have a long way to go.)

Besides, I have more immediate concerns. I asked Mother if she had shared this stunning revelation with Bill. She replied that she was leaving that task to me. Bill and I are invited to Mother's new home for dinner on Saturday, at which time we will meet Professor Casey. Mother is sure we will all get along splendidly. I'm sure to need industrial-strength antacids. And Bill will probably have to be shot with tranquilizer darts.

Because of Dad, I had already contemplated the idea of a stepmother. I'm not sure I can handle the prospect of *two* of them, though.

With love from an old-fashioned girl
(apparently),
Elizabeth

CHAPTER 4

On the day of her husband's death, Lucy Todhunter was visited by the local sheriff, a courtly, silver-haired politician, and told in the politest possible terms that she should not consider leaving town. Indeed, the law would take it most kindly if she would stay within the house itself while the authorities conducted investigations into her husband's demise. Neither Dr. Humphreys nor Dr. Bell was prepared to sign a death certificate, the sheriff explained. Until the test results arrived, he suggested that she remain calm. He added that he hoped an attorney would be among those who dropped by to pay her a condolence call. Meanwhile, he would like her formal permission to question her houseguests about the events surrounding her husband's final illness.

Lucy, already attired in mourning of the deepest black-dyed satin, complete with veil, nodded her assent and reached for her black-edged handkerchief.

Two days later the chemist's report was telegraphed to Royes Bell from Richmond. He took the report with him to Richard Humphreys's office to discuss its implications. "Well, here it is," he said, sinking down into his colleague's consulting-room chair. "Interesting results. According to Richmond, the samples of regurgitation from Philip Todhunter—the ones collected before we administered the *nux vomica*, mind you—

were free of arsenic, but the autopsy samples tell quite another story." He opened the telegram and handed it to the other physician.

Humphreys's eyebrows rose as he read the report. "Trace amounts of arsenic found in Todhunter's intestines. One thousandth of a grain in the kidneys, and a full one-eighth grain in his liver. Hair samples also indicate the presence of arsenic."

"I wonder how the devil she did it," said Royes Bell.

That statement was to become the refrain of the entire Todhunter case. On the basis of the chemical analysis, Lucy Todhunter was charged with poisoning her husband. Ascribing a motive for her actions was not easy, but finally the district attorney settled on Lucy's anticipated inheritance of Todhunter's wealth as her incentive for murder.

She made a lovely defendant, sitting on the witness stand in her widow's weeds, so becoming to her pale skin and dark eyes. Her attorney, Patrick Russell, an auburn-haired Irishman with a gift for courtroom histrionics, heightened the illusion of Lucy's frailty by escorting her to and from the defense table as if she were made of spun glass. He had other tricks, too, for the benefit of the twelve solemn farmers and shopkeepers who sat in the jury box.

"Now, Mrs. Todhunter," he would say, softening his voice to the point of reverence. "In the matter of your departed husband, the former Union Army Major Todhunter—"

Several of the war veterans on the jury would stiffen each time he used that phrase, and Gerald Hillyard, the young prosecuting attorney, would mop his brow with his handkerchief—and hope that he had enough evidence to carry the day.

He was to be disappointed in that hope.

The medical evidence was clear enough regarding the symptoms of arsenic poisoning that Philip Todhunter had certainly displayed. Both doctors were adamant in their assertions that the dying Philip Todhunter had every sign of someone poisoned with arsenic: clammy skin, uncontrollable vomiting, esophageal pain, blood-tinged diarrhea, and finally a coma followed by death. The postmortem testing confirmed their opinion: arsenic in the internal organs—even in hair samples and nail cuttings taken from the deceased. Hillyard had felt confident that he was winning the case, despite Russell's theatrics, until the defense began to present its own case.

The servants were questioned first. With each of them, Russell was charming and confidential. "Now here's the person who knows what goes on at the Todhunters'," he said to a stern-faced Mrs. Malone. "I always say that the cook is the heart of the house."

The portly woman sniffed disdainfully. "I don't know about that," she said, but Russell's exuberance was boundless.

"Now, Mrs. Malone," he said, with a winning smile. "You were in charge of the kitchen, of course."

"And you'll find no tainted meat or bad mushrooms in my larder!" she informed him.

"Naturally not. And did Mrs. Lucy Todhunter give you instructions about what to cook?"

"Now and again," the cook conceded. "But not what you'd call regular. She never seemed to care what she ate."

"And was she much of a help to you in the kitchen? Buying the food? Or chopping vegetables, perhaps? Preparing the pastry?"

Mrs. Malone's incredulous stare suggested that Patrick Russell and his senses had parted company. "Not while I know it!" she replied. "I can't remember the last time I saw Miz Lucy in the kitchen. And if I saw her do a hand's turn of work, that *would* have been a day."

"So she didn't prepare any meals for former Union Army Major Todhunter during his last illness?"

"No more did I. He wouldn't take so much as a bowl of gruel. Said his stomach wouldn't stand for it."

"But a cup of tea, perhaps? Or a glass of spirits?"

"Not that I ever saw." A thought struck her. "Except his beignet."

"Ah, the beignet!" Russell nodded encouragingly. "His breakfast pastry—an acquired taste from New Orleans. Could you tell us a bit more about that?"

"She used to take him one of my fresh-baked beignets every morning. It was a custom of his. He didn't want anybody else to bring him his pastry, only Mrs. Todhunter. And she always did, except the couple of days he was sick. That day he was mortally stricken, she took him a beignet to keep up his strength, but it was no use, rest his soul." Despite the piety of her words, she did not seem unduly grieved by her employer's demise.

"And she never took him anything else during his illness?"

Mrs. Malone shook her head. "She wouldn't leave his bedside, most times, unless she was so tired that she collapsed in her own room. So mostly I took up broth and juices, or I sent one of the girls up with it. Not that he'd touch a mouthful of it."

"Was Mrs. Todhunter herself taken ill during her husband's final days?"

"No, sir. She wore herself out sitting up with him, but she was fit enough."

"And the other members of the household? All hale and hearty?"

Mrs. Malone's lips tightened. "We were sound as a bell, all of us! I told you that no contagion came out of my kitchen, and there's your proof!"

Russell thanked the cook profusely and excused her from the witness stand. He followed her testimony with that of the housemaids, who whispered agreement to Mrs. Malone's version of the events. "And did Mrs. Todhunter ever take the broth or pastry, or whatever you brought, and add anything to it?" Russell asked gently.

"No, sir," said the terrified kitchen maid. "That is, I couldn't say for most days she didn't, but that last day, she surely did not."

"Well, perhaps she took the tray from you and sent you back downstairs so that she could give the broth or pastry to Mr. Todhunter herself?"

"No, sir." The girl shook her head: a definite no. "She always made me stand there and wait so I could take the tray and dirty dishes back to

70

the kitchen. And the slop bowl, too, like as not."

"Caring for invalids is an arduous task," said Russell sympathetically. "But I'm sure you were a great help in the family's hour of need."

"Besides, Mr. Todhunter wasn't taking any nourishment by then, anyhow. Dreadful ill, he was."

The other maid said much the same, but with considerably more terror in her voice at the prospect of being on display in such a menacing place as a courtroom. Patrick Russell called Dr. Humphreys and Dr. Bell to the stand, with a deference suggesting that they were on loan from the Oracle of Delphi. They were popular men in Danville, and Russell knew it. He did not challenge their statement that the patient had succumbed to arsenic poisoning.

"Now, Dr. Bell, I'll ask you the same as I've asked Dr. Richard Humphreys. Did you ever see Mrs. Lucy Todhunter administer anything potable to her unfortunate husband?"

Bell's eyes narrowed. "I did not. But I suspected she had. During my stay with the patient, I searched the rooms, and sure enough, finally after Todhunter's death, I found arsenic—"

"You did find arsenic, Doctor? Tell us the circumstances."

"It was white powder in a small glass jar. I suspected what it was, of course, and I took a sample away to be tested."

"Oh, yes. And the results confirmed your suspicions, did they not?"

"They did. The substance in the jar was arsenic trioxide, a fine white powder that puts one in mind of sugar."

"Humphreys says the same," mused the

attorney. "And one of you was with the patient at all times until the end?"

"Yes. Or Norville or her cousin Mary Compson."

"Yes. And do you know, Dr. Bell, Mrs. Mary Hadley Compson of Maysville, North Carolina, has testified to the same statement—that at no time did she see Lucy Todhunter administer anything to her ailing husband, the late Union Army Maj—"

"You haven't asked Norville yet!"

"Let me remedy that at once, Doctor," said Patrick Russell with a courtly bow.

Richard Norville came to the stand, wary of justice among strangers, but willing enough to tell what he knew. "Yes, I escorted Mrs. Todhunter to her husband's room the day he took sick," he told the court. "She wanted to take a tray up to him from the breakfast table, and I wouldn't allow her to carry it."

"And they say the Union had no gallant officers!" said Patrick Russell solemnly.

Norville seemed discomfited by snickers from the spectators, but he resumed his testimony. "I took the tray up to Philip's room and went in with her. She handed him the plate of beignets and he ate most of it. Then he sank back as if he were taken ill again."

Russell heard the buzz from the back of the courtroom, but he did not turn around. "He had an attack at once, did he? Well, that could have been the pastry, but it seems unlikely that it would work so quickly. What happened next?"

Norville squirmed in his seat and muttered something.

"I beg your pardon, Mr. Norville? I couldn't quite hear what you said."

"I said: 'And then she ate the rest of the beignet herself!' "

Russell raised his eyebrows, giving a convincing imitation of someone who is hearing startling news for the first time. "You say that Mrs. Lucy Todhunter *herself* consumed a piece of the same pastry her husband had eaten? The very same one?"

"Yes. There were half a dozen on the plate. He chose himself one at random. We had all eaten one."

"And did you see her add anything to that particular pastry? More powdered sugar, perhaps?"

"I did not. Never took my eyes off her for a moment. She didn't add anything. I'll take my oath to that."

"So you have, Mr. Norville," said Russell, smiling. "Mrs. Todhunter gave her husband a beignet, and he became ill and died. But she ate from the same pastry and was not affected. Perhaps some secret antidote to the fatal dose?"

Norville shook his head. "There's more to it than that. I told you: we had all eaten a pastry from that plate at breakfast before she took the tray up to his room."

"You don't tell me!" said Russell, slipping a bit of brogue into his performance.

"I do," said Norville grimly. "All four of us— me, the Compsons, and Mrs. Lucy Todhunter— ate one of those baked goods from that very plate before it was taken upstairs to Philip Todhunter."

"And this plate of pastries ..." Russell leaned close to the witness, measuring his words by the syllable. "It never left your sight from the time you all ate one until the time Philip Todhunter took his last mouthful of sustenance on this earth from its contents?"

Patrick Russell gave a deep sigh and turned to face the jury. From the prosecution's table, young Gerald Hillyard watched with a heavy heart. "There it is, gentlemen," he said, without a single note of triumph in his voice. Hearing him, you might have believed that he was sorry to have to point out the inescapable conclusion to the as sembled seekers of truth. "There it is, indeed. We have two eminent physicians who assure us that poor Philip Todhunter went out of this world on account of a few grains of arsenic that sickened his body. And I'm sure I don't doubt the word of two fine, learned gentlemen such as these." He nodded courteously at Bell and Humphreys, both scowling at him from just behind the railing. "And my earnest colleague Mr. Hillyard there—why, he would have you believe that the frail young lady whom I am defending, Mrs. Lucy Todhunter, did willfully poison her husband with that arsenic. There's even been testimony by Dr. Bell that a jar full of the deadly substance was found hidden in the upstairs of the home. And yet, the beignets were tested. The kitchen sugar was tested. And the stomach contents of Mr. Todhunter were tested. All proved to be arsenic-free. Well, gentlemen of the jury, I suppose that leaves us with but the one question...." He looked at the jury, at Hillyard, and then stared down the crowd who had come to watch the trial.

"Can you tell me how in heaven the lady managed to do it?"

"How's your case going?" Bill MacPherson asked his law partner, over spurious morning coffee. He tried to sound casual about it.

"I've just begun," said A. P. Hill, turning a page of the *Danville Register & Bee*. "I'm still gathering information. Haven't even decided on an angle for the defense yet really."

"I had a question," said Bill diffidently. "Just a hypothetical thingamabob, you know. Just a thought that occurred to me. Thought I'd run it by you."

Powell Hill was reading the editorials now. "Um-hmm," she said. "What is it?"

"Well, supposing that Jeb Royden hadn't divorced Eleanor. I mean, supposing he just up and announced that he'd had—oh, say, a message from God—and that he had been instructed to take a new wife. So instead of tossing Eleanor out to the wolves, suppose he had just brought in a third party. Wife number two."

She lowered the paper slowly until her eyes met Bill's. "What do you mean, brought a new wife home? You mean *bigamy*?" A. P. Hill's voice could have frosted beer mugs.

"Well, not technically. I mean—just say, for example—that he had exchanged vows with the new wife privately, without benefit of the state licensing procedure."

"This is a legal question, right, Bill?" Powell Hill gave him a cold smile. "I mean, I know what *I'd* do."

Bill crossed his legs. "Yeah, but you'll have to pay Edith a quarter if you tell me."

A voice from the receptionist's area called out, "Are you all talking about Manassas Three again?"

"No!" Bill yelled back. "Just some legal theorizing."

"What *are* we talking about?" asked Powell, giving up on the *Bee*.

"Oh, all right. I took a new case while you were in Roanoke, interviewing Eleanor Royden."

"A case about bigamy? You found a bigamist in *Danville*?"

"Well, sort of." Bill explained about Chevry Morgan's directive from God. A. P. Hill listened in silence, but her expression suggested that she would not be converting to that particular brand of religion. In fact, if an angel had appeared to her, she might have sent him back for the fiery sword while she made out her hit list. And lo! Chevry Morgan's name would lead all the rest.

Powell sipped her tea, discovered that it was cold, and set it down again. "I can't believe it," she said softly. "There is actually a woman alive today who would fall for that crap?"

"Two of them, to be exact," Bill pointed out. "And you can't blame it on an unenlightened generation, either, because both of the Mrs. Morgans seem to have accepted the news of their husband's divine mission without too many qualms. Remember wife number two is a teenager." He looked at his partner's forbidding expression. "Of course, that isn't to say that *most* women of any age would be taken in. Er—I don't suppose you're his type, Powell."

"Probably not," she agreed. "I am neither adolescent and gullible, nor old and helpless. I'm trying to think what we can do to help these poor women."

"I don't think the second Mrs. Morgan wants any help. When I saw her last night, she looked like the cat in the cream jug."

"You *saw* her?"

Bill reddened. "Did I forget to mention that? Edith and I went to church."

"I hope you didn't put anything in the collection plate," snapped A. P. Hill.

"Edith wanted to contribute something, but it wasn't monetary. I talked her out of it. I don't think there's much we can do about Mrs. Morgan the Younger, unless we can think of something to charge Bluebeard with, and get him sent to jail. She might wise up once he's gone. Right now they're like birds hypnotized by a snake. You should have seen him at the service. He was very charismatic. Sort of an ecumenical Elvis, prancing around with his microphone."

"I can imagine. And nobody questioned his lunacy? What about the girl's parents?"

"Members of the congregation. He convinced them, too."

Powell Hill shook her head. "I hope the tabloids don't get wind of this. You haven't lived down the Confederate Women yet." Bill winced at this mention of his first case—a real-estate transaction that had become a nightmare. "Tell me, why did the other Mrs. Morgan come to you?"

"Glimmerings of common sense, I think," said Bill. "Every so often Chevry Morgan's spell

77

wears thin. Then she realizes how absurd the whole thing is. When hubby comes back, she's trapped again. For all I know, she may call off the case any day now. If he finds out she's been seeing a lawyer, he'll pressure her until she gives in."

"Get her out of there, Bill."

Bill looked uncomfortable. "Well, it's tricky. She claims she doesn't want a divorce."

"She doesn't want a divorce?"

"Doesn't believe in them. They belong to a very strict fundamentalist sect. Mrs. Morgan the Younger has a long list of *thou shalt not*s to follow. No short skirts; no dancing; no lipstick."

"Oh, right," said A. P. Hill, emptying her teacup into Bill's philodendron. "This teenage honey isn't allowed to dance or wear make-up, but her folks let her go off and have sex with a married man old enough to be her grandfather. Right."

"Maybe you ought to take this case," said Bill, rooting around on his desk for the pertinent manila folder. "You have exactly the right tone to highlight the folly of it all. I can just picture you cross-examining Chevry Morgan."

"Sorry, partner," she said, pushing back her chair. "I'm doing a murder case, and I don't handle domestic matters. But if someone *murders* old Chevry, I'll defend them for free."

"Well, do you have any suggestions on what I might do?"

"Check the statutory-rape laws. The girl is probably too old for that to work, though. Give Chevry credit for being sly enough to escape the obvious pitfalls. Then see if laws pertaining to alienation of affection or criminal conversation are still on the books." Powell Hill grimaced. "I never thought I'd hear myself recommending that one."

"Criminal *conversation*?" echoed Bill.

"Legal euphemism. It means that you can sue someone for committing adultery with your spouse." She shrugged. "It's a form of property damage, I guess. The early silverbacks put it into law to keep their wives off-limits. It would be nice if you could use that old legal chestnut the other way, to ensure the fidelity of the male spouse."

"You mean, Mrs. Donna Morgan could sue Mrs. Tanya Faith Morgan for husband-napping?"

"More like sexual trespassing," said Powell. "Possibly, yes. You'll have to crack the law books to find out for sure. It's an old law, seldom if ever used today."

"I wonder if Ivana Trump thought of it."

A. P. Hill picked up her briefcase. "If that doesn't work, let me know. We can dredge up something else." She grinned. "Maybe we can fix up Mr. Morgan with a knife-wielding manicurist from Manassas."

From the other room, a voice called out, "You owe me a quarter!"

"Amy P. Hill, what an unexpected pleasure! What brings you up here to Roanoke?"

"Hello, Bob. Just visiting a client." A. P. Hill remembered Bob Creighton from law school. He had been a class ahead of her, and she hadn't been particularly impressed by his legal skills or his clumsy attempt to add her scalp to his belt in after-hours student socializing. She wondered if he was as obvious in court as he had been as a prospective suitor. He still looked like the fraternity social chairman, she thought: blow-dried hair, navy-blue blazer, and a tie that looked frivolous to the uninitiated. The law-school Ken Doll. She decided to ignore the fact that he had called her *Amy*. "You're in the DA's office, aren't you, Bob?"

He checked to see if his shoes were shined. "Got me there, Amy girl. How'd you guess?"

"Women's intuition," said A. P. Hill with what passed for a smile.

"Can I buy you a Coke?"

"Sure. Why not?" She realized that this was not a casual meeting. Bob Creighton represented the DA. Old school pleasantries aside, her adversaries were about to fire the opening salvo. Still, she wanted to hear what the prosecution thought of the Eleanor Royden case, and this might be a civilized way to find out. She decided to play along.

Bob Creighton led her to the snack bar, a collection of small tables flanked by a row of vending machines. He chatted amiably about the weather, his golf game, and how much he enjoyed his work. He asked very few questions of A. P. Hill, but, in her experience, that was not unusual. Creighton was the sort of man who used women as sounding boards, preferably mute and adoring. Powell Hill thought she could just manage the former; the latter was past praying for.

They settled in metal chairs, sipping diet soft drinks and smiling warily at each other. "So," said Bob, who had run out of small talk, "I hear

80

you're up here talking to that Royden woman."

"I'm thinking of taking the case," said Powell Hill, trying to sound casual. "I'd have thought it would be considered quite a plum. Major publicity. Possible movie interest. I can't think why nobody in Roanoke wanted it." She gave him an innocent smile. "Or am I just being modest? I assumed I wasn't the first attorney Mrs. Royden contacted."

Bob Creighton winced. "The *first* Mrs. Royden," he said. "Those of us who knew Jeb like to think of poor Giselle as the *real* Mrs. Royden. I'm sure Jeb would shudder if he could hear Eleanor referred to by that honorific."

"To which she is still legally entitled, of course," purred Powell Hill.

"But morally," said Creighton, frowning, "morally, it pains me to hear it. Consider the circumstances. Calling Eleanor that is an affront to Mrs. Royden's memory. Jeb's wife, I mean. His true soul mate, till death—a.k.a. Eleanor—did them part. You didn't know Giselle, of course, but she was such a ray of sunshine in Jeb's life."

A. P. Hill preserved her reputation for humorlessness by not remarking, "I expect she was a hot little number, all right."

"Jeb and Giselle." Creighton sighed. "They were such an ideal couple. It was the most touching thing to see them together. So in love."

A. P. Hill looked puzzled as the name finally registered. "Giselle? That's not the name on the documents—"

"Oh, no." Bob gave her a sad smile. "Her real name was Staci, but she once studied ballet,

81

and Jeb thought she was so graceful, with her big brown eyes. Like Bambi. So the pet name went from Gazelle to Giselle. *Giselle* is a famous ballet," he added, in case A. P. Hill were culturally challenged.

She returned his smile with a cold stare. "A ballet? Really? Is it about adultery?"

"I see that woman has poisoned your mind," said Bob. "That's because you didn't know Jeb and Giselle. Eleanor couldn't run that game on any of us around here, which is why she had to import a lawyer."

"Maybe she just wanted an unbiased trial," A. P. Hill replied. "Clients are funny about that."

"Oh, we'll be fair, all right," said Creighton. "But we take it very personally when an hysterical middle-aged woman guns down her ex-husband out of jealousy and spite."

A. P. Hill made a mental note to look again into a change of venue for the trial. "I hear he wasn't exactly benevolent in the divorce," she said.

Bob Creighton hesitated for a moment. Deciding which argument to pick, thought A.P. Finally he smiled at her and said, "He was a lot like you, Amy. I know you wouldn't expect some old flame to support you for the rest of your life. And I know you wouldn't care to have one sponging off you, either."

"I might choose a spouse more carefully to begin with."

Creighton shrugged. "Hindsight doesn't win football games."

"So tell me about this divorce," Powell prompted. "I have my client's side of it, of course, and I can get the documents, but I'm sure the legal community here saw a good bit that I won't find in either account."

"Oh, for sure. Everybody knew Jeb. He was a pillar of the community. Symphony fund-raiser, great golfer. Famous for his dinner parties."

"Oh, he cooked?"

"Well, no. For the last couple of years he's hosted his dinners at La Maison, because Giselle didn't cook that sort of fare."

"But before that?"

"I suppose that woman handled the cooking," Bob Creighton said grudgingly. "Eleanor. Probably it was all she was good for."

"You were going to tell me about the divorce."

"It was just one of those things, Amy. Jeb and Eleanor Royden got married very young, and over the years they grew apart. It happens—and it certainly isn't uncommon these days."

"Not among people who can afford a trade-in, no," said Powell Hill sweetly.

"I told you. He met Giselle and then he couldn't see spending the rest of his life being middle-aged and bored. Then none of them would have been happy. He tried it for a while, though. He and Staci—Giselle — used to be seen around town together. She'd go with him on trips sometimes, but he still went home to Eleanor like a good boy. I think he tried to keep his marriage intact."

"How very noble of him."

"Yeah." Creighton sighed. "Eleanor Royden found out about it, though. She was out with Jeb at a charity event one evening, and they ran into an attorney who was new in town. The

83

attorney asked Eleanor if she was Mrs. Royden's mother."

"No doubt it was awkward," said A. P. Hill. "I'm sure he felt just like Aldrich Ames."

"Who?"

"The CIA fellow who got caught spying for the USSR. It's always unpleasant to be caught."

Creighton raised his eyebrows. "I know it's good form to identify with one's prospective client—publicly, at least. But such hausfrau sentiments are a little out of character coming from you, Amy."

A. P. Hill's civility had worn thin. "Nobody calls me Amy, Creighton."

"You're *talking* like an Amy, Counselor. All bourgeois horrified at the wicked ways of the world. Surely you aren't so naïve, whatever your client's failings."

A. P. Hill gave him a mildly attentive stare, the look she used to give fetal pigs in high-school biology lab. "So, Bob, you are saying that if something is a common occurrence, one should not be upset when one encounters it. Child abuse is fairly common. Drunk driving is routine. Torture goes on in most parts of the world. Should we take all that in stride merely because it happens a lot? I thought morality depended on what was right, not on what was popular."

Creighton looked over his shoulder. Then he turned around and peered at the empty chairs of the snack bar. "Is there a jury in here?" he asked. "I don't see one. Or were you just grandstanding from force of habit?"

"Just presenting the rebuttal for that smug

little editorial of yours. Now get back to the Roydens' divorce. What happened after Eleanor found out about Staci?"

"Oh, she became completely irrational. Probably something to do with menopause."

"An interesting defense," said A. P. Hill. "What did she do?"

"She stormed out into the parking lot to Jeb's new car. He had just bought a white Nissan 3002X."

"Probably something to do with male menopause," she said solemnly.

"Why shouldn't he? It was *his* money. Anyhow, Eleanor got into the trunk, took a tire iron, and did a pretty thorough job of smashing that car into an unrecognizable wreck."

A. P. Hill thought that she might have been tempted to do much the same, but she only nodded. "I see. So the battle lines were drawn."

"Actually, Jeb was pretty sympathetic. He didn't move out. Didn't even seem too upset. He probably told Eleanor that she was imagining things, or that he'd break it off. And then he tried to be more discreet."

"I do like an honorable man," said A. P. Hill with a sour smile. "But tell me about the divorce."

"Well, as I said, Jeb tried to be discreet. Eleanor, however, had a nasty suspicious mind, and she behaved like an absolute bloodhound. No matter how he covered his tracks, she simply wouldn't believe that he was being faithful. Her endless badgering grew tiresome, so, of course, he moved out."

"Well, poor old Jeb. And in the divorce proceedings, I suppose he cast her as the Polish cavalry?"

85

World War II metaphors were wasted on Creighton, whose intellect was even more limited than his imagination. He ignored the remark and launched into a detailed account of Jeb Royden's legal maneuvers in his efforts to humiliate his ex-wife and to deprive her of every vestige of financial security. He described the campaign as dispassionately as he might have discussed the strategies of the Trojan War. To Creighton, any human suffering incurred in the legal battle was a minor side effect of the technical process. A. P. Hill detected a note of admiration in her colleague's description of the suits and countersuits in *Royden* v. *Royden*.

"Jeb was remarkably patient with her," he said. "He was always a lawyer first and a litigant second. Eleanor really lost it a few times. She stormed into his office and started relating her version of the divorce to his clients, so Jeb quietly had her arrested and charged with trespassing."

"How noble of him."

"He was fed up. Anybody would be. She took out an ad on the Possibilities page of the *Roanoke Times* — that's the dating section. It said: *Prosperous Roanoke lawyer, long on financial assets, short on physical ones, seeks gold-digging bimbo to jazz up his briefs. Preference given to sluts named Staci.*"

A. P. Hill raised her eyebrows. "What did the happy couple do about that?"

"They just laughed. Eleanor was becoming the town loony by that time. Everybody could see why he wanted to get away from her. But Jeb got even with her by donating their furniture to Goodwill, and giving her a check for half its appraised value as used household goods. About two hundred and fifty bucks. The stuff was brand-new James River furniture worth nearly twelve grand, but Jeb said he could afford to take the loss, just for the pleasure of hearing Eleanor scream about losing it. The next week he took Giselle to North Carolina and bought almost exactly the same stuff for their new home. Boy, was Eleanor steamed!"

A. P. Hill stood up. "This has been fascinating," she said. "But I've got to meet with my client now, Creighton. Before I go, let me give you one of these. A woman's group in Roanoke had them printed up, and they sent me a stack." She reached into her purse, and handed the assistant DA a red-and-white bumper sticker: FREE ELEANOR ROYDEN AND SEND HER OVER TO MY EX-HUSBAND'S PLACE.

CHAPTER 5

Lucy Todhunter sat at the defense table, swathed in mourning, but dry-eyed, watching the jury with a tremulous smile that widened slightly when the judge told them that they could not convict a defendant of murder unless they were able to work out how the crime was committed. In his summation for the defense Patrick Russell had said much the same.

"Mind you, gentlemen, you cannot say that the defendant somehow managed to administer arsenic to the victim—you know not how—and is therefore guilty," Russell told the jurors. "You must be certain beyond a reasonable doubt, when and by what means the fatal dose was administered. If you are unable to decide that—and I cannot say that the prosecution has been much help to you in the matter—it is your bounden duty to acquit the defendant, Mrs. Lucy Todhunter. It does not mean that you believe her to be innocent; only that by strict legal standards you cannot *prove* her guilty. In a court of law, we can be concerned only with whether or not the facts presented can support the verdict. The state of Mrs. Todhunter's soul is the province of Almighty God, not the Commonwealth of Virginia."

"You might have shown more faith in my innocence," Lucy Todhunter murmured as her attorney sat down.

"Never mind what I think," Russell told her. "It is the opinions of those twelve men that count. I hope I have left them little choice in the matter."

Apparently he had succeeded in this aim, for in less than an hour the solemn jurors, looking rumpled and sweaty in unaccustomed suits and cravats, filed back into the courtroom and resumed their places.

"Gentlemen, have you reached a verdict in the matter of the *Commonwealth of Virginia v. Mrs. Lucy Todhunter?*"

"Reckon we have," said the foreman, a tobacco farmer, who later remarked that the formality of courtroom procedure made him itch. He handed a folded sheet of paper to the bailiff, who passed the verdict to the judge.

His Honor peered over his spectacles at the message—lengthier than the usual jury decision.

"It is unnecessary to explain your decision, gentlemen," he said mildly as he passed the paper back to the bailiff. The verdict read: *Not Guilty. We can't figure out how she did it.*

Patrick Russell shook his client's hand and formally congratulated her upon her victory. He sent her an exorbitant bill and never spoke to her again.

As the crowds made their way out of the courtroom, Royes Bell turned to his fellow physician Richard Humphreys and said, "Now that Mrs. Todhunter has been acquitted of her husband's death, in the interests of science, she ought to tell us how she managed it."

She never did, though. Lucy Todhunter went back to her late husband's opulent home, where she remained, declining visitors, until three months after the trial—when a pair of events brought Lucy once again to the forefront of the Danville gossip mill. First, Philip Todhunter's relatives from Maine arrived to contest Lucy's possession of her husband's estate; second, the young widow's pregnancy became evident, despite the camouflage effect of the long full-skirted dresses that were currently in fashion.

The Danville grapevine estimated the widow Todhunter to be about four months along in her pregnancy, and after considerable finger counting, they grudgingly allowed that the child was probably sired by her husband. It was just as well the jury hadn't decided to hang her, everyone conceded, but impending mother-hood did not endear her to the community. The Todhunter relatives were not impressed by this last legacy from poor dear Philip. They wanted the house, but not the heir, until attorneys for both sides pointed out to them that the baby would inherit a share in its father's fortune.

"They'll get that house over my dead body!" Lucy Todhunter told her few remaining friends.

They did.

She was never a robust young woman, and the strain of pregnancy, perhaps complicated by the rigors of the trial, exhausted her strength. She went into labor several weeks early and died of complications in the ensuing birth. It wasn't to be wondered at, said the matrons of Danville. Didn't she have all those problems with her earlier confinements? She even had to go to the spa to recuperate. Her funeral was well attended, since those who forbore to speak to her after the trial resumed their friendship with her at the graveside. Her headstone gave only her name, the dates of her birth and death, and verse 15:51 from the Book of Corinthians: BEHOLD I SHEW YOU A MYSTERY. Royes Bell attended Lucy to the last and regretfully reported to his colleagues that Mrs. Todhunter's secret, whatever it was, went with her.

The child, a boy named after his late father, lived, and was raised in his Southern home by two of Philip Todhunter's spinster aunts. The maiden ladies had decided that they preferred child raising in Southern prosperity to the status of poor relations in the homes of their New England kin. In time they grew accustomed to the conventions and the climate of Virginia, and they never returned to the North. Philip Todhunter, Jr., was raised with Calvinist strictness, and complete silence on the subject of his mother. He managed to fritter away most of his inheritance by the turn of the century, but he left a son, in whom no trace of the stern, cold Todhunters remained, in either accent or temperament. That young man, born in 1900, became a millworker, married a local girl, and lived in comfortable poverty, enlivened with country music, stock-car racing, and that old-time religion, a stranger to the ways of both his patrician grandmother Lucy and his ambitious grandfather, the murdered Major Todhunter—if murdered he was. No satisfactory explanation for the crime had yet been found.

By the time Philip Todhunter's great-granddaughter was born in 1940, the family was entrenched in the lower middle class, so thoroughly Southern nationalists that they would have been grieved to learn of Major Todhunter's wartime affiliations. His murder was a dimly recalled family legend. Whether Lucy's bloodline left a fatal legacy remains to be seen.

DO YOU KNOW WHERE YOUR EX-WIFE IS TONIGHT? "Some of the local women's group had that bumper sticker made up," A. P. Hill told her client. "They asked me to bring you one."

Cackling with laughter, Eleanor Royden held up the sign for the guard to read. "Tell them I love it!" she said to A. P. Hill. A week's stay in the county jail had taken its toll on her appearance, but her raucous high spirits were intact. She looked haggard now, and the lines on her face seemed deeper. The harsh prison shampoo had stripped most of the blonde from her gray hair, giving her a faded look that added a decade to her age.

A. P. Hill rummaged in her handbag. "I brought you the Rancé soap you asked for. The guard said it was all right to give it to you. Would you like some special shampoo for tinted hair?"

Eleanor Royden pulled down a lock of coarse gray hair and inspected it. "Not much point in that, is there? I think the tint is kaput. I must look like the prom queen from hell. I hope Jeb doesn't see me like this."

A. P. Hill studied her client carefully for signs of disorientation. "Jeb is dead, Eleanor, remember?"

"Well, sure he is. I spent three bullets making sure. Damn the expense of the extra ones, I said. He's worth it. I just meant I wouldn't want him to see me in case he's haunting the courthouse or something."

"I don't think that's one of your problems," said A. P. Hill.

"Probably not. He and Mrs. Bimbo are probably haunting the Pinehurst golf course, or else they're in Satan's tanning parlor, getting a *really* bronzed look." She chuckled.

A. P. Hill made a mental note to deny all journalists' requests for interviews with her client. Eleanor Royden was irrepressible and highly quotable. She could easily become so notorious that a fair trial for her would not be possible anywhere in the hemisphere. At least she wasn't hysterical and frightened. Remorse in an accused murderer was a desirable trait, but A. P. Hill wouldn't have wanted to handle a client afflicted with the loud, wet variety.

"I brought you the bumper sticker in case you needed cheering up," she told Eleanor Royden. "Apparently, the gesture was unnecessary."

"I appreciate it, though, Sunshine. I may not be sorry I shot those two reptiles, but being in this place is absolutely the pits. So, yeah, I think I needed a day-brightener." She smirked mischievously at the young attorney. "Thank you for sharing, dear."

A. P. Hill winced, catching the sarcasm. "Don't mention it," she muttered. "Upon consideration, I'm not sure it's anything to be cheerful about."

"I heard there's another bumper sticker, too. A guard told me. One that says: *Free Eleanor Royden So She Can Shoot More Lawyers!*"

"That's *definitely* not good," said Powell Hill. "If you become notorious, you might inspire a lot of jokes, and maybe some tabloid headlines, but the stereotyping is risky. If people see you as a cartoon Annie Oakley, they won't feel any sympathy for you. If the jury decides that you are a pistol-packing vigilante, they will have no qualms about sending you to jail. Do you want to be famous or free?"

"Can I think it over?"

"Yeah, for about a nanosecond. This is the sound-bite era, when broadcast news sums up an issue in a sentence, and you don't get a second chance to project a favorable image. Nobody feels sorry for a gloating killer. What if the media's take on this story is that Jeb and Staci were two tragic lovers, gunned down by a raging jealous witch? Or to put it in your terms, suppose the movie version stars Harrison Ford and Demi Moore as Jeb and Staci?"

"They weren't like that," said Eleanor Royden. "They ought to be played by the *Jurassic Park* dinosaurs. Raptors. They were stupid, selfish, greedy raptors, and I was their prey."

"Your life depends on our ability to convince the jury to see them that way. If those twelve unimaginative people think you gunned down Harrison and Demi in Technicolor, they'll put you away for a very long time."

Eleanor Royden considered this prospect. "I still think Sally Field ought to play me," she said at last. "That's my idea of a defense. What strategy did *you* have in mind?"

"We need a *plausible* defense. I thought about temporary insanity, but that's a very hard sell to a conservative jury."

"Good," said Eleanor. "Because frankly, Sunshine, I hate the idea. I'm not going to stand up there and say I was crazy to shoot those two pit vipers. They tormented me for a couple of years, and they had every legal and financial advantage over me. I took it for as long as I could. Finally, the only thing I could use to even the score was my trusty nine-mm. Taurus."

"Let's talk about the gun, then," said A. P. Hill, abandoning philosophy. "It was registered to you. How did you happen to have it?"

"For protection," said Eleanor, shrugging. "I worked in real estate, remember? A couple of years ago here in Roanoke, a woman realtor went to show a house. The prospective customers robbed and killed her and left her body in the vacant house. After that, we all got nervous. I went down to the local gun store, and picked up the Taurus on the clerk's recommendation. I even went to the shooting range a few times to learn how to use it. How to load, shoot quickly, fire at targets in dim light, and so on. I must say it came in handy—especially that last bit."

"No," said A. P. Hill. "You must *not* say things like that. Haven't you been paying attention? I want to see a woman pushed over the edge by mental cruelty, and now racked with guilt and remorse over what she's done."

Eleanor Royden shook her head. "I'd have to *be* Sally Field to pull off that performance."

"I was afraid you'd say something like that." Powell Hill sighed. "I want you to be examined by a psychiatrist. Will you agree to that, Eleanor? The medical evaluation might consider a defense that hasn't occurred to me yet."

"How about 'Pest Control as a Public Service'?" said Eleanor with a grin.

A. P. Hill was not amused. "*Will* you talk to a psychiatrist?" she demanded.

"I suppose so." Eleanor sighed. "It would be a pity to spoil the festivities by going to an unsimpatico place like prison. I promise to behave. Now, will you get me some cigarettes and an Egyptian cotton towel, Sunshine? Benson & Hedges cigarettes, and a two-hundred-and-twenty-thread-count, undyed cotton towel. I'll definitely go crazy if I don't get some creature comforts around here."

"Good," said A. P. Hill. "If you're crazy, I can defend you."

Bill MacPherson had offered his client some coffee. Much to his consternation, she had accepted, forcing him to admit that cocoa and Earl Grey were the only beverages available in the office. "But I could run out and get you coffee," he told her. "No trouble at all."

"I can't stay that long," said Donna Jean Morgan. She looked nervous to be in a law office, even one as shabby as Bill's. She sat there in her shapeless brown dress looking like someone who is too polite to mention that her chair is on fire.

"Well, I'm glad you stopped by," said Bill. "I wondered how you were getting along."

She shrugged. "Tolerable, I guess. Things are about the same at home, but you can get used to anything after a while."

"You don't have to get used to it," said Bill, fighting the urge to raise his voice. Honestly, Donna Morgan was the modern counterpart to "The Boy Stood on the Burning Deck." "Your husband cannot get away with having two wives. Trust me on this. Here, I've written a couple of drafts of a stern letter to Chevry, explaining the errors of his ways and the possible legal ramifications. I wanted you to take a look at it before I type up a final copy for mailing."

Donna Morgan took the letter and read it slowly, blinking and whispering an occasional word aloud in her bewilderment at the intricacies of legal phrasing. "I'm sure it's very nice," she murmured politely, handing it back.

Bill slid the letter into the Morgan folder, along with local newspaper clippings about the case and a few photocopied pages from law books. He could tell by Mrs. Morgan's expression that she had not understood the contents. "In short, what it says is that we wish to warn

Reverend Chevry Morgan that he is in violation of the state law against criminal conversation—that's being unfaithful to one's spouse. It's actually *illegal*. I wonder if people realize that." He broke off for a moment, thinking about MacPherson *père*.

"I never heard of anybody getting taken to court on account of it."

"Neither have I," Bill admitted.

"Mostly, they get shot," said Donna Jean.

"Yes, well, there are other ways of handling it," Bill assured her. "The letter informs your husband that he may have broken several other laws as well as the one covering infidelity. It further states that if he does not cease his relationship with Miss Reinhardt, we plan to threaten him with legal separation, which will cost him support money on your behalf, and we conclude by saying that we may bring the local law-enforcement people into the picture, to see if they feel like arresting him for anything."

"That seems harsh, Mr. MacPherson. Not like a wife ought to speak to her husband."

"Well," said Bill, "you didn't write the letter. I did. Lawyers are trained to be harsh. Most people who are willing to listen to reason don't hear from us, and we have to be stern to get the attention of the rest."

"I don't know if that letter will help or not," said Donna Morgan. "You see, there's been a development."

Bill clutched the edge of his desk. "Not another wife?"

In spite of herself, Donna Morgan smiled. "No, sir. It's just that Tanya Faith and me had a big fight the other evening, and she set

Chevry against me, so he's decided to move out with her."

"Your husband has left you?" Bill pictured a sensational divorce trial and wondered if he ought to invest in a new suit.

"Not exactly *left* me," Donna Jean replied. "He said he'd had a new revelation from the Lord, telling him that he wasn't meant to keep two wives under one roof. Chevry says a woman's home is like a hen's nest, and that every hen has to have one of her own. He wants to give Tanya Faith a place that belongs just to him and her, and he'll move back and forth between her house and mine, every other day, or some such plan."

Bill blinked. "He's buying another house?"

"No, but there's an old one that belongs to the church. They bought it for taxes years and years ago, when they purchased the adjoining land to build the new parking lot. The old place was used as the original parsonage. It was built about 1860, same as the church was, but the church has been modernized through the years, and this place hasn't. It's big and imposing. I expect it was pretty once, but it's in a sorry state now. Still, Chevry is real handy with tools and drywall, and of course he can get the carpeting wholesale, so he thinks he can put it to rights. He's been working on it in the evenings after he finishes his day job. I'll take him over his dinner and a change of clothes for evening services, and then he'll go back and work another hour or two before bedtime. He's been feeling poorly lately. I tell him he oughtn't to overwork himself, but he's burning to get the place fixed up so that Tanya Faith can have it."

"How do you feel about that?" Bill was fascinated by this new development.

"I don't know," said Donna. "At first I was relieved to get shut of Tanya Faith, prissing around my house and giving herself airs. She won't hardly lift a finger to help in the kitchen, you know. Bone lazy. And she goes whining to Chevry if I try to make her do her part. If she had her own place, I wouldn't have to put up with her, and maybe Chevry would see what a useless little tart she is."

Bill MacPherson sighed. He had never wanted Phil Donahue's job. After more than the usual number of years in law school, all he wanted was a nice steady income, helping people draft their wills, drawing up deeds for home buyers, and defending the occasional teenage vandal or careless motorist as they faced the terrors of the legal bureaucracy. Now it had come to this. He was the fundamentalist Dear Abby, advising the parties in a bigamous marriage about how to promote their domestic tranquillity. He knew he was supposed to be on Donna Morgan's side, but he found it difficult to see life from her point of view. Every time Bill tried to put himself in Donna's place, he imagined rage and an urge for colorful revenge. These qualities were notably lacking in Mrs. Morgan the Elder. It was most perplexing. Bill felt further than ever from understanding women.

Bill tried to reason with his client. "Whether or not Tanya Faith does housework is not really the issue, Donna Jean. I don't think getting her out of your house is going to solve the problem. The problem is that your husband is committing adultery. Bigamy. Almost statutory rape. He's a sexual outlaw, Mrs. Morgan, and having two zip codes is not going to fix any of that."

Donna Jean Morgan nodded. "You go ahead and send Chevry that letter," she said. "I hope it will persuade him to send Tanya home. I just wish he'd hurry up and finish that house so that Tanya can move out."

"How long is it likely to be?" asked Bill.

"He's got the lights rewired, and last Saturday some of the men of the church helped him fix the pump on the old well so he'd have running water. Now what he's doing is mostly painting and prettifying." She gave a disapproving sniff. "He's letting *her* pick the color of the carpet. He didn't let *me* pick the color of anything in *our* house. Said the Lord meant for the man to be the decider in all things."

"Well," said Bill, "let's see if we can settle this matter before Chevry gets struck by lightning."

"Are you free for lunch?"

Bill MacPherson saw his sister, Elizabeth, in the doorway, looking tense and weary, as she usually did these days. He had been planning to invite Jerry Lawrence to lunch at Ashley's, in hopes that the assistant district attorney would be willing to trade legal second opinions for a buffet lunch. Bill wanted to know how strongly the state felt about formalized fornication, *in re* the Chevry Morgan ménage. That inquiry would have to wait, though. He could see that Elizabeth was in need

100

of company, and he felt guilty that MacPherson and Hill had been unable to provide any assignments to occupy their new investigator.

"Sure," he said, with a perfunctory glance at his appointment book. "I'm free until—well, until Thursday, actually, but something will probably turn up. Let's go to lunch."

"How are things with you?" Bill asked, when they had settled into a booth at the restaurant. He hoped that his sister would say, "Fine," as convention demands, but since those who are ill or otherwise preoccupied with themselves always take this pleasantry as a serious inquiry, Elizabeth spent several minutes answering his greeting in clinical detail.

"I wish you had something for me to do," she finished plaintively. "I think too much—and there's really no point in brooding over things I can't change."

"Powell has a murder case," said Bill. "But her client has confessed, so I don't suppose there's much to investigate. She may want you to track down character witnesses, though." He brightened at the thought. "I'll ask her."

"A murder case? Anything interesting?"

"Nothing you ought to mention to Mother," said Bill. "Powell is defending Eleanor Royden, the ex-wife of a Roanoke attorney. She shot and killed her husband and wife number two."

"Sore loser?"

"Apparently there was some provocation. I don't know too many of the details."

Elizabeth lost interest in the domestic murder in Roanoke. "What are you working on?"

"I have a bigamist," said Bill. "And a bad-check case. A house closing next week. Sorry."

Elizabeth nodded. She had not expected much drama to come out of Bill's practice. "The bigamist sounds interesting," she commented. "I trust you're not defending him?"

"No. I'm trying to get him to quit," said Bill. "His original wife is a nice dowdy woman in her fifties, who shouldn't have to put up with his shenanigans. I hope I don't turn all peculiar when I hit fifty. You don't suppose it's hereditary?"

"Maybe they'll have a cure for it by then. By the way, have you talked to Mother lately?"

"I guess so," said Bill, trying to remember. "She's all right, isn't she?"

"She's quite cheerful," said Elizabeth, not precisely answering the question. "She has a new roommate, and she'd like us both to come over for dinner so that we can get acquainted."

"A new roommate?" So great was Bill's distress that he put down his fork to pursue the subject. "It's not a man, is it?"

"Um. No."

"Well, that's a relief. So who is it?"

"An English professor named Phyllis Casey. I haven't met her yet myself, but Mother said they get along... um... like a house afire."

"That's good to hear. I'm glad the old girl's perking up again. Maybe they can take macramé classes together. Form a couple for duplicate bridge."

"A couple. Yes." Elizabeth seemed inordinately preoccupied with her salad. She hardly looked at him at all. "So, can you make it for dinner on Saturday? I promised I'd let her know."

"Oh, I guess so," said Bill. "It'll be dull, but I'll bet they're both great cooks."

Elizabeth raised her eyebrows. "The evening may surprise you."

"Well, I'm glad Mother has found a nice woman friend to spend time with, instead of some predatory man in a midlife crisis," Bill said with a happy smile. "I should have known we could trust Mother to be sensible. But you know me: I always expect the worst."

Elizabeth gave him a sad smile. "No, Bill. You don't."

Chevry Morgan set down his hammer, leaned against the old oak mantelpiece, and wished he had a cold beer. This was not a desire he would share with his parishioners, many of whom felt that Jesus had been unnecessarily frivolous when He turned the water into wine at the wedding at Cana. ("Surely grape juice would have been sufficient, and perhaps some cookies," as Mrs. Harville of the Senior Ladies' Circle phrased it.) Still, carpet laying was thirst-making work, and Chevry did not feel that the Lord intended for His servants to avoid the pleasures of the flesh. Who else had He made them for, after all?

A prophet lacking both honor and distilling facilities in his own country, Chevry saw that he would have to make do with well water instead of spirits. Donna Jean had given him sandwiches, but nothing to drink with his evening meal. She had mumbled a gruff apology for forgetting to bring a drink, and he'd let it go—but he suspected that the oversight was intentional. For a meek and God-fearing woman, Donna Jean certainly had been huffy lately. Every time he saw her, she looked like she was about to spit nails. There was no pleasing her. First, she had a hissy fit about chores, demanding that he get his sweet baby Tanya out of the house, and then when, after prayerful consideration, he took steps to do so, Donna Jean fumed about the time and expense of fixing up the new residence. He said he thought she was undergoing a crisis of faith about the Lord's new revelation, and he suggested that she pray about it. This spiritual counsel was not well received.

Chevry mopped the sweat from his brow with a big cotton handkerchief. It sure was hot in the old house, being after sunset like it was. The tin roof soaked up the sun's heat and held it for hours. He hoped that boded well for keeping the place warm in winter. He struggled to his feet, trying to ignore the aches in his legs and back. He would have to go to the kitchen and get his own drink. Wasn't that a hell of a note? A man with two wives has to get his own dad-burned glass of water.

He stumped into the kitchen, feeling sorry for himself, remembering all the envious leers he'd gotten lately from the men in the community. He knew that they must have dirty movies running in their minds when they thought of him and his domestic situation. He was glad they didn't know better. The truth was, he hadn't been getting his ashes hauled at all lately. Why, there were probably men in prison who saw more carnal action than he had seen these past few weeks. That wasn't much of a change as far as Donna Jean was concerned: sex had been boring her shitless for decades, and now that she was furious with him, she was even less inclined to perform that wifely chore. Once, long ago, he had tried to convince Donna Jean that oral sex was a marital variation of Holy Communion, but two days later she had countered with a few pertinent verses from Leviticus. Furthermore, she had threatened to bring up the matter for discussion in church if he persisted in his arguments. Billy Graham took her side in the matter, too; at least, Chevry had always suspected that the letter to Billy Graham's column in the *Roanoke Times* had come from Donna Jean.

He took a jelly glass from the sparsely stocked cupboard, blew the dust off it, and turned on the tap. The water ran rusty for half a minute, and he waited for a clear stream before filling his glass. He downed it in one gulp and filled the glass again. Then he splashed cold water on his sweaty face and hands. His backache was worse now. It occurred to him that a man could work so hard on wife maintenance that he could be too tired to reap the pleasures of connubial bliss. He'd be finished renovating this house soon, though, and then his procreative powers would return. Damn, he needed a beer.

The thought of frosty bottles of beer brightened his mood. That was one advantage to having a second home: he could keep beer in it, something Donna Jean would not permit back at the house on Pumpkin Creek. She didn't hold with imbibing liquor, not even for medicinal purposes. He'd once thought of introducing snake handling into the church services so that he would have an excuse to keep whiskey on the premises, but

Donna Jean had put the quietus on that plan, faster than the Lord had deconstructed the Tower of Babel.

She knew him entirely too well, did Donna Jean. That came of their having been married since time immemorial. She had been a pretty, shy little thing in '59, big-eyed with admiration at his white-walled red Fairlane and his Wildroot Cream Oiled hair. He had some ambitions of becoming a singer, based on a weak but pleasant baritone and a passing resemblance to Elvis Presley; but that hope had come to nothing. He lacked the drive as well as the talent to make it in country music. He was too easily distracted by revelry.

Chevry had been a wild one in those days, bad to drink and quick to throw a punch at anybody who crossed him. When you break up the furniture in a roadhouse brawl, they don't ask you back again to sing. He'd even done a month or two in the county jail for his recklessness, but Donna Jean had stuck by him. She'd never said a hard word to him, even when he drank up his pay or gambled it away in some smokehouse card game. And finally he had outgrown all the tomfoolery of sowing wild oats. He turned thirty-five and found the Lord.

Donna Jean had been so proud when he'd announced that he had felt the call to preach. She'd looked at him with shining eyes and believed that he had been summoned to the pulpit from On High. Well, maybe he had, but he could not quite block out a stubborn memory of the young, sly Chevry Morgan, sizing up a trusting congregation and thinking: This gig is easier than show business.

Sure, it was. You didn't have to be drop-dead handsome and you didn't have to be able to carry a tune. Anybody could holler. The rest of it was patter and snake-oil showmanship, and he had been born with more than his share of that. He knew the Bible well enough from childhood Sunday school (*thank you, Mama!*), and he read up on it in the evenings, looking for new material. There was some good stuff in there, too. In his opinion, the Song of Solomon was a showstopper, and anybody who thought that its meaning was metaphysical had grits for brains. He'd got himself a black suit with the trousers one size too small, and a string tie, and he'd preached fire and brimstone with a little Presley swivel to his hips, and the women — congregations are mostly women and hostages— had moaned with righteous fervor. He was hotter than Elijah's chariot.

Within a year, he had become the minister of his own little rural church, a respected man in the community, and a happy performer, with his own flock of pious fans. He wished that preaching paid well enough to let him give up carpet laying, but he was realistic about his prospects. Moses might have been able to get water from a rock, but he couldn't have got a Cadillac from a minimum-wage congregation. So be it.

The years had rolled on, and he'd stayed strong and passionate, and—with the help of Grecian Formula—young; while Donna Jean had just faded more and more each day, until her face was as gray as her hair, and her waist and ankles thickened with age and indifference. She had let herself go, all the time claiming that the Apostle Paul didn't want women to dye their hair and paint their faces. Which was fine when they died at thirty, like they mostly did in biblical times. He didn't argue with her, because fundamentalists mostly discourage vanity and artifice, but it saddened him to think of himself saddled with an old lady. She was a good woman—yes, she was; but she hadn't gotten his motor out of first gear in years.

Sex. That was the gulf between them. He thought young, and he lusted young. Donna Jean faded and didn't even care.

He reckoned Donna Jean could last until Judgment Day without another roll in the hay, and never miss it, but he was getting hornier by the hour. That's when he'd started noticing Tanya Faith at services. She was fifteen then, but she had a ripening body and a sultry look about her that could have sold apples to the seraphim guarding postserpent Eden. He'd found himself at the pulpit, preaching straight to her and gauging the success of his sermon on her reactions. The time she got up and started speaking in tongues, slumping back against him in a swoon afterward, he thought he would sweat a bucketful. How could he live out his life in tapioca nothingness with Donna when he burned for Tanya Faith?

Maybe the Lord had put the idea in his head. Chevry had got to thinking about roosters and stallions, and it suddenly occurred to him that man was not meant for monogamy. Didn't the biblical King David have scores of wives, and didn't his son Solomon have a gracious plenty, too? And God had liked both of them well enough. Surely, a modern prophet like himself was entitled to one over the limit.

The revelation of multiple wife taking had been a miracle, as far as Chevry was concerned, but, of course, Donna Jean was furious over it, and now Tanya Faith was being cold and stubborn, claiming she couldn't be a real wife until he gave her a home of her own to be a wife in. If he didn't finish these renovations soon, he'd catch pneumonia from cold showers. And now he was getting frosty letters from some lawyer in Danville, threatening him with legal action for sexual improprieties. Chevry sighed with the weariness of the unhonored prophet in an unwired kitchen. He wished the Lord had given him a little help in persuading the rest of the planet that this idea was divinely inspired, that was all.

His reverie was cut short by a howl of pain, and he bent double, clutching his abdomen and gasping for breath. His gut felt like somebody was inside him with a weed-whacker. In a wave of dizziness, he lowered himself to the kitchen floor. What the hell had Donna Jean put in those sandwiches? he thought as the decor of the room faded to black.

In the whiptail lizards, everyone is female—and the hatchlings have no biological fathers. But reproduction still requires heterosexual foreplay—the formality of copulation with males of other, still sexual, lizard species, even though they cannot impregnate the females—or a ritual pseudo-copulation with other females of the same species.
—CARL SAGAN AND ANN DRUYAN,
Shadows of Forgotten Ancestors

CHAPTER 6

Bill MacPherson hesitated as he gazed through the windshield at his mother's new home. "I didn't expect to see so many cars here. Do you think I'm dressed properly for the occasion?" he whispered to his sister. He fingered his second-best necktie and attempted to look at his reflection in the rearview mirror of his car.

"Oh, I don't think anyone will take much notice of you, Bill," Elizabeth MacPherson murmured sweetly.

"That's a great dress," he said generously. "It looks like a party frock. It's stylish. Basic black, right? I mean, it makes your point without being obtrusive."

Elizabeth raised her eyebrows. "If you mean that I'm not wearing jet beads, elbow-length black gloves, and an opaque veil, then, yes, in a simple black dress I'm not being *obtrusive*.

It doesn't matter to me whether anyone knows that I'm wearing black for mourning. *I* know."

"Sorry I mentioned it," muttered Bill. "You won't brood about it all evening, will you?"

"I never brood." Elizabeth made a mental note to disparage Bill at her next session with Dr. Freya.

They had driven out from town to attend their mother's Saturday dinner party at the home of her new roommate, Casey. Elizabeth had described it to Bill as a get-acquainted party, arranged to introduce Margaret MacPherson's family to her new set of friends. She had not managed to be more specific than that about the nature of their mother's new life, so Bill was happily unaware of anything unusual. He's so amazingly dim in social matters that he may not even notice, Elizabeth told herself. She resolved to keep a watchful eye on him, though, for the duration of the evening.

Margaret MacPherson's hand-drawn map had led them down a pleasant country road into the rolling green hills of the county, and finally up a long, graveled drive to a two-story white farmhouse, gleaming in the last rays of the evening sun. "This looks quite homey," Bill remarked as he maneuvered the car onto the grass beside half a dozen vehicles belonging to the other dinner guests. "Very nice. Two women on a farm, managing on their own. Reminds me of a book by somebody or other."

"D. H. Lawrence?" Elizabeth suggested.

"No, that wasn't it," said Bill, frowning with the effort of recollection. "I think it was a chapter in *Huckleberry Finn.* Or was it *Anne of Green Gables*?"

"Never mind," said Elizabeth. "It isn't a working farm, anyhow. Mother says they plan to have a small herb-and-vegetable garden, and maybe a few free-run chickens, but nothing in the way of major crops or livestock."

"Good, because Mother never took any agriculture courses at the community college, did she? Just conversational Spanish and macramé."

"I believe she's been branching out lately," murmured Elizabeth, thinking of the unfortunate white-water rafting episode the previous spring.

"But not into farming, I hope," said Bill. "I was afraid that sooner or later we might be invited to a barn raising."

"No," said Elizabeth. "Since Phyllis Casey is an English professor, specializing in nineteenth-century literature, I doubt you're qualified to give her any help whatsoever."

They got out of the car and walked to the front porch. "Maybe we should have brought a housewarming gift," Elizabeth murmured, with a last anxious glance at the lawn full of strange cars.

"I have some root beer in the trunk," said Bill. "Some pork and beans, too. Actually, I forgot to unload the groceries this morning."

Elizabeth shuddered. "Never mind. We'll bring flowers next time."

"Okay. Well, is there anything else I should know about this party?"

Elizabeth's hand froze in midair on its way to the door knocker. "Why? What do you mean?"

"Oh, you know. Taboo subjects? Is the new

roomie a Republican, or a vegetarian, or a fan of pro wrestling? Any conversational hints?"

His sister shrugged. "I've never met her," she said truthfully. She hit the knocker against the brass plate. "You might not want to say anything caustic about k.d.lang. Otherwise, just be your usual charming self."

Bill was still trying to place k.d.lang within the ranks of nineteenth-century authors when, moments later, the door opened, and a beaming Margaret MacPherson ushered them in. "Just in time!" she said. "The hors d'oeuvres have just come out of the oven. Come in and meet everybody."

She led them into a cozy parlor with a freshly polished pine floor, overstuffed sofas covered in rose chintz, and a collection of large, well-tended plants, all of which were visible only in glimpses around various clumps of people. The guests were congregated in groups of three and four, laughing and talking over Celtic harp music in stereo, most of them holding glasses of white wine or balancing paper plates on their laps.

"Do you know anybody?" Bill whispered to Elizabeth.

"No," she hissed back through an unmoving smile. "Just wing it."

"There certainly are a lot of women here," Bill muttered. "You don't think Mother's trying to match me up with someone, do you?"

"I think it's... unlikely," Elizabeth assured him.

A hasty round of introductions told them that the guests were all members of the college English department or professors from neighboring colleges or local artists. Elizabeth tried to keep track of the names and faces as they gathered around while her mother plowed through the traditional sound-bite résumés of such gatherings. "Bill and Elizabeth, my children—everybody. He's a lawyer, and she's a forensic anthropologist, currently unemployed."

"Mother!"

"But she has a Ph.D. Bill, Elizabeth, I'd like you to meet Megan Holden-McBryde, of the English department. She's working on feminist critical theory in the works of Jack London, and this is her husband, Skip Holden-McBryde, who is a poet."

Elizabeth shook hands with the willowy couple in matching running suits. "Ah. A poet," she murmured, hoping that he was in the dormant phase of the condition.

"Here are Sadie Patton and Annie Graham-Robeson, feminist deconstructionists." She nodded toward two heavyset women in their early fifties.

"Architects!" said Bill with a happy smile.

There was a brief pause while everyone tried to think of a quick way to explain literary theory on a third-grade level. Simultaneously, everyone gave up. "Something like that, dear," said his mother, shrugging. "Miriam Malone, a kinetic sculptor. She does the most marvelous things with bathtub toys floating in blue mouthwash. And Tim Burruss, who coaches wrestling. They're not together—his lover can't be with us this evening."

Elizabeth was about to mention her own

bereavement-presumptive, when Tim said, "He's driving a stock car at the speedway tonight. I said, 'You can break your neck if you want to, but don't expect me to go and watch.' "

"—And this is Virgil Agnew, who's in theatre and dance."

"He's our token heterosexual," said Sadie (or possibly Annie).

"I'm in therapy for it, though," Virgil informed them. He thrust his hands into the pockets of his tweed jacket and frowned at nothing in particular.

Elizabeth ignored Bill's elbow in her ribs. "Token hetero—wait!" she exclaimed. "I thought you said Megan and Skip were married."

Megan Holden-McBryde nodded happily. "We are. But actually I am a gay man trapped in a woman's body. I had past life regression and discovered that I used to be a medical student in turn-of-the-century London. I was a friend of Oscar Wilde. It explained so much."

Skip put his arm around his spouse's shoulders. "So we feel that we really count as a gay couple."

After a short, leaden silence, Annie (or Sadie) remarked to Bill, "I have a son who practices law."

"You have a son?" Since Bill's brain was completely occupied in reformatting a mental image of his mother, he was in no condition to think before he spoke.

"Oh, yes. And two grandchildren."

"Three if you count the step-grandchildren from your third marriage," her partner observed.

"Third marriage?"

She nodded. "Sadie and I have only been together two years. Between us, we've had five husbands."

"Political lesbians?" asked Elizabeth, who thought she was beginning to get it all sorted out.

"No. That would be D. J. Squires, over by the fireplace, talking to Barnie Slusher, the chemistry professor." She nodded toward a scowling young woman with close-cropped blonde hair, a leather biker's outfit, and riding boots. She looked like the title character in a postmodern production of Shaw's *Saint Joan*. "D.J. is a feminist historian, and she said that when she realized as an undergraduate that all seductions are a form of rape, and that marriage would mean sleeping with the enemy, she just broke off her engagement to the star quarterback. She contends that she's never looked back."

"It has done wonders for her career," Tim Burruss remarked. "She'll be one of the youngest tenured professors ever. If she makes it, I mean."

"She'd better make it," grunted Sadie. "The university couldn't afford to fight the discrimination suit she'd bring if they turned her down."

"And this is Casey," said Margaret MacPherson, with an air of saving the best for last.

Phyllis Casey, who had just come in from the kitchen, was a small, tanned woman who appeared to be in her late forties, handsome in a well-scrubbed and athletic way. She was wearing a tunic and long skirt of natural linen, and her long hair was woven into a thick braid.

She set down the tray of canapés, and gave Bill and Elizabeth each a hug. "Margaret's children. So nice to finally meet you."

Bill kept trying to make eye contact with Elizabeth, but she was studiously avoiding him. "Nice to meet you, too," he said with an anxious smile.

"It's a lovely house," said Elizabeth.

"Yes, it has a lot of space. Margaret and I have turned the spare bedrooms into home offices."

Before Bill could figure out where the conversation was going next, someone tapped him on the arm.

"Your mother said that you are a lawyer," said the earnest-looking young woman. She had long, crinkly brown hair, adorned with a white flower over one ear and dangling earrings in the shape of dolphins nose to nose.

"A lawyer. That's right," said Bill, with an inward groan. He hoped that the inevitable legal question was going to be one that he could answer with some measure of confidence. He balanced his paper plate on one palm, in case she was the earnest handshaking sort. "And you are... ?"

She blushed. "Oh, my name is Miriam Malone. I'm called Miri. I'm from Florida, but I've moved up here to teach in the art department. I sculpt. Didn't your mother mention me? I thought she might have."

Bill shook his head, wondering if he had time to eat a stuffed mushroom before he had to speak again. He risked it.

"I wanted to consult you, in a general sort of way, about a legal matter. Your mother suggested it, actually. She says you're a specialist in family law. Would you like to go out into the garden?"

What Bill truly wanted was to stay close to the refreshment table—and to rely upon the adage of safety in numbers. He thought briefly of clutching the piano leg to keep from being dragged away into the silent, threatening garden by this earnest and humorless Amazon, but a glance around at the chattering guests, oblivious to his plight, told him that it was no use. He might as well go bravely to the doom his mother had obviously arranged for him, and get it over with. "Certainly," he said, feeling like the pig at the luau.

She led him through the kitchen, out the back door, and onto a wooden deck surrounded by scraggly rosebushes. Bill wished he'd had the presence of mind to remember his drink. He leaned against the wooden railing of the deck and gave her his most attentive and professional young-attorney smile. "What can I do for you?"

"I want to get married," said Miri Malone.

"Where is Bill?" asked Margaret MacPherson. "I've hardly seen him since he got here."

"Mingling, I expect," said Elizabeth, without any noticeable concern for her missing sibling. "I hope he's remembering to pass out business cards."

"Well, perhaps he's enjoying himself. I think it's going rather well, don't you?"

"It is," said Elizabeth, glancing around the

room. "It's certainly different from the get-togethers you and Dad used to host. All the men would congregate around a televised football game, or else they'd take over the living room and fill it with smoke and loud guffaws."

Her mother nodded sadly. "Yes, and the women would gather in the kitchen and talk about the children, or the weather, or linoleum—God knows what we talked about. I don't know that I was listening."

"Were you unhappy?" asked Elizabeth, surprised at this revisionist account of her childhood. "*I* thought you all were incredibly boring, but I didn't know that you minded."

"Perhaps I didn't at the time," said Margaret thoughtfully. "I didn't have much to compare it with. Men don't generally talk to women, you know. They simply listen until they can figure out what one sentence will end the discussion. Then they say, 'Buy it,' or 'Take another aspirin,' or 'Whatever you decide will be fine, dear.' That said, they dismiss you from the universe entirely, and go back to the newspaper, or the instant replay, or whatever constitutes reality to them at the moment."

"And now you have someone who will talk to you?"

"Well... there is always something to talk about in new relationships, so I can't be sure that things will turn out differently this time, but it's all very *interesting*." She wandered away then, picking up empty glasses and exchanging a word or two with each guest as she passed.

Elizabeth began to mingle, or at least she stood

hesitantly on the fringe of one group after another, trying to find a conversational opening. Most of it, though, escaped her completely. Barnie Slusher was telling Virgil Agnew and Annie Graham-Robeson about his difficulties in getting anyone to install asymmetrical slate flooring in his newly redecorated kitchen. The Holden-McBrydes and Sadie Patton were debating the merits of the Montessori school versus home teaching; and D. J. Squires and Tim Burruss had taken beers and a basket of tortilla chips into the other room to watch a Cincinnati Reds game on television. Everyone else was talking about university politics. Elizabeth sat down on the sofa and began to leaf through the latest issue of *Vanity Fair.*

"Married," said Bill, clutching the railing of the deck for support. "Yes, well, that's refreshing, but... you see ..."

"Not to *you*." Miri Malone rolled her eyes in exasperation. "I wanted to *consult* with you about it. You do specialize in family law, don't you?"

"I don't seem to be able to escape from it," said Bill. "What did you have in mind? Prenuptial agreements? Community property laws?"

"It isn't a question of money," the young woman said. "We love each other and we want to get married. But some states have laws against it."

"Interracial laws?" said Bill. "Not anymore. Those statutes were done away with years ago. *Loving* v. *the Commonwealth of Virginia* was the Supreme Court decision making that dis-

120

crimination illegal. So you and your fiancé—er, your fiancé is male, isn't he?"

Miri smiled. "Very much so."

"And you are female?" *The Crying Game* had taught Bill that it isn't safe to make any assumptions, regardless of what common sense tells you.

"Yes, I'm definitely female. Would you like to see my driver's license?"

"I'm not sure the DMV is in a position to testify on the matter," murmured Bill. "Well, never mind. So he's male, and you're female." Another thought struck him. Not the Morgan Family Trio again! "He's not *already* married, is he? And planning to stay that way?"

"No. He's a dolphin. I met him when I was living in Florida."

"Great!" said Bill. "Do you think they'll make the play-offs this year? Does he know Larry Czonka?"

Miri's stare was withering. "Not a *Miami* Dolphin," she said. "A *delphinidae* dolphin."

"You mean like Flipper?"

"That's a demeaning stereotype. Dolphins are extremely intelligent and sensitive. They have a spiritual nature which is quite beautiful. They are not, of course, vegetarians, but aside from that they are in perfect harmony with our New Age philosophies of ecology and sharing the planet."

"Well—can't you just be friends?" stammered Bill.

"Why can't I marry a dolphin?" she demanded.

Bill smiled. That was an easy one. "He can't walk. He can't talk. And he can't sign the papers."

"Neither can Stephen Hawking, but you'd let me marry *him*."

Bill was shocked at her flippancy toward the disabled physicist. "Oh, look here, you mustn't—"

"Don't be so patronizing," she said. "Anyhow, let me tell you about Stephen Hawking. I know he's paralyzed with ALS and for the past decade he has only been able to move the little finger of his left hand. *But* a couple of years ago, he left his wife for another woman!"

"How?" said Bill, momentarily diverted from the legal problems of maritime mammals.

She threw up her hands. "How should I know! He just rolled away. He took off with his nurse. It was in *Discover* magazine a while back. When I read about that, I said: this is absolutely the last straw! If you can't trust a man even when he's paralyzed from the neck down, you don't have a cat's chance of getting any of them to be faithful. I said to hell with it, and I decided that if feminists can become political lesbians, then an animal-rights person like myself ought to be able to become a political delphinogamist. Human males are no damned good."

"Now you're stereotyping *my* species."

"Oh, rubbish. It's a fact. Men remind me of those poor male spiders who keep trying to mate even after their heads have been bitten off. I mean, it is your entire *raison d'àtre*. No, I'm through with Homo sapiens. From now on, give me a dolphin."

Bill was beginning to conclude that modern relationships for men very much resembled trying to mate while having your head bitten off, but he wisely returned to the original topic. "Even so, I'm afraid you can't marry a dolphin. Not legally anyhow. I suppose you could get a scuba-diving Unitarian to come to the holding tank and—"

"I want it to be legal. It's a matter of principle."

"But dolphins aren't intelligent. I mean, they sort of are, but—"

"Marie Osmond is married, isn't she?" snapped Miri. They both laughed. "And all joking aside, intelligence is not a criterion for matrimony."

"Good thing, or none of us would be here," said Bill.

"I mean, learning-disabled people can marry, can't they? Even if they can't read or write?"

"Yes, all right, I concede that point," said Bill. He was beginning to think that the law had lost a great trial attorney when Miri Malone took up art with bathtub toys. "But there are laws, you know, against having sex with a helpless creature. I know there are statutes on the books concerning sheep, and chickens, and who-knows-what-else. I think those proscriptions could apply to dolphins."

She let out a whoop of laughter. "You don't know much about dolphins, do you?"

"Not a great deal, no. But my brother-in-law is — *was*—a marine biologist." For more reasons than one, Bill wished that Cameron Dawson were present. He was running short of arguments, and he had exhausted his limited supply of knowledge about seagoing mammals.

"Ask your brother-in-law then," said Miri. "It's common knowledge. Dolphins are notorious for trying to mate with their trainers at marine parks like Sea World. Believe me, it wouldn't be rape. In fact, our whole relationship was originally Porky's idea."

"Porky?"

"My intended. It was just a physical thing on his part at first, but I was able to learn some of his language, and so our relationship progressed into a much deeper friendship."

Bill knew that if the words *Free Willy* flashed into his mind one more time, he would fall to the floor, shrieking helplessly. A movement from the kitchen doorway caught his attention, and he turned to see his sister, beckoning for him to come back inside. Bill reached in his pocket and drew out a business card. "Here's where to find me," he told Miri. "I charge sixty bucks an hour. If you really want to pursue this matter legally, give me a call."

"Thanks for rescuing me," he said to Elizabeth as he closed the door behind him. Miri was walking in the garden. "I seem to attract them. That woman wants to marry a dolphin."

"I expect she's a Pisces," said Elizabeth. "But I don't know that I've rescued you. Edith is on the phone. She said that A. P. Hill asked her to call you."

"That's odd," said Bill. "They're never that anxious to reach me. I gave them this number in case of some emergency. We've never had one, but Powell is always prepared for every contingency. What does she want?"

"Well, she asked if I could interview some

124

witnesses tomorrow for A.P.'s murder case, but that wasn't the main reason she called. Ask her yourself." She handed Bill the telephone and went back to join the party.

"Edith?" said Bill, half expecting to hear the crackle of flames in the background. "What's wrong?"

"Calm down," said his secretary. "Nobody is repossessing the copy machine. A.P. asked me to phone because there has been a development in one of your cases."

"Which one?"

"The Morganatic Marriage case."

"Not *another* wife!" wailed Bill. "Listen, I've had a very trying day here, and—"

"A trying day is exactly what your partner reckons you're in for. You see, the old buzzard himself, Chevry Morgan, keeled over dead last night, and wife number one says the police are asking all sorts of awkward questions about it. They seem to think it's a case of murder. Your client is understandably nervous about the implications of that."

"How did he die?"

"They've pumped for poison," said Edith. "He's been sent off for an autopsy. Wonder if they'll find a brain?"

"Now, Edith, the man is dead."

"Yeah. This time I believe he *did* get a message from the Lord. But apparently the Almighty had a little help in deporting old Chevry from the world."

"They think somebody deliberately poisoned Mr. Morgan? They haven't charged Donna Jean, have they?"

"No. She's at home, but we got the impression that she'd be awfully glad to see you."

"I'm on my way," said Bill.

After delegating the tracking down of Bill MacPherson to the secretary, A. P. Hill had set off to Roanoke to interview a possible character witness in the Royden murder case. Most of the Royden acquaintances she would leave for Elizabeth MacPherson, but she wanted to hear firsthand what Marizel Farrell had to say about her former best friend.

At Eleanor Royden's suggestion—grudgingly given—A. P. Hill had contacted Marizel Farrell by phone. After endless reassurances of confidentiality, Mrs. Farrell had provided the attorney with directions to her home in Chambord Oaks. The upscale subdivision was much as A. P. Hill expected. A bronze sign in Old English lettering mounted on one of the stone pillars marked the entrance to the development. The two-story brick houses all looked as if they had been designed by the same architect, differing only in the placement of the Palladian windows, or in the facade: phony Colonial, sham Tudor, or faux château.

Marizel Farrell's house turned out to be a white brick faux château, set among clumps of azaleas and strategically placed dogwood trees. A bas-relief of mallards in flight graced the simulated wood mailbox. A. P. Hill pulled into the drive, vowing for the umpteenth time in her life that suburbia would never take her alive. She retrieved her briefcase from the backseat and went up the patterned brick walkway to interview the murderess's best friend.

Marizel Farrell did not seem altogether

impressed by the diminutive young attorney standing on her doormat. Powell Hill was wearing low-heeled shoes, no makeup, and tiny pearl earrings. "You're Eleanor's lawyer?" Mrs. Farrell said doubtfully, as if she suspected that the leather attaché was a sampler case of Girl Scout cookies. "Well, come in, then, Ms.—er—Hill. Sorry," she said, with an anxious smile, "I was kind of expecting a grown-up."

Women twenty years older than A. P. Hill might have taken this feeble witticism as a compliment, but tributes to Powell's youthfulness were wasted on a woman who took offense at waiters who requested an ID before bringing her a glass of wine. She knew better than to antagonize a potential witness, however; so she managed a semblance of pleasantry as the slender, blonde woman in the Donna Karan suit led her into the house.

"I just can't believe that Eleanor actually did it," said Marizel Farrell, after they had settled in the white-and-gold living room. "Shot Jeb, I mean."

"Why can't you believe it?" asked A. P. Hill, noting the date and time at the top of her yellow legal pad. She also wrote down Mrs. Farrell's name and address, estimating her age at an accurate, but unflattering fifty-five.

Marizel spread her hands in a helpless little shrug. "Well, because it's such a trashy thing to do. I mean, people shoot each other in trailer parks, for God's sake, not in Chambord Oaks."

"I see," said A. P. Hill, deciding to forgo the lecture in sociology that was probably called for. "Tell me about them as a couple. How did you meet them?"

"How does one meet anyone?" said Marizel Farrell with her wide-eyed stare. "Our husbands were not colleagues. Jeb was a lawyer; Arthur is a surgeon. But we were in that professional social set—in some ways, Roanoke is a very small town. I suppose we attended the same dinner party, or got put at the same table at a charity event. I can't really remember. We've known them for a dozen years at least."

A. P. Hill's eyebrows maintained a steadfast neutrality. "Eleanor Royden says that you were her closest friend."

"How terribly sad," said Marizel Farrell, shaking her head, more in anger than in sorrow. "You know, she was once quite a nice person, always fun to be around, and very energetic. We co-chaired a couple of symphony fund-raisers together back in the mid Eighties, and at the Homeless Shelter Gala, we shared a table with the Roydens. Let me see... and bridge and tennis. I mean, I *saw* a lot of Eleanor, you know—the way one does; that is, until lately, when she had to get a *job*, and became very arch and brittle about her reduced circumstances, and then, of course, one simply had to stop seeing her. One was embarrassed."

A. P. Hill looked up from her notes. "So she didn't confide in you about her frustration over the divorce?"

"I'd hardly call it confiding," said Marizel Farrell with a little laugh. "She certainly complained about it constantly to anyone who would listen. And she tried to be amusing about it. I'll give her that. But, really, what could one do? She didn't belong to the club anymore, and she couldn't afford the usual outings of the old set, and her job kept her from the women-only socializing in the daytime. I went to lunch with her a couple of times downtown when she started working, and once I took her to the ballet on Arthur's ticket when he had an emergency at the hospital, but I felt quite awkward around her. What could one *say* to her? Of course, we all thought Jeb's behavior was dreadful."

"I understand that it was a bitter divorce."

"Oh, it was! But Eleanor was partly to blame for that, too. Jeb Royden was a cold, calculating attorney who had gotten his own way all his life. He could be completely charming as long as no one stood in his way. And of course he had a fling with a younger woman. I mean, it's utterly *commonplace*. Men are quite childlike, really. The minute their hair starts thinning out and their eyes require reading glasses, they start looking for Band-Aids for the ego. You just ignore it as long as you can and hope it wears off. We tried to tell Eleanor that at first! Much good it did."

A. P. Hill, who came from a different generation than Mrs. Farrell, was privately in sympathy with Eleanor Royden's attitude. In fact, she thought, her own behavior in similar circumstances could be used as a training film for terrorists; wisely, she refrained from expressing this opinion. "So you all thought that Mr. Royden would have his fling without resorting to divorce?"

"Well, they usually do," said Marizel. "I got a new Mercedes after Arthur's little indiscretion, but then I earned it. I was sweet as pie the entire time and I never once reproached him or let him see me cry."

129

This was Martian to A. P. Hill, but she merely nodded for Mrs. Farrell to continue.

"I told Eleanor not to throw tantrums over it. We all learned how to suffer in silence, but, oh no!—Miss High-and-Mighty Eleanor was too proud to be sensible. She made scenes in public. She confronted the bimbo and she screamed at Jeb and argued with him, until he had to leave her. Jeb Royden wasn't the sort of man to let his wife tell him what to do. She made him furious and he walked out." Marizel Farrell shrugged. "Then, of course, he set out to punish Eleanor with the divorce court's version of the siege of Leningrad."

"So you thought that Mrs. Royden's ex-husband was being vindictive?"

"My dear, he *was*! Jeb wanted to have his own way, without any arguments, and when Eleanor wouldn't agree to that, he set out to destroy her for being uppity. They're all like that. Anybody could have told her. Of course, he thought he would ruin her financially, and send her off to work as a waitress and live in a trailer, while he built a palace for the new playmate. I suppose he underestimated Eleanor, though."

A. P. Hill nodded, suppressing a smile. "She refused to take the thunderbolt lying down."

"Yes—and of course, we're all terribly sympathetic with poor Eleanor, even though she brought it on herself. At first we thought of having a benefit luncheon at the club to raise money for her defense fund, but then we were afraid that our husbands might not care for the idea. You will give her my best, though, won't you, dear?"

"I'll give her *my* best," said A. P. Hill.

CHAPTER 7

It wasn't something that he would admit to another adult, but sometimes when he was getting ready for work, Bill MacPherson would watch *Mister Rogers* on his tiny black-and-white television. Occasionally when he was meeting with clients, Bill found it comforting to think of the calm and sensible Mister Rogers, who never seemed to be shocked or angered by anything. A succession of petty criminals, sullen teenage vandals, and vicious divorcing couples had convinced Bill that he and Mister Rogers did not live in the same neighborhood; today he had begun to wonder if they lived on the same planet. Dolphin weddings and dead polygamists seemed beyond the scope of any wisdom within Fred Rogers's power to impart. Bill was on his own.

Now, as he followed Edith's telephone directions to Donna Morgan's house, he tried to think where to go from here, but he knew it was too soon to make any decisions on the matter. Chevry Morgan was dead, which meant that he no longer needed to pursue a case of possible bigamy against the man. Whether Donna Jean Morgan would have further need of his services in a criminal capacity remained to be seen.

He found the house without difficulty. It was a one-story white frame house, with a green-striped awning over the front porch. It sat back from the blacktop road, flanked by a grove of pine trees. Donna Jean Morgan was in the front yard, near the plaster deer, weeding the bed of pansies set out in the whitewashed truck tire. She was alone.

Bill eased the car up the bumpy dirt driveway, sighing with relief that a contingent of police cars was not in evidence. Donna Jean, straw hat and gardening trowel in hand, came to meet him. Her dumpling face was splotched from crying, and her gray hair was scraggly and uncombed. She wore a faded housedress and men's high-top sneakers.

"I just had to do something," she said, pointing to the flower bed. "I thought that if I sat in that house one more minute, listening to the phone ring, I'd go right out of my mind. It's not that I don't grieve for poor darlin' Chevry. You understand, don't you?"

Bill nodded. All except the grieving part, he thought. "If you are saddened, then I'm very sorry that your husband is dead," he said, choosing his words carefully. As humanity went, he privately thought the world could spare Mr. Morgan and never miss him. He wondered if Chevry had possessed the forethought to prepare a will, but decided that it would have been out of character. Just as well for Donna Jean, too. A court fight could eat up an estate in no time.

"Where's Tanya Faith?" he asked.

"Over to her parents." Donna Jean dabbed at her eyes. "She left as soon as we heard."

"Can you tell me what happened?"

She led him to a shaded circle of lawn chairs in back of the house. Bill had to decline lemonade, coffee, homemade pound cake, and a footstool before he could get her to sit down in the canvas chair and focus on the problem at hand. Finally, after a quick trip into the kitchen for a box of tissues for herself, Donna Jean was ready to talk. "Chevry went off last night, like he always did these days, to fix up that big old house next to the church for him and Tanya Faith. He came by here first, because I always packed him some supper to take along while he worked."

Bill had vowed not to interrupt, but he heard himself say, "Why didn't Tanya do that?"

Donna Jean gave him a tearful smile. "Oh, honey, Tanya Faith can't hardly *spell* cook. Anyhow, I packed his food, and—"

"Wait." Bill pulled out his pocket notepad. "I'd better get this down. Exactly what did you give him to eat?"

"Well, I had some ham left over from Sunday dinner, and I made him some potato salad, because he's always been partial to it. I put in some bread-and-butter pickles that I made back in the summer, and I gave him a plastic margarine tub full of leftover baked beans. There was four or five fresh-baked biscuits, too, and a baby-food jar with homemade grape jelly in it. And a couple of homemade doughnuts. Chevry always said that working gave him an appetite."

"Did anyone else eat this food?"

"Only me," said Donna Jean Morgan. "And

133

there's just my word on that. Tanya Faith is what you call a picky eater. She had ice cream for dinner, and then she went next door to baby-sit for the neighbor's little girl. So she didn't see what I ate."

"Okay. Then what?"

"Well, he didn't come back last night. I went on to bed early, same as always, and Tanya Faith sat up awhile, wondering why he hadn't come home, but she couldn't drive, so she just fretted about it until nearly midnight. Finally she called her daddy, and he drove over to the old house, and found Chevry laid out in the kitchen, soiled with his own upchuck—"

She broke off here and covered her face with a clean tissue.

Bill waited until the sobs subsided. "Was he dead?"

"Not then. Reinhardt called the rescue squad, and they took him off to the hospital in Danville, but it wasn't no use. He kept on being sick right along, and finally his heart gave out from the strain of the convulsions. He died around six this morning. The sheriff's department was here by eight."

"What did they say?"

"The sheriff's deputy—a Mr. Brower; nice, polite-spoken feller—he told me that Chevry had died under suspicious circumstances. The doctors in Danville were insisting on an autopsy and saying that they thought Chevry might have been poisoned. Mr. Brower knew all about Chevry's marital situation, and he seemed to think that had a bearing on the case."

"Well, Chevry's behavior would inspire many wives to poison."

134

"I preferred prayer," said Donna Jean. "So, anyhow, they've sent his body off to the medical examiner and they're testing all the leftover food that was in the kitchen. Now we have to wait and see what the report says."

"Maybe it was food poisoning," said Bill, putting away his notebook. "If you made the potato salad with mayonnaise, it could have easily gone bad and caused the poisoning symptoms. I don't think you have anything to worry about, Mrs. Morgan."

"Yes, I do," said Donna Jean. "My maiden name was Todhunter."

A. P. Hill was in conference with her client. She was by far the more apprehensive of the two, pacing back and forth, her fists clenched at her sides. Eleanor Royden, looking wan but alert in an unflattering green prison shift, was buffing her nails and watching her attorney with an expression of polite interest.

"What's eating you, Sunshine?" she finally asked.

"This case," said Powell Hill, through clenched teeth. "I'm wondering if I ought to resign."

Eleanor raised her eyebrows. "Was it something I said?" she murmured.

"It's something everybody said! The district attorney's office sent a wreath to your husband's funeral. None of them can say your name without grimacing. And your so-called friend Marizel wouldn't spit on you if you were on fire, so don't expect to build any defense on *her* support. And then there's you! You sit here gloating about committing two murders, and collecting case-related bumper stickers! And I'm supposed to *defend* you. How am I supposed to contend with all that?"

Her client shrugged. "Considering your hourly rate, what did you expect? An easy acquittal? Charlie Manson's fingerprints at the crime scene?"

"It's not that." Powell Hill sighed. "I don't mind hard work. I don't even mind the fact that you shot them, and that you've admitted it. I'm just worried that my best work won't be *good* enough in this case. The state is going to ask for the death penalty, and I'm afraid the jury will give it to them. I don't know if I can live with that."

"*I* certainly can't," Eleanor observed.

"There you go again, Mrs. Royden. Making jokes about your situation as if it were a community theatre production instead of literally life and death. You may not take all this seriously, but I do. And I wonder if somebody else could do a better job of defending you. Someone with more experience."

Eleanor Royden smiled. "Do you propose that I be defended by a—what was that picturesque term you had for my husband's more *distinguished* male colleagues?"

A. P. Hill hung her head. "A silverback," she muttered. "But silverbacks *can* be awfully effective. They have the experience, the connections, and the know-how to beat the system—if they choose to. Maybe you'd be better off with one of them defending you. Mrs. Royden, I'm almost as much of an outcast as you are."

"That seems fitting to me," said the defendant. "At least I know that I can trust you. You won't make secret deals behind my back, or urge me to plea-bargain for the sake of your own fee schedule or your legal reputation. If we go down, it's together. I like that. Marriage used to work that way; now you have to try to find an attorney who'll promise to be with you till death do us part." She nodded. "Yes, I do like that."

A. P. Hill managed a faint smile in return. "That's very brave of you, Mrs. Royden, but I'm not sure I want to play the Sundance Kid in your production. You're the one who might be sentenced to die. Will I be able to prevent that? I just got out of law school last year. My grades were excellent, but my trial experience is minimal, and I keep thinking that you deserve better representation."

Eleanor Royden put down her nail file and looked up at her attorney with an expression bordering on seriousness. "Amy Powell Hill, on your honor as an officer of the court, do you swear that you personally believe that I killed Jeb and Staci Royden *with provocation?*"

A. P. Hill stopped in midstride, her mouth open. After a moment she continued. "Provocation? Yes, I guess I do."

"Good. Then you ought to be able to convince a jury of that, Sunshine. Till death do us part, then?"

A. P. Hill extended her hand. "Till death do us part."

"Todhunter," said Bill MacPherson, puzzled by his client's worried expression. What did Mrs. Morgan's maiden name have to do with her husband's sudden death? "That's rather an unusual name."

"It's pretty famous around here," said Donna Jean.

Bill mulled it over, trying to figure out why the name sounded familiar. Finally it hit him—and his stomach lurched with a sudden, unpleasant realization. "Not old Lucy Todhunter! Lethal Lucy?"

Donna Jean Morgan nodded mournfully. "That's what they call her. Only the poison was supposed to have been in a doughnut, I think. Lucy Todhunter was my great-grandmother. Of course, she had been dead for years and years, so nobody in the family ever knew her, but the fact that she poisoned her husband was common knowledge. The menfolk in the family used to joke about it at weddings. I remember they said something about it to Chevry at the reception when I married him. Funny, isn't it?"

Not if they can find somebody who remembers them saying it, Bill thought. Aloud he said, "But I thought Lucy Todhunter was acquitted of murdering her husband." His knowledge of the case was hazy, based more on hand-me-down references than on any familiarity with the trial records. He knew she hadn't been hanged, because A. P. Hill kept track of such things.

"She got off, all right. But people always said it was because she outsmarted the law. Nobody ever doubted that she did it."

Bill MacPherson nodded sympathetically. "Like Lizzie Borden. No one remembers that she wasn't convicted. Of course, I think she

138

was guilty, too. But the Lucy Todhunter case was more than a century ago. What difference does it make now?"

"My great-grandmother was a notorious poisoner. People think she killed her husband," said Donna Jean patiently. "My husband Chevry just died of poisoning. Don't you think a jury will put those two facts together?"

"I hope not," said Bill. "I know for sure that the information about your great-grand-mother absolutely cannot be introduced into the evidence at the trial. If there is a trial, I mean. They don't even have the autopsy report yet. Your husband may have died of nat-ural causes."

"Not Chevry," said his widow mournfully. "He never was one to take the easy way out. I just know what folks will be saying. If they can't prove how Chevry was poisoned, they'll reckon that Lucy Todhunter passed her secret down to me—how to poison your husband and get away with it. Maybe nobody will come right out and say it in court, but the word will get around. Small towns have long memories."

"All right," said Bill. "I'll have our inves-tigator look into Lethal Lucy's trial. Maybe she was innocent, too. And you promise me that if any law-enforcement people come by to question you, you will ask for permission to call your lawyer—and you won't answer any-thing until I get here. Is that understood? Before you even offer them pound cake, you call me."

"You think they'll be back, then?" asked Donna Jean.

"Oh, maybe not," said Bill. "I'm just taking every precaution to ensure your safety." Privately he would have bet a year's rent that she'd be seeing badges before the week was out.

"I am not a distrustful or cynical person," said Elizabeth MacPherson, eyeing a pizza deliveryman who looked suspiciously like her brother, Bill. "But when you turn up at my door at ten in the evening bearing pepperoni and mushrooms, with a look of canine eagerness on your face, I am bound to ask you what inconvenient task you want me to perform."

"May I come in?" asked Bill, wisely deciding to defer the debate until after the bribe had been taken.

"Oh, all right," his sister grumbled, standing aside. For her indeterminate stay in Danville, Elizabeth had taken an apartment in the same building as A. P. Hill, although they saw little of each other as neighbors. Elizabeth was not feeling very sociable most of the time. Still, when she heard the knock at her door that evening, she was glad of the company—not that she would have admitted such a thing to her older brother, who was standing there exuding pizza fumes with a fatuous smile.

She ushered him in. "I suppose you want to talk about this emergency that called you away from Mother's party. Since you came bearing high-calorie gifts, I suppose I'll listen to your unreasonable requests. Lucky for you that Mother has decided to forgo the serving of actual food at her parties these days."

"Really? I'm sorry I missed it—intellectually, I mean. I'm sure my stomach profited by my absence. What did you have for dinner?"

Elizabeth scowled. "Library paste. Put the pizza box on the coffee table while I get us some Cokes from the kitchen. Actually, I had decided for the sake of my diet, not to mention my cholesterol, not to eat for the remainder of the evening." She set a tray of plates and glasses down beside the pizza. "And I was just regretting it. You are an angel unawares."

"How gratifying," said Bill, helping himself to the largest slice. "I thought you didn't trust me."

"I don't. I am under no illusions as to which sort of angel you represent. The tropical kind, I am sure. If you tell me what you want now, will it put me off my food?"

"I doubt it," said Bill. "It may be another answer to prayer. You've been pestering us to give you some investigating to do, and now I have two related cases that demand your attention."

"Go on," said Elizabeth warily. "I'm listening." She had not forgotten the time she'd been obliged to track a covey of absconding old ladies to Georgia for one of Bill's cases.

Between slices of pizza, Bill managed to outline the Morgan case—and to tell Elizabeth as much as he knew about the century-old notoriety of Lethal Lucy Todhunter, ancestor of the present suspect. Elizabeth's expression became increasingly forbidding as the conversation progressed. Finally, after divulging everything he could think of, he lapsed into silence, his former enthusiasm in tatters. "Doesn't it sound fascinating?" he finished weakly.

Elizabeth sighed. "Fascinating? Try impossible. I'm not sure what you think is entailed in the abilities of a forensic anthropologist, but I can assure you that those skills do not include solving century-old murder cases, involving the unautopsied remains of long-decomposed corpses. And I can't do anything about the Morgans until somebody makes a ruling on how Chevry died. I doubt if they'll give me the body and invite me to see for myself."

"Don't worry about the Morgans yet. I just wanted you to be aware of the situation in case things start to happen quickly. I think they might. As for Lethal Lucy, you could look into it, couldn't you?" asked Bill. "Maybe there is some evidence that you could reevaluate in the light of modern science."

"But what's the point? Mrs. Morgan hasn't even been charged yet. Why are you investigating her great-grandmother?"

"Look," said Bill. "You're the one who has been complaining that you have too much time on your hands. You're the one who's been pleading with us to find you something to do. I'm offering you one of the most famous cases in Virginia criminal history—a woman who was acquitted because no one could figure out how she did it. Now, do you want to work on it, or do you want to sit around brooding about your loss—and your mother's new lifestyle?"

Elizabeth blinked at him. There had been very few times in Bill MacPherson's life when he had been assertive. Most of the time people forgot what an intelligent fellow he was, because his unassuming nature allowed them to do so. In the South, "simple country boys" are often the sharpest and most dangerous people—it is a pose particularly favored by aspiring politicians. Elizabeth began to be afraid that her brother, the simple, modest country boy, might be planning to run for the Senate someday. The idea made her shudder. "Yes. All right," she said quickly. "I work for you guys, right? If you want me to investigate an 1860s wrongful death, then I'll hop right to it."

"Great," said Bill, lapsing back into his usual Bertie Wooster demeanor. "Only don't take too long about it, okay? As soon as the Morgan autopsy comes back, I think you'll have a more recent murder to worry about."

Elizabeth's eyes widened. "Bill! You think your client is guilty?"

He shrugged. "Not exactly. But Chevry Morgan richly deserved to be murdered. I can't believe that no one took him up on it."

Donna Jean Morgan would not have known the Emily Dickinson poem that contained the line "the bustle in the house the morning after death"; but she was familiar with the custom. The dining-room table was laden with neighbors' offerings of peach and apple pies, three kinds of potato salad, cold cuts, and half a dozen plates of deviled eggs. Certain dishes were "fitten" to take to a house of mourning, and most people stuck to tradition. In anticipation of this onslaught of friends and parishioners, Donna Jean had been up since six, giving the already spotless house yet another cleaning. At a quarter to nine, she had changed her faded housedress for her navy-blue Sunday best. She had set a stack of paper plates and napkins on the sideboard, then deposited herself in Chevry's lounge chair to wait.

Her kinfolk turned up promptly at nine—the men gravely shaking her hand and expressing a restrained sympathy before they stumped out onto the back porch to talk among themselves about cars and quarterbacks, while the women, after perfunctory hugs, set about rearranging the table and adding their own contributions to the buffet. They roamed around the house with brooms and dishcloths, looking for ways to make themselves useful, chattering brightly all the while. But nobody really *talked* to Donna Jean.

By noon, clumps of visitors arrived, families together or women in pairs. The men joined the male contingent on the porch and the women bustled or scattered about the parlor to gossip, their hushed, mournful tones gradually giving way to the usual sunny babble of idle conversation. No one said much about Chevry, beyond the first sentence or two of condolence, although an elderly second cousin of Donna's attempted to console the widow by observing that Donna Jean was "a sight better off without the rutting hound." Since Cousin Elsinor was popularly assumed to be senile, no one paid any attention to this untactful remark. They heartily concurred, of course, but no one would have dreamed of *saying* so. Apparently the void he left in the community was neither large nor permanent.

No one mentioned the suddenness of Chevry Morgan's death or speculated on the cause of it. Donna Jean knew that this was a bad sign.

People were avoiding a touchy subject, one that they had discussed at length elsewhere—not in her presence. The community had already held its own unofficial grand-jury hearing, and its own arraignment, conducted by telephone and in the aisles of the Food Lion. Donna Jean wondered what private verdict had been reached. She avoided the topic as well, because she was too numbed by the fact of Chevry's death to worry about anything else. She wanted friendly company, not an informal inquest.

Tanya Faith Reinhardt (Morgan) turned up at one. Swathed in a sheath of black chiffon, with a matching hat and gloves, she emerged from the backseat of her parents' Ford Tempo, tottering a little on newly purchased spike-heeled shoes. Her parents, clad in Sunday clothes and looking ill at ease, trailed along behind her; Tanya's mother was carrying a foil-wrapped pot of yellow chrysanthemums.

Donna Jean, who had observed the mournful procession from her picture window, met Chevry's second widow at the door. "I might have known you'd come late," she said, her voice heavy with scorn. "Now that all the work has been done around here."

Tanya Faith tossed her head, causing her wide-brimmed hat to lurch suddenly toward her ear. "Some of us are too grief-stricken to think about stuff like cooking and housekeeping," she declared.

"Some of us are too lazy *ever* to think about cooking and housecleaning," Donna Jean replied. "Did you come to pay your respects?"

"I don't have any respect for you," said Tanya Faith. "I'm here because I loved Chevry, and I don't want you going through all his things and keeping the best for yourself. He wouldn't want that. I know he'd want to see that I was taken care of."

"Oh, bull turds!" Donna Jean Morgan was oblivious to the shocked murmurs from her guests. This was clearly not how they thought a bereaved woman should behave. On the other hand, the provocation of meeting one's husband's *other* widow did seem to call for extreme measures. Donna Jean was no coward — you had to give her that. In the dining room, one woman murmured to another, "Todhunter blood."

"You think Chevry would want to see you taken care of?" said Donna Jean, with an unpleasant smile. "Why, honey, where he went, I reckon the lusts of the flesh drop right off you when you shed your earthly form, so I doubt if you cross his mind much at all anymore. Taken care of! Well, if you want me to, I can go out on the back porch and see if any of the old men out there are in the market for a sluttish extra wife."

In the shocked silence that followed her offer, Tanya's father decided that it was time to stand up for his little girl. "Now, Donna Jean, you know that you accepted the situation while Chevry was alive. And now you've got no call to talk that way to—"

"I have both the call and the right," said Donna Jean Morgan. "While Chevry was alive he called the shots, because I had no skills and no income. I had no more say than his coonhound. He could ram this piece of trash down my throat and claim they were married in the eyes of God—the devil must be laughing over that one!—and I had no choice but to go along with it. Well, Chevry is dead now, so all that is over and done with. Now, you Reinhardts, listen good! As of now, this is my house and my land, and Chevry has nothing to say about it anymore. If you don't want to be arrested for trespassing, you'll get out of here right now, and take your trashy young'un with you."

Tanya Faith took the potted chrysanthemums from her mother's slack grasp and threw them with careful precision at the newly vacuumed living-room rug. The plastic container shattered on impact, spilling clumps of moist brown dirt and severed petals across the ivory carpet. "Part of what Chevry left is mine by rights," she said. "And, Donna Jean *Todhunter* Morgan, if you killed our mutual husband, which I reckon you did, then *all* of it is mine."

In her first act as investigator for her brother's cases, Elizabeth MacPherson paid a morning visit to the Sutherlin House, Danville's local history museum. The elegant two-story brick house, justly billed as the Last Capitol of the Confederacy (for one frantic week in 1865), was maintained with period furniture and exhibits related to the history of the house itself, as well as other items of local interest, such as maps, displays of crafts, and artifacts of area notables.

Elizabeth knew that Lucy Todhunter would not be featured in a Sutherlin exhibit, because she did not represent the image of graceful gentility or successful capitalism favored by local preservation groups in their displays of regional pride. To outsiders, a famous murderess may be the town's most celebrated citizen, but locally such a person is considered best forgotten.

Once, in Fall River, Massachusetts, Elizabeth and her cousin Geoffrey had gone in search of a Lizzie Borden museum, or at the very least *Lizziebilia*, souvenirs in the form of tiny hatchet key chains or T-shirts announcing ACQUIT ME: I'M AN ORPHAN. The nineteenth-century ax murderess was, in fact, the entire reason for their visit to Fall River, but they soon discovered that interest in the infamous Lizzie was not encouraged locally. No signs assisted the traveler in finding the infamous house in which she had axed her father and stepmother; in fact, the house number had been changed and the building was now home to a print shop which did not advertise its landmark status. Elizabeth and Geoffrey had managed to find the house and they had retraced Andrew Borden's fateful walk home from the bank on the morning of his death, but to their chagrin, they found not so much as a postcard commemorating Lizzie. (Geoffrey later remarked that he supposed there wasn't going to be a Lorena Bobbitt exhibit in Manassas, either.)

No, there would be no memorial to Lucy Todhunter in Danville—but Elizabeth was banking on the fact that some resident historian had been unable to resist the temptation to document the case. If so, the best place to look for an account of Lucy's career would be in the basement of the Sutherlin House, where the museum kept a craft shop and bookstore, offering such locally printed pamphlets as

In a Rebel Prison, or Experiences in Danville, Virginia by Alfred S. Roe, late private, Co. A, Ninth New York Heavy Artillery Volunteers.

It was there. Tucked in between *Recipes of the Confederacy* and *The Gibson Girl in Danville* was a softcover chapbook of a little more than one hundred pages, bound in black construction paper, and featuring as its cover illustration an antique arsenic label complete with skull and crossbones. The book was unimaginatively titled: *The Trial of Lucy Todhunter, Suspected Poisoner from Danville.* Elizabeth picked it up and flipped through the first few pages for copyright information. The volume had been typeset and assembled at a local print shop, and its publication consisted of the author—according to the title page, one Everett Yancey—taking a stack of copies around to the local drugstores, gift shops, and other tourist-oriented establishments. The book, published in 1972, was in its thirteenth printing (at approximately two hundred copies per printing, Elizabeth guessed). This would be the perfect resource with which to begin her immersion in the Lucy Todhunter case. Elizabeth handed the clerk ten dollars for the purchase, thinking that there was nothing amateurish about the author's pricing instincts. She hoped his research would prove equally good.

"Is the author still alive?" she asked the smiling young woman behind the counter.

"I hope so," the volunteer clerk replied. "He's our volunteer docent here at the Sutherlin House on Thursday mornings."

"Good," said Elizabeth. "I may come back then and take the tour. After I've done my homework."

CHAPTER 8

"Have you lost weight?" asked Elizabeth MacPherson. Ordinarily that remark between women is tendered as the highest compliment, but in this case it was an expression of concern. A. P. Hill looked not only thinner, but also slightly green. Bottles of Maalox were lined up on her bookshelf, and a spiderweb glistened across the top of her coffee mug. Her clothes seemed a size too large. Elizabeth wondered if Powell Hill had accompanied Bill to any of their mother's recent dinner parties.

"I haven't felt much like eating," said Powell Hill, with an indifferent shrug. "The Royden case could put Julia Child off her food. That woman is impossible!"

"You mean Eleanor Royden? In what way?" Elizabeth was being briefed on the case in her capacity as the official investigator for the firm of MacPherson and Hill. "Is the client unintelligent?"

"I wish," said Powell bitterly. "Stupid defendants are wonderful to work with. They do what you tell them, because they can't think of anything else to do. You know the saying that a trial is like a chess game. Well, it is, but we lawyers *like* it that way, and we don't want the red king to look up and say, 'Rook to Queen Three,' while the game is in progress."

"But it's Mrs. Royden's trial," Elizabeth

pointed out. "Not to mention her life. Of course she'd want some input."

"She's had that. She exercised her freedom of choice and hired me. Now she should shut up. Usually, even clever people accused of first-degree murder are as cooperative as the dimwits, because they are completely terrified. A silverback trial lawyer once told me that killers make the best clients, because they have too much at stake to argue with you. And, of course, most murderers are not overly intellectual, anyhow. Eleanor Royden is the exception on both counts."

"What has she done?"

A. P. Hill reached into a drawer on the side of her desk and brought out a thick legal-sized folder. "This, for starters," she said, passing the file to Elizabeth.

"The *Roanoke Times*, the *Washington Post*, the *Richmond Times-Dispatch* ..." Elizabeth let out a low whistle as she leafed through a sheaf of clippings. "This case is getting tremendous coverage. Eleanor Royden seems to be quoted a lot in these articles. Good picture of her!"

"She made me take some L'Oréal to the county jail. And the local women's group put her in touch with a beautician who went in and did her makeup before the photo session. I wanted a *remorseful*-looking defendant. I wanted someone who looked shattered about the fact that she had taken two lives. Eleanor looks like she's trying out for Diane Sawyer's job."

"She may get it," said Elizabeth. "These are great quotes. 'I should be charged with killing vermin without a license. How much is the fine?' Oh, dear. And this one in the *Post*: 'I'll do community service at the Battered Women's Shelter—if they'll open a pistol range!' " She set the folder aside. "I see what you mean."

"I thought you would." A. P. Hill reached for an antacid tablet from the candy dish on her desk. "She's making a fool out of herself. Evil Eleanor, the Clown Queen of Crime. The media loves it, of course, and she thinks that means the reporters are on her side. She can't see that they're only using her to get outrageous, sensational stories, and that when they tire of her ranting, they'll turn on her."

"I see. You'd be better off defending a sweet, timid, drab little woman with moist eyes and a catch in her voice."

"I dream about it," said A. P. Hill. "When I sleep at all, that is. I envision myself defending Donna Reed, or Saint Bernadette, in a little navy-blue dress with a Peter Pan collar and sensible shoes. Once in my dream, it was Oliver North in drag, looking moist-eyed at the jury and saying he was terribly sorry. Anyone but Eleanor!"

"It must be tough to dislike your client. Or do you, Powell?"

"That's just it." A. P. Hill sighed. "I do like her. She's bright and witty and tough. And I think that Jeb Royden was an arrogant monster who underestimated the temerity of his victim. I don't condone what she did, of course, but I can see how she was driven to it. But she is making it very difficult for me to mount a defense. Every time I see one of those damned bumper stickers, I cringe!"

"And you want me to find some people in Roanoke who will testify that she was really a nice, shy person before she snapped?"

"You can try," said A. P. Hill. "I doubt if we'll convince a jury of that, but it's worth a shot. What I really want is witnesses who will vilify Jeb and Staci Royden. I want all the dirt I can get on them. Every act of arrogance; every example of pettiness; anything that will make them seem like cruel, shallow people. Get the divorce records—start with that. Since Eleanor is behaving like a stand-up comic, the only thing I can do is to make the victims look worse."

"But they're dead!"

"I can't help that," said A. P. Hill grimly. "They're still going on trial."

"You said to drop by if I wanted to pursue the matter," said Miri Malone, with a smile that to Bill looked more like stubbornness than good humor. His mother's housewarming party had taken place some time ago, but his conversation al fresco with Miri Malone had not faded from memory. "You know, about the connubial rights of dolphins?" she was saying. "My wanting to marry one, I mean. We talked about it at Casey and Margaret's party."

"It's not the sort of thing that would slip my mind," said Bill, wishing that the city of Danville would arrest more jaywalkers so he wouldn't even have to consider cases like this one.

"Good. I'm glad you recall our discussion. There's been a development."

Bill managed to look solemn. "You're pregnant?"

"No," said Miri, scowling. "I wish I could pull that off, though. It would certainly strengthen the argument, wouldn't it? But I shouldn't have to. Men with vasectomies get remarried all the time. Procreation is not an issue."

"There's a pun in there somewhere," Bill pointed out.

Miri Malone was not to be deterred by frivolousness. "I just went down and applied for a marriage license," she informed him.

"I'd like to have seen that," murmured Bill. "How did it go?"

"Did you know that you get marriage licenses in the Courts and Jails Building?"

"Some people consider that appropriate," said Bill, thinking of various divorce clients. "It does look a little grim, doesn't it? All that concrete and smoked glass."

"I asked a man in a gray uniform where one applied for marriage licenses, and he grinned and said, 'Upstairs. Right over the jail.' Ugh."

"Next to the circuit courtroom." Bill nodded. "I know it well."

"I went up to the long counter, and when it was my turn, I asked the clerk if I could apply for a marriage license without my fiancé being present, and she wanted to know why he couldn't come with me."

"And you said?"

"Well, I thought about it," said Miri. "I could have said that he is disabled, but if you're a dolphin, it isn't really a disability not to be able to walk, is it? In fact, for a dolphin that condition is quite normal. He might consider me disabled, because I can't sleep in the water."

Bill wasn't sure that his prospective client was the best judge of what constituted "quite normal," but he nodded to speed up the narrative. "What did you tell the clerk?"

"I said that my fiancé was unable to walk, and she expressed her sympathy, and I decided right then that I didn't want to prolong things by misleading this clerical worker, so I just came out with it: 'My intended husband is a person who happens to be a dolphin.'"

"Well," said Bill. "Well. I'll bet Mrs. Mingus didn't have an answer to that."

"No. She was looking sort of like a trout herself. Her mouth kept opening and closing, but nothing was coming out. Anyhow, she refused to let me apply for the license, so now we have grounds to sue the state for discrimination."

"You might have," said Bill, trying to force his neurons into untried pathways. There are things that even the youngest lawyers cannot explain. "I suppose that—what's the dolphin's name?"

"Porky. He may change it, though. That's his tank name. I'm sure his mother called him something else, except it's a whistle sound, and there's no orthography for it."

"Porky, then," said Bill. "Porky may have been discriminated against—if we can prove that he is entitled to any legal rights, but Porky hasn't consulted an attorney."

"He has now. We want you to represent both of us."

"I'd have to"—Bill couldn't believe he was going to say this—"interview him to verify that he wishes to go through with this."

"Fine. I'll give you his address in Florida."

"I don't speak dolphin!" Bill burst out, closing his eyes and hoping for an alternate universe.

"You'll have an interpreter. Rich Edmonds, who works at the sea park, communicates with their marine mammals almost as well as I do. I told him we're coming."

"We?"

"Of course. I'm going with you."

On the next Thursday morning, Elizabeth MacPherson took a tour of the Sutherlin House, 975 Main Street in the historic district of Danville. She had spent the past two days in Roanoke, obtaining divorce papers for the Royden case and going through the list of the friends of Jeb and Eleanor, in search of friendly witnesses. So far it had been slow going. Several wives had agreed to speak to Elizabeth off the record, provided that they didn't have to testify in court. She took them up on their offers, thinking that at this stage in the investigation, such interviews would provide useful background.

It had been depressing work, though, listening to anxious older women. Surely, thought Elizabeth, I'll find someone who is willing to speak on the record for an ill-treated woman, but the women she interviewed were either afraid to claim Eleanor Royden as a friend, or too put off by her outrageous lack of remorse. Perhaps, too, they were afraid of ending up like her. When two subsequent calls ended with the statement "I'm testifying for the prosecution," Elizabeth began to wonder if Eleanor Royden had any chance at all.

At least she didn't have to worry about A. P. Hill's case today. The Sutherlin House tour was a prologue to her chat with Everett Yancey, the local historian. She stood in the tiled entrance hall with a group of school-children who were waiting to be shown around the mansion.

At a quarter past ten, a silver-haired man in a cape strolled into the hallway, pointed his cane at the gaggle of youngsters, and drawled: "Those who chatter will be evicted from the premises. Those who wander will be censured. Those who touch things will be shot."

The students tittered nervously, and edged away from him.

He nodded approvingly at their wariness. "How very perceptive of you," he observed. "I am Mr. Yancey, your guide to the historic treasures within these walls. I am not overly fond of children *tartare*. I will answer questions if you can think of any, but I prefer complete silence so that the information that I impart can be heard by all. Let us proceed."

Elizabeth fell in behind the first cluster of students and listened in respectful silence as Everett Yancey began the tour. He had obviously given the lecture many times, because his narrative never faltered, and he quoted names and dates with a clipped precision born of long familiarity. He talked about the fateful week in April 1865 when the Sutherlin House served as the capitol building for the Confederacy, and he was eloquent in his description of the frenzied Confederate leaders, hurrying to escape the approaching army. When he told of the wooden box constructed in Danville to hold the gold bars salvaged from the Confederate treasury, the audience seemed to be holding its breath. Elizabeth thought of adding her own comments about the eventual disposition of the Confederate gold, but since she had no proof to offer, she kept quiet. Everett Yancey was not the sort of guide who encouraged audience participation.

She did note that as Yancey's history of Danville neared the twentieth century, the guide became less ardent in his recital of events. In 1912, the Sutherlin House became Danville's public library, and Everett Yancey seemed to lose interest in the house and in Danville as a whole. His discussion of industrial progress after World War II was positively perfunctory, and the students began to fidget, no longer caught in the spell of a storyteller. He shepherded them to the basement gift shop, pointed out copies of his self-published pamphlets on local history, and volunteered to autograph their purchases, but no one took him up on the offer. The students, dazed with boredom and information overload, drifted away, leaving Elizabeth MacPherson alone with the guide.

"Excuse me," she said. "If you're not in a hurry, I'd like to talk to you."

Everett Yancey looked at her speculatively. "I charge twenty dollars an hour for ancestor research," he said without notable enthusiasm.

"It's not that." Elizabeth smiled. "At least, I hope she's not an ancestor. I wanted to talk to you about Lucy Todhunter. Can I buy you lunch?"

"As long as we don't order beignets," he replied. "You might be a Todhunter reenactor."

Twenty minutes later they were settled into a red paneled booth at the Long River Chinese Restaurant—Everett Yancey's choice. Elizabeth was relieved that it was not the booth she shared during that fateful luncheon with her mother; the modern scandal might have kept her mind off the nineteenth-century femme fatale.

"I've read your book on Lucy Todhunter," Elizabeth told Everett Yancey. "It was fascinating."

His response was wary. "You're not the sort of romantic who wants to prove that Lucy was innocent, I hope?"

"No, I'm a forensic anthropologist. The case interests me because it's technically an unsolved crime. Lucy was acquitted of the murder of her husband. Your book convinced me that she did poison her husband, but I do wonder about two other questions: *how* and *why*." Elizabeth decided not to mention the more modern connection to the case: the mysterious death of the husband of Donna Jean Morgan, descendant of Lucy Todhunter.

Everett Yancey busied himself with his bowl of hot-and-sour soup. Presently he said, "It makes me uneasy when young women come up and ask how Lucy Todhunter managed to kill her husband. I'm not sure I'd tell that to anyone, even if I knew."

"I told you, I'm a forensic anthropologist," said Elizabeth patiently. "I don't have any plans to dispose of a husband." She took a sip of green tea, to keep herself from telling this forbidding stranger all about Cameron, and how much she wished she had him back. That

159

was not germane to the matter at hand. Better think about the case.

"Well, I'm not sure you can solve the case from a distance of more than a century, but I'd be glad to help you try. That could be a very nice sequel to my original history of Lucy. Er— you weren't planning to publish anything yourself, were you?"

Elizabeth assured him that she was not.

"You asked why she did it," said Yancey thoughtfully. "I don't know. Wish I did. I took my best guess in the book: perhaps she hated Major Todhunter for threatening to sell her family farm. Doesn't that seem logical to you?"

"Not entirely," said Elizabeth. "She sounded like the sort of woman who would have tried persuasion rather than poison to get her way. Something about your explanation didn't ring true. Never mind, though. That was idle curiosity. I really need to know how she did it. Do you think the account of the case given at the trial was accurate?"

"You mean, are the facts of the poisoning as impossible as they seem? It is tempting to suppose they are not. If the doctor was mistaken, or the cousins lied, or the servants were bribed, perhaps the Todhunter poisoning wasn't such a great mystery after all. Perhaps Lucy simply poisoned her husband's pastry with arsenic-laced powdered sugar, and got away with it through the collusion of her household. I don't think so, though."

"Why not?"

"Because one of the key witnesses *wanted* her to be guilty. Major Todhunter's old comrade in arms, Richard Norville. He had never met Lucy before that visit, and he never saw her afterward, but still he swore that she had finished off the beignet she had given to her husband, and she suffered no ill effects. Surely, if this strange woman had murdered Norville's good friend, he would do all that he could to see her hanged for it."

"I suppose so," Elizabeth conceded. "I can't think of any reason for him to protect her."

"By all accounts that beignet was the only nourishment taken by Philip Todhunter within days of his death; yet on autopsy his system was found to be filled with arsenic. The remaining beignets and the sugar were untainted, however. And while the entire household ate from the same batch of pastry, no one else became ill."

"All the testimony agreed on that point, didn't it? I don't suppose *everyone* would have lied to protect Lucy," mused Elizabeth.

"I doubt if anyone would have," Everett Yancey replied. "Her cousins disapproved of her for marrying a Union officer. The servants didn't care for her. And neither doctor appeared to be smitten by her charms. No one would have minded in the least if she'd been convicted. They told the truth quite grudgingly, I thought, judging from the trial transcripts."

"All right," said Elizabeth. "We'll assume that the scenario was reported truthfully. Lucy Todhunter gives her husband a home-made pastry, and he dies. I don't suppose he was allergic to it?"

"Arsenic in the corpse," Yancey reminded her. "Besides, he ate one nearly every morning."

"I don't suppose his death could have been an accident of some sort?"

"Philip Todhunter didn't think so. Almost his last coherent words were: 'Lucy, why did you do it?' But the question is: What did she do?"

"And all the guests ate sugared pastry from the same tray; Norville says Todhunter chose one at random from those remaining; and Lucy ate a few bites from the same one her husband ate, so that lets out the idea of the murderer being immune," said Elizabeth. "I was thinking of a Dorothy Sayers novel, in which the murderer and his victim share a poisoned meal, but only one dies because the other has a tolerance for the poison. That would hardly work with a collection of strangers, though. Norville had only recently arrived, so he could not have built up a tolerance to a fatal dose of arsenic."

"If Lucy had been trying to get a houseful of people immune to arsenic, there'd have been vomiting stories from half of them, since their tolerance levels would vary. That's the tricky thing about arsenic: the fatal dose varies greatly, according to the individual. But nobody reported being sick during their stay at the Todhunter home. I think we'll have to pronounce them *unpoisoned.*"

Elizabeth frowned. "That doesn't get us anywhere, though."

"Would you like to read my source material on the case?" asked Everett Yancey. "I don't think you're going to solve it over lunch. I still have my trial transcripts, and photocopies of letters, diaries, and so on. Perhaps you might find something in there."

162

"I'd like to try," said Elizabeth.

"Certainly. As long as I get to publish your results." Everett Yancey smiled, and twirled a forkful of shrimp lo mein. "There is no such thing as a free lunch."

The two officers from the sheriff's department were sitting in Donna Jean Morgan's living room, attempting to look genial, without actually accepting the repeated offers of coffee, pound cake, or butterscotch fudge. Both as a courtesy to the widow, and perhaps as a strategy toward a possible murderess, they were pretending that their visit was little more than a social call. The suspect, Donna Jean Morgan, was also pretending that their visit was a formality, because she was too embarrassed and frightened to consider any other possibility.

"You're sure you wouldn't like a doughnut?" she twittered again.

The older deputy responded with a plaster smile, while the young, nervous one got out his notebook and looked expectantly at his partner.

Alvin Brower decided that it was time to get down to business, but he wasn't going to be unpleasant about it, because this was still an interview, not an interrogation. In an interview, you put the witness at ease, acted friendly, and let him do most of the talking, because you didn't know all the answers yet, and you wanted all the information you could get, including, you hoped, any inconsistencies or demonstrable lies the witness might care to tell. The interrogation came later, when you *did* know all the answers, and you wanted the suspect to admit guilt. That discourse was far less courteous, and would not be held in the suspect's living room. Brower thought he was one step closer to an interrogation now: the autopsy report had come back.

"Now, Mrs. Morgan, I don't want to have to charge you with assault on my waistline," he said, smiling again. "So don't tempt me with baked goods." Actually, the offer wasn't all that tempting, since the last recipient of Donna Jean's cooking was dead of arsenic poisoning. "Let's go back over the evening of Mr. Morgan's death again, as best we can."

Donna Jean sighed. "It won't change with retelling, Mr. Brower. He came here, and I fixed him a supper to take with him while he worked. I always fixed his supper. Maybe he thought Tanya Faith would take over that task, and she was welcome to it as far as I was concerned, but I don't think it ever would have happened. Catch Tanya Faith cooking!" She smiled at the absurdity of it.

"But you were angry with your husband, weren't you, Mrs. Morgan?"

"Chevry could be a stubborn man," his widow admitted. "And I think he heard more instructions from the Lord than the Lord ever gave."

"My wife agrees with you there, ma'am," said Brower genially. "She had heard about your previous trouble over polygamy, and I'm sorry to tell you that she laughed out loud when she heard of your late husband's demise." He watched the widow closely for a trace of a smile.

"He didn't deserve to die for being a graven fool," said Donna Jean solemnly. "To my way of thinking, he deserved to live so that he could repent at leisure after he found out what a bad match he made with that teenaged slut."

The deputies looked at each other. A new possibility had presented itself. "Was Tanya Faith helping your husband work that night?"

"She was not," said Donna Jean.

"And she wasn't supposed to go over and eat with him, by any chance?"

"No. Tanya Faith didn't go out there much. I don't think she liked the fact that it was next to the old church cemetery. She'd have had nightmares if they'd moved in, you mark my words. Anyhow, the old place wasn't fancy enough for her yet. She was waiting for her wallpaper and her carpeting to be installed." The older woman frowned. "She stayed here with me."

"Did she help you fix Chevry's dinner?"

"No more than she could help." Donna Jean sniffed. "She may be a handmaiden to the prophet in the bedroom, but she made herself scarce in the kitchen." She thought for a moment in the ensuing silence. "Reckon that would have changed in time. She'd have been scarce both places, but Chevry wasn't ready to see that. I wish he could have lived for the disillusionment."

Alvin Brower frowned at the other deputy. Donna Morgan wasn't sounding like any bona fide killer that he'd ever met, but he'd be the first to admit that he wasn't an expert on homicides—especially not on homicides per-

165

petrated by women. She could be too sly to gloat about her husband's death—or maybe she did regret his passing, but that didn't necessarily mean that she hadn't helped him leave this world in a fit of jealous rage.

"Was Tanya Faith ever alone with Chevry's dinner box that evening?"

"I didn't pay her any mind." Donna Jean sniffed. "I was too busy working."

"I sure wish you could remember details about that night, ma'am," said Brower. "Because, you see, the fact is we got the autopsy report back, and it shows arsenic in your late husband's system."

"I didn't poison him," said Donna Jean. "He'd been saying that he felt poorly off and on for more than a week. Even Tanya Faith had a touch of it for a day or so."

"And what about you, Mrs. Morgan? Did you ever feel sick?"

"No."

"Well, there may be explanations we haven't even thought of yet," said Brower, standing up and shifting into his *brisk* mode. He talked faster when he wanted suspects to agree to something without thinking too much about his request. "We need to clear this up, though, Mrs. Morgan. You don't want this business hanging over your head for who-knows-how-long. You know how people talk in a small town. If we don't clear it up soon, you'll be subjected to trial by bridge club."

"Card playing is sinful," murmured Donna Jean.

"So is gossip," Brower agreed. "So I say let's shut 'em down. If you'll let Wade and me search the house now, and if you'll show us how you made that dinner, that will go a long way toward clearing things up. I have a report to write, you know."

It always amazed Brower that people didn't tell him to go to hell right then and there. There was no way that he could legally impel a suspect to allow an informal search or to reenact part of a suspected crime, but most people didn't seem to realize that. Maybe they were afraid that they'd look guilty if they refused, or maybe they thought he'd never find anything incriminating. Maybe they just didn't want to inconvenience him. *I have a report to write, you know.* It was his best line, practically surefire. Sure enough, Donna Jean Morgan was smiling and nodding just like all the rest of the poor fools who had given Brower just about an inch too much rope.

But then, she said, "Certainly, Mr. Brower. I'll just call my attorney, and if he says it's all right, why, then you can do whatever you please."

It was 5:04 P.M., and Margaret MacPherson was experiencing the familiar sensation of waiting for the emissary from the outside world. She remembered it well from her married life: she stayed home day after day, sending children to school, and a husband off to the city, while she waited in the tidy brick house, like a domestic Prisoner of Zenda, cooking and cleaning and waiting to hear about everyone else's adventures that day. Because, of course, *she* hadn't had any.

She thought she had left behind that existence,

167

when she filed for divorce upon finding out about Doug's pubescent bimbo, but now the feeling was back: the five o'clock vigil. She had busied herself all day with her photography, trying out new exposure times in the darkroom on some of the black-and-white portraits. She had even mopped the kitchen floor, because it needed doing, and she'd set some green beans and new potatoes on to cook, because she was home and Casey wasn't. It wasn't a division of labor or anything. She wasn't a *housewife* anymore. She just happened to be home, so it seemed like the sensible thing to do.

At least she didn't have to comb her hair and put on makeup anymore just because it was five P.M. *Some* things had changed, after all.

Phyllis Casey turned up at 5:30, slinging her briefcase onto the dining-room table with a groan. "If anyone wants to know what it was like in the Borgia court, they have only to ask me," she declared, heading for the wine decanter.

"English faculty meeting?" Margaret guessed.

"What else?" Casey kicked her shoes off and sank down in the armchair across from Margaret. "I think we should put a metal detector at the door to the conference room, because, I swear, one of these days an untenured peon is going to kill Stanley Johnson. It may be me."

"I know a good lawyer," said Margaret, with a lazy smile.

"Actually, it wasn't as bad as usual," Casey said. "I think word of our party had got around. All through the meeting, Johnson kept eyeing me nervously, as if he expected me

168

to jump up and spit tobacco juice into his coffee mug."

"Yeah, you militant lesbians are dangerous, all right," said Margaret solemnly.

Casey nodded. "It was very gratifying. We started discussing the teaching schedule for the fall term, and I spoke right up and said that I didn't want to teach the Transcendentalist poets anymore. I wanted the James Joyce/D. H. Lawrence course. *And* I said that I wanted to add Virginia Woolf to the course for a feminist perspective on sexuality."

"Good for you! How did they take it?"

Phyllis Casey laughed. "First, there was a charged silence in the room, as if everyone were thinking furiously at once, and then Dr. McClure started to wheeze, which means that *he'd* heard the rumors. And Johnson just nodded, and went on to the next item on the agenda. I couldn't believe it, Margaret! After all these years of being well-spoken and polite, during which time they ran roughshod over me, and gave me the courses nobody else wanted, now suddenly I let it be known that I'm a lesbian, and they treat me like a conquering Visigoth. It was wonderful."

Margaret MacPherson nodded happily. "My children are shocked into absolute silence. We should have thought of this *years* ago!"

"And the best part of it is, they just take your word for it!"

"Well," said Margaret reasonably, "it's not the sort of thing you can check up on, is it?"

Casey said, "Do you think I ought to buy some leather outfits, anyway? Just in case?"

CHAPTER 9

Eleanor Royden's eyes glittered at the unexpected novelty in an otherwise boring day of
confinement. "So," she said, sitting down at
the conference table. "I get to spend an hour
or so with you. This will be a nice change
from Still Life with Bars. I hope you're better than daytime television. I can't say much
for the decor, though." She glanced appraisingly around the small, bare interview room.
"Why does the criminal justice system have
to paint everything beige? Maybe you ought
to analyze *them*. I'd say it's a symptom of
repression—don't they strike you as being
rather anal-retentive—but then, you're the
expert." She looked at him with an expression
of sparkling expectation.

Exactly like the hostess at a cocktail party,
thought the psychologist pityingly. I wonder
if she has any notion of reality left?

"Well, enough about them," said Eleanor,
seeing that her opening gambit was not a
success. "Let's talk about you. You're a
psychologist! How fascinating! Have you done
anybody famous?"

"Famous?" echoed the young man in his best
Freudian manner.

"Well, perhaps *notorious* is the better word.
You're an expert witness in criminal psychology,
so you must lead a pretty interesting life. Have
you met Jeffrey Dahmer? James Earl Ray? A
Menendez brother?"

Eric Stanfield's face was impassive. He had

170

been warned that Mrs. Royden was somewhat eccentric, and he had resolved not to be provoked by her behavior.

"Now listen to that," Eleanor went on, without waiting for his reply. "I haven't mentioned a single woman in that list of notorious murderers. Do you think women aren't as well suited to spectacular crimes, or do we just not get enough press? In your professional opinion."

Stanfield blinked at this conversational U-turn. "Now, Eleanor," he said in his courteous monotone, "I'm here to talk about you. As you know, your attorney has asked me to evaluate your condition so that I can testify at your trial."

Eleanor Royden looked appraisingly at the bespectacled young man in the polyester-blend navy jacket. He gazed back, absently fingering his yellow paisley tie. He blinked first. Eleanor sighed and gave up. Another anal-retentive, just like everyone else she had been dealing with for lo, these many weeks. "I'm going to have to do a lot of background for you, Skippy," she told the psychologist.

He stiffened. "Mrs. Royden, my name is Dr. Eric Stanfield. I hold degrees from—"

"Right, Skippy. And you probably still have your Smurf cocoa mug. Give it a rest. I need to make you understand what you're dealing with here. Now, I'll bet you studied the battered-woman syndrome in grad school, but, frankly, what we're talking about in my case is much more sophisticated than that. You are taking notes, aren't you?"

Despite his resolution to remain impervious, Eric Stanfield glared at the madwoman in the orange prison fatigues. He took out his Cross pen and began to scribble on a yellow legal pad. "You were a battered wife, Mrs. Royden?" he said, attempting to regain control of the interview.

"Jeb didn't beat me up, no," Eleanor replied. "I told you, my case is more subtle than that of the drunken bully who uses his wife for a punching bag because he's a loser. Jeb Royden was not a loser. He was probably *the* most successful lawyer in southwest Virginia. If he could have kept his pants zipped, he might have run for attorney general." She snickered. "Hey! Maybe he would have run for president if I hadn't conducted my little exit poll in his bedroom." She pantomimed the firing of a pistol.

"Your husband was unfaithful."

"Show me one that isn't," snapped Eleanor. "Are you married, Skippy? Or do you still watch Winona Ryder movies and drool?"

"Mrs. Royden, your husband is dead. It is your mental health that we need to focus on."

"He is the key to my mental health! You know what doctors tell you about allergies? Remove the offending substance from your life. It works with mental-health problems, too!" She laughed.

"Tell me what you mean." It was all Stanfield could manage in the way of a response.

Eleanor spent ten minutes pacing the room and summarizing her marriage in an ironic invective that could have played at the local comedy club without a rewrite. Stanfield would have laughed if he hadn't kept reminding himself that he was in the presence of a multiple murderer. This articulate, outspoken woman had killed two people in cold blood, and she didn't seem the least bit remorseful for her crime. His notes were observations of her behavior, rather than a summary of her complaints. *Uses punch lines when relating anecdotes.*

"I didn't kill him because he was unfaithful," said Eleanor. "Write that down. I killed him because he made a blood sport out of our divorce. And I killed the Bitch—she gave a whole new meaning for the term *golden retriever*!—she was certainly determined to retrieve Jeb's gold, let me tell you. Anyhow, she had to go with him, because she enjoyed the process. My husband set out to destroy me, and she cheered him on."

"When you say that she—the second Mrs. Royden — had to go with him, do you mean that you had to fatally shoot her as well?" Stanfield thought it was time he injected some plain speaking into her narrative.

"That's right," said Eleanor cheerfully. "I blew the slut to kingdom come. Maybe it will deter other gold-digging home wreckers, but I doubt it. Not until more wives... go ballistic."

"Did you attempt to counter your husband's legal maneuvers through the court system?" He had to speak loudly, because she was laughing at her own pun.

Eleanor stopped laughing, and made a face at him. "You really don't get it, do you?" she said. "Take Jeb to court? That would have been like trying to fight a tiger with a toothpick. Jeb was a golf buddy to all the judges in the district, and every lawyer in town was his pal. Besides which, they all truly believed that he was right to dump me, and that I ought to go away quietly with *no* settlement, and get a job in a hash house. His last threat was that he'd convince the world that I was crazy, and have me locked up in a mental institution. The more I protested, the more evidence he had of my *derangement*, as he called it. I had no alternative. A bullet was the only thing that Jeb couldn't bribe or bully into being on his side."

"I see what you mean," Eric Stanfield said, nodding.

"I don't think you do," said Eleanor. "You are supposed to think how tragic it is for a woman to be driven to the point of believing that she could only solve her problems with a pistol. That's the state of desperation I had reached on the night Jeb died. I was a victim of emotional abuse and psychological brutality. You do see that, don't you?"

Bill MacPherson had never before interviewed a prospective client while wearing madras Bermuda shorts and tasseled loafers, but since the client in question was *au naturel* and leering at him from the edge of the pool, Bill felt that the honors of formality rested with him. At his elbow hovered Miri Malone, in a black swimsuit and sunglasses.

They had taken an early flight to Florida and proceeded to the marine mammals park in a rented Plymouth. Bill had been apprehensive about a possible trespassing violation, but Miri assured him that the owners did not object to *visitation*, since she was a former employee. "I go back all the time to see the gang," she explained.

He wondered how they would react to the notion that she might soon be using illegal maneuvers to kidnap one of the gang, but since Miri was his client, he abandoned that train of thought. Maybe it's a far, far better thing we do, he reasoned, and followed her through the gate to the large saltwater pool.

"Bill MacPherson, I'd like you to meet Porky Delphinidae," Miri was saying.

Nearby, a nervous young man, wearing a wet bathing suit and a Sea Park towel, consulted his watch. "This isn't going to take long, is it, you guys? Porky is on in half an hour."

"I doubt if we'll get too caught up in the conversation," Bill told him solemnly. He still couldn't believe that he was doing this at all. "I have a thing for you to sign here, Mr. Edmonds, certifying that you are a disinterested party in these proceedings, and that you understand what the dolphin is saying."

"Porky wants Rich to be best man," said Miri, stroking the dolphin's head.

Whereas, Porky will be best what? thought Bill wildly, still trying to figure out how to proceed. Perhaps he should have brought a tape recorder. "Look, before we go any further here, I need to know how the owners of this marine park feel about—er—Porky's personal life. I mean, what if you win the lawsuit, and they refuse to part with him?"

Miri Malone smiled sweetly. "If they refuse, they will have the public-relations nightmare of the decade. I will go on every talk show on

175

the planet, telling how the cruel dolphin-slavers are keeping true lovers apart."

"She would, too," Rich assured him. "She's quite a woman."

Bill looked at the pair of them appraisingly. "Hmm," he said. "Miri, what about you and Rich here—"

"I told you how I feel about primate males!" said Miri.

"Whereas those are my mates of choice," said Rich, grinning. "Besides, I couldn't cut in on a pal, could I, Porky, old buddy?"

Porky favored them with his maniacal smile, and bobbed in agreement.

"So you'd better talk to this guy about getting engaged," said Rich. "Because I'm not available. And you'd better hurry, because in twenty minutes it will be show time, and then we're outta here."

"Right," said Bill, consulting his notes and turning to the male half of the couple he had come to think of as the starboard-crossed lovers.

"Er—how do you do, Porky?" he said to the dolphin, who was still leering at him with an expression of antic cheerfulness.

"Give me a kiss, Porky," said Miri Malone, puckering her lips and making smacking noises at Porky. Obligingly, the dolphin touched her lips with its own.

"Don't lead the witness, Miri," said Bill. "Lots of guys will kiss you, but it doesn't mean they're willing to get engaged. Does Porky kiss just anybody?" he asked.

Miri smiled. "Want to give it a try?"

"Can't kiss clients," said Bill, shaking his

head. He turned back to Rich Edmonds. "He'd kiss just anybody, wouldn't he? You, for instance?"

"Well, Porky's a pretty friendly guy," Rich agreed. "But he's certainly more affectionate toward Miri than toward anybody else. He— how can I phrase this?—put the moves on her a few times in the pool. That's only to be expected, of course. You can ask him yourself, you know. He understands human speech pretty well."

Bill knelt down beside the dolphin. "Porky," he said, resisting the urge to speak loudly. Where were its ears? "Miri says that you would like to leave the ocean park here, and go to live with her. Is that what you want?"

Porky whooped, and bobbed his head.

Bill looked to the dolphin's trainer for a translation. "I'd say that was a yes," he said.

"Watch this, and see what you think." Rich went to a bucket near the tiers of seats and took out a fish. "Want a snack, Porky?"

Porky whooped again, bobbing his head vigorously. Bill thought the reactions were identical, but in proper legal fashion he remained skeptical. Perhaps the dolphin reacted that way toward any string of phrases addressed to him, regardless of their meaning. He leaned forward and said in a hearty tone: "Porky, would you like to end up in a can of tuna?"

Several minutes later, when Bill had gone through a stack of towels and was now reasonably dry again, he looked up at Miri Malone with salt-reddened eyes and shrugged. "All right, let's assume for argument's sake that he *does* understand what people say to him.

How do we know that he understands the concept of marriage? And, by the way, there's very little chance we'll get any of this past a sober judge. But just supposing. How do we know he understands what you're asking?"

Miri thought about it. "The conditions are spelled out in a conventional marriage ceremony, aren't they? You could go point by point and ask him."

"Sure, why not?" said Bill, dumping a small puddle out of his tasseled loafer. "Dolphin law. It could be a whole new area of specialization. We have to give him the benefit of the doubt, don't we?" Solemnly he turned toward the pool. "Do you, Porky, take this woman to have and to hold? In sickness and in health?"

Elizabeth MacPherson sat on the rug in her living room surrounded by a stack of old books and dog-eared photocopies on loan from Everett Yancey. Bill was off in Florida on a daft case for one of their mother's friends. She had finished dinner; now she planned to spend most of the evening listening to classical guitar on the stereo while she read material on the Lucy Todhunter case. She was only about a quarter of the way through the documents after an hour of reading, and making notes of comments that seemed relevant to the case, but already she had a much clearer image of the Todhunters, having seen them characterized by friends, servants, and physicians.

From what she learned, Elizabeth did not regret missing the chance to meet them herself. In fact, she thought she *had* met versions of them

178

several times in couples of her parents' acquaintance. Philip Todhunter was the hearty, crass fellow, whom everyone suspected of having a terrible temper, although no one had ever seen it. Lucy was the smiling slender belle, with the Miss Georgia good looks, the brand-name vocabulary, and the decorator-magazine decor. As a couple, they would socialize with people important to the husband's business interests, or the "right" people from the neighborhood or the country club, but no one would know them very well, because their conversation was confined to trivial pleasantries. Perhaps it was all they were capable of. Such people made Elizabeth feel five pounds heavier, and colt-awkward, because try as she might, she could not think of anything to say to them. She was glad that the Todhunters had been dead for more than a century, thus relieving her of the task of interviewing them in person.

Elizabeth turned to the transcript of Lucy Todhunter's trial, but she found that the court record added little to the summary provided by Everett Yancey in his history of the case. Next she turned to a photocopy of a lengthy newspaper interview with Richard Norville. Since the case had been a cause célèbre in Danville, considerable coverage had been given to the trial, to the background of the unhappy couple, and to interviews with the principal witnesses. A pen-and-ink sketch of Norville, captioned WARTIME COMRADE: FAITHFUL UNTO DEATH, accompanied the article.

According to Richard Norville, his friend the major was something of a dandy, meticulous about his clothes and his possessions, but he was not a man of robust health. Philip Todhunter had suffered from neuralgia and stomach complaints during the war, and he was accustomed to dosing himself with patent medicines, in hopes of relieving his discomfort. Norville maintained, though, that despite his health problems, the major had been a good officer and, later in civilian life, a hardworking businessman.

"He was a hypochondriac and a carpetbagger," Elizabeth remarked aloud. "I expect he was tiresome, but I wonder why anyone would want to poison him? Especially, why Lucy? If wives poisoned spouses just for being tiresome, entire *continents* would have to be used as prisons." She added, "No offense, Cameron!" in case any angelic presences were passing through the room.

The journal of Dr. Richard Humphreys went into greater detail about the medical tribulations of the Todhunters. According to Humphreys's narrative, Philip Todhunter was a cornerstone of his medical practice, forever calling in the physician to treat his headaches, his sleeplessness, and his aching joints. Humphreys noted that his patient was in the habit of dosing himself with patent medicines obtained from the cities he frequented on business. Despite the physician's warnings about these nostrums, Todhunter was forever trying some new elixir guaranteed to cure all ills. Elizabeth thought she detected a note of asperity in the doctor's description of his perpetually ailing patient. Apparently, he considered Todhunter a hypochondriac.

Humphreys's attitude toward Mrs. Lucy

Todhunter was altogether more sympathetic. He chronicled the difficulties of her pregnancies, and the sorrow and suffering that accompanied her miscarriages. *She will not live to stand many more assaults on her constitution,* Humphreys wrote. *To my mind it is odd that the Major is so mollycoddling of his own health, and so indifferent to that of his wife. I have warned him that his determination to get an heir will make him a widower, but my counsel falls on deaf ears. I have told Miss Lucy as well, and she wept a bit and implored me to speak to Todhunter. Finally, I sent her off to White Sulphur Springs. The rest will do her as much good as the waters, I daresay.*

Elizabeth read this passage three times, before finally putting the photocopy aside and staring at the white ceiling for some time. She resumed her reading with an air of determination. "Maybe Lucy wasn't guilty," she said aloud, turning a page. "I wonder if it can be that simple."

Her next path of inquiry was to study Mary Hadley Compson's version of the events. Everett Yancey had written a notation at the top of the page: *The Compsons were Lucy Avery Todhunter's North Carolina cousins, visiting at the time of Philip Todhunter's death.* Mary Compson's account of that fateful visit was contained in a series of letters written to her married daughter in New Bern. The letters spanned the period of time both before Todhunter's death and later during the trial. Because they dealt with a Danville cause célèbre, a descendant of Mary Hadley Compson had donated the letters to the city's histori-

cal society. Everett Yancey had dutifully photocopied the lot of them, occasionally penciling
in missing words where the copperplate script
had faded into illegibility.

"He's thorough; I'll give him that," said
Elizabeth, settling down under the stronger
light of the table lamp as she attempted to deci-
pher the spidery writing.

*Though she has much in the way of material wealth
to make her proud, I cannot think that Cousin Lucy
is a happy woman,* Mary Compson had told
her daughter, in a letter dated the week before
Todhunter's death. *Her recent confinement has
left her much weakened, and there is an air of
strain between husband and wife that saddens me
greatly. Mr. Todhunter seems to be neither a brutal
man, nor a drunkard, but he seems more concerned
with his own trifling ailments than with the health
of his young wife. It grieves me to see them, Louisa,
and I trust that you will count yourself fortunate
to have been spared such a fate. You have not your
cousin's finery or possessions, but you will be the
happier for it, I am certain.*

"I wonder if she thought Lucy solved her
marriage problems with white powder,"
murmured Elizabeth, reading on.

*Cousin Lucy's husband has been taken dread-
fully ill,* Mary Compson wrote her daughter.
*At first we feared that it was some outbreak of fever
that would imperil us as well, but that does not
seem to be the case. It cannot be bad food, as the
Major has taken nothing in several days. Both
attending physicians have been most stern in
their questioning of the household, but we could
tell them nothing. Nor would we, if we knew anything to the detriment of that poor young woman,*

our cousin. She tends her stricken spouse like an angel of mercy, but I cannot say I have seen her in much distress over his condition.

The little maid—the clever one—told me that the poor Major was heard to say, "Oh, Lucy, why did you do it?" But this may be put down to the ravings of a delirious man. Indeed, I have given the matter much thought, and I have decided that if Lucy Avery made away with her husband, she is a cleverer woman than I take her for, for I cannot see how she could have accomplished it.

The Compsons stayed on after the death of Major Todhunter, ostensibly to give aid and comfort to their bereaved kinswoman, but also perhaps because the local law-enforcement people wanted them to be available for questioning, and to testify at the forthcoming trial.

I told them all I knew, Mary Hadley Compson recalled. *Which was that Lucy seemed a dutiful helpmeet, and a sympathetic nurse to the dying Major. She had voiced no complaint to me about her marriage, and at no time did I see her behaving in a sinister fashion, with potions or anything of the sort. She gave him a pastry, I told them in court, and I know it was not tainted, because we all ate from the same plate. Any one of us could have chosen the one he ate. So there! Mercifully, Lucy has been acquitted, and we have not spoken of the unpleasantness, although she knows that we are anxious to leave. We think it might not be wise to eat too many Virginia... pastries.*

"Ha! Mary Compson suspects Lucy, too!" said Elizabeth, tapping the paper. "But she isn't sure of her guilt, because she can't figure out how it was done. Neither could anybody else, which is the only reason Lucy was acquitted.

How do you poison a man with a doughnut, when you didn't have the opportunity to tamper with it? I wish I knew. But, clearly, nobody thinks the major did it to himself. And why did he cry out, 'Lucy, why did you do it?' I have to figure out what it was that she could have done."

By the time Elizabeth had finished reading the Compsons' testimony about their visit to the ill-fated household, and then the medical reports of the deceased, she was fairly certain that she knew the motive for the murder of Major Todhunter, and she had a suspicion about what might have caused his death, but now she needed to do some reading on nineteenth-century medicine—or nineteenth-century ailments.

If I'm right, this will be one of those good news/bad news situations, thought Elizabeth. I hope Bill looks on the bright side. I think his client's great-grandmother committed murder, but not in a way that Donna Jean Morgan could duplicate. Now I suppose I'll have to figure out *that* poisoning, too.

Elizabeth looked at the clock. Just after ten, but this was urgent. She found Edith's home phone number scribbled on the erasable message board in the kitchen, and dialed the number. "I know it's late," she told the secretary, "but I remembered that Bill said you had gone with him to Chevry Morgan's church one night. I wondered if you could give me directions on how to get there. I need to look at the place as part of my investigation."

"You sure do," said Edith. "We got a call from

the widow Morgan late this afternoon. They've arrested her for murder. I thought I'd wait until she was convicted to notify the Nobel Prize people."

"I thought she claimed to be innocent."

"Just modesty, I expect," said Edith. "But I realize that Bill has to get her off, because her husband has done enough harm to her without inconveniencing her with a prison sentence, so you just let me know how I can help."

"Can you tell me how to find the church, Edith?"

"Well... it's not the end of the world, but you can *see* it from there. Anyhow, I can't remember all those three-digit state road numbers that they use for those cow paths. It would be easier just to show you where it is. Do you want to go tomorrow?"

"Yes, but I was planning to go early. I also need to drive to Charlottesville tomorrow to consult the UVA medical library. How long will it take us to find the church?"

"Let's allow two hours for the round-trip and the poking around," said Edith. "Meet me at Shoney's at six, and we'll have the breakfast buffet before we drive out there."

"Thank you, Edith," said Elizabeth. "I really appreciate your taking the time and trouble to do this for me."

"You're buying breakfast," said Edith, followed by a dial tone.

Elizabeth replaced the receiver, still thinking about the poisoning cases. She supposed that she ought to go to bed if the day's research was going to start so early. Somewhat startled,

185

she realized that she had not thought about Cameron Dawson for nearly two hours.

"What do you mean, my lawyer's in Florida?" asked Donna Jean Morgan, her eyes red from crying.

"He's getting depositions for another case," said A. P. Hill. She was uncomfortable in the presence of strong emotion, and she hoped she wouldn't be expected to bestow comforting hugs, or to cope with hysterical outbursts from this poor, drab woman.

"But I've been charged with murder, ma'am," wailed Donna Jean. "How could he leave me at a time like this?"

"Don't call me ma'am," murmured A. P. Hill automatically. "I answer to *Powell,* or *A.P.,* or just about anything, except *honey.*" A guard had just tried that last one, and received a blistering lecture on the deportment of law-enforcement personnel, delivered in an icy tone from four inches below his shoulder patch. Bill hadn't been able to get an evening flight back into Danville, because the connecting flights were full, so he'd phoned to say that he was taking the red-eye to Charlotte, and the puddle jumper he'd be on from there would get him to Danville about ten in the morning. That seemed fine until an hour later, when Donna Jean Morgan had used her traditional jailhouse phone call to summon her lawyer, as she had just been charged with her husband's murder. A. P. Hill hoped that nothing would delay her partner's return: she couldn't cope with two murder cases at once. Eleanor Royden was more trouble than a shoe full of fire ants.

"They said they got the autopsy back, and that Chevry had arsenic in him. They're saying I poisoned him. I just knew they'd blame me!" Tears trickled out of her swollen eyes.

"But you didn't do it?" asked Powell Hill. She asked merely out of curiosity; it was Bill's case, but, personally, she would have taken an ax to the old trout weeks earlier, and she marveled at Donna Jean Morgan's self-restraint. (Had the woman not been a client of the firm, A. P. Hill would have characterized her behavior with words less charitable than *self-restraint*.)

"I did not kill my husband," said Donna Jean. "Not that anyone will believe that, on account of my great-grandma being a famous poisoner and all."

"Oh, yes, Lucy Todhunter. Well, don't worry about that, Mrs. Morgan. The sins of one's ancestor are not admissible as evidence in a court of law. What Lucy did or didn't do has no bearing whatsoever on your case. Besides, MacPherson and Hill have their best investigator working on your husband's murder. We may find evidence that will give the DA something else to think about." She forbore to mention that MacPherson and Hill's "best investigator," Elizabeth, was in fact the firm's *only* investigator. The poor woman needed reassuring, after all.

"I don't see how anybody else could have done it. Tanya Faith sure had no reason to want him dead." Donna Jean looked thoughtful. "I expect she would have, you know, in a few years' time. When she realized what-all she missed of her youth, and what a dull, sorry life she'd be leading as an old man's darling, I reckon

187

she'd wish him dead fast enough, but right now she was as high as a wave on a slop bucket. So don't think you can pin this on her."

"We don't have to *pin it* on anybody," said A. P. Hill. "All we have to do is to provide a reasonable doubt about your guilt. Rounding up other suspects is the sheriff's job, not ours."

"Do you think that Mr. MacPherson can convince them I didn't do it?"

"He believes in you," said A. P. Hill, with what she hoped was an encouraging smile. "We'll do everything we can. Starting with a bail hearing." She glanced at her watch. "You may have to trust me to handle that for you. Bill's plane is delayed."

Donna Jean Morgan nodded politely. "I'm sure Mr. MacPherson has taught you everything he knows."

Professional loyalty kept A. P. Hill solemn. "I guess he has," she agreed. "Now let's see if they feel like letting you out of here."

CHAPTER 10

"I suppose you're related to the general?" said Eleanor Royden, when her attorney joined her at the conference table. She nodded toward A. P. Hill's navy-blue suit and tailored blouse. "You look like you're in uniform, too."

A. P. Hill sighed. "Leave it to you not to want to talk about your impending murder trial," she said.

"Well, it isn't as if it's coming anytime soon,"

Eleanor pointed out. "Besides, I just found out that there was a Confederate general called A. P. Hill. I'd heard of the Boy Scout camp by that name in northern Virginia. I suppose that's named for him, too. He was no Boy Scout, though." Eleanor chuckled. "Imagine catching syphilis while you're a West Point cadet. I hope you didn't inherit that, too."

"I didn't." A. P. Hill scowled. "That was a few generations back. Where did all this historical trivia come from?"

"I have been reading," said Eleanor triumphantly. "I never had much time for it before, but now that I am a lady of leisure, I have taken to cultivating my mind. Unfortunately, the jailhouse library consists of dog-eared Louis L'Amours, and a full collection of tomes about the Civil War, donated by the widow of the judge who collected them. That's one way to clean house. Of course, it's fairly tedious for me, having to sit around my cell day after day, reading about that tiresome war."

"I expect it is," said A. P. Hill. As a reenactor, Powell Hill's idea of heaven would be to sit around all day with nothing to do but read books about the War. Maybe I should shoot someone, she thought. Time to get back to business. "Are you ready to talk about the battle in progress, Eleanor?"

"Not yet. I had a question. Are you, by any chance, a bastard?"

Powell blinked. "I beg your pardon?"

"Well, your last name is *Hill*, but I was reading a biography of the general, and it mentioned that all his children were daughters, which means that they should have ended

189

up with different surnames, so, of course, I wondered—"

The attorney sighed. Everybody wondered. Sooner or later real war buffs always got around to delicately phrasing that question. "It's like this," she said. "I'm descended from the general's youngest daughter, Ann Powell Hill, who was born June sixth in Culpeper, a few weeks after her father's death. She married Randolph Junkin and, since there were no other descendants, the couple decided to preserve the general's name by calling themselves Randolph and Ann Hill-Junkin. When the family moved to southwest Virginia in the 1930s, the male heir thought that the name was too pretentious sounding for a rural law practice, so he dropped the Junkin part. Personally, I'm glad they kept Hill, because of the historical connection, and because I like the sound of it. So I *am* descended from Confederate general A. P. Hill. Okay?"

"God," said Eleanor. "You're so straitlaced, you can't even be a party to a scandal once removed. Enough about your ancestors! You're almost as boring as the jail library."

"How gratifying," said her attorney. "Then you'll be thrilled by a change of subject. Dr. Stanfield has given me his report."

"Who? Oh, you mean Skippy, the Boy Shrink. That must have been fun reading. What'd he say about my little legal problem? That I should have reloaded and fired again?"

A. P. Hill frowned. "No. Remember that you want him to find psychological problems in your personality, because that's what will keep you from being convicted for first-degree murder." She opened her briefcase and withdrew a computer printout. "He says you're narcissistic, overly dramatic, and... repressed."

Eleanor Royden cackled. "Did you keep a straight face through that one?"

A. P. Hill did not smile back. "I admit it sounded a bit odd, but Dr. Stanfield explained what he meant by repressed. He says that you put on a show of being funny and charming so that people won't know how you really feel."

Eleanor nodded. "It's called being Southern," she said. "You *paid* him for this pronouncement?"

"He seems to think you put on such a show for people that you have lost touch with how you really do feel."

"I was pretty clear on Jeb and the bimbo," Eleanor pointed out.

"Yes, but that was in a private setting, and the people involved hardly had time to think harshly of you." It was as close to sarcasm as A. P. Hill ever came. "In public, you make a great show of concern for others, and you seem obsessed with what they think of you. Like just now when you *thanked* the guard for holding the door open for you. He was just doing his job."

"I was raised to be pleasant, Sunshine. It's supposed to make life easier for all concerned."

"You overdo politeness, Eleanor. You are perky on automatic pilot so that no one ever knows how you really feel about anything—including yourself."

"Is that a defense?"

"Well, it does suggest someone who might

191

not realize the depths of her rage. It means that people couldn't tell how you really felt about anything, which would mean that their testimony regarding you was unreliable. We might be able to argue a sort of Dr. Jekyll syndrome—that you thought you were all right, but the carefully concealed rage inside you took over, and killed the Roydens with out conscious effort on your part." Powell Hill shrugged. "Diminished capacity due to an emotional disorder. It could work."

"I still like unauthorized pest control," said Eleanor. "Ha! You almost smiled. I knew I could make you laugh, Sunshine!"

"Yes," said her lawyer sadly. "You can always make people laugh, can't you?"

Elizabeth MacPherson had to slow down at every country intersection while Edith, her navigator for the expedition, strained to read the three-digit numbers on the county-road signs. Stretched out on Edith's lap was a map of Pittsylvania County, with the route from Danville to the scene of Chevry Morgan's death outlined in yellow Magic Marker.

"We're in the wilds of Pittsylvania County now," Edith remarked. "Some of these places are so remote, they're only on the map two days a week." Yet another blacktop proved not to be their turnoff.

"Don't worry," said Elizabeth. "I have a full tank of gas, and a compass in the glove compartment."

"Sure," said Edith. "And the hunters will find us, come fall. Oh, wait—there it is. Make a right. Well, if you'd stop driving so all-fired fast! This isn't an interstate. Okay, back up and make a right; there's nobody behind you. It should be about a mile down this road, and then a right turn. Bill and I came out here after dark, so I'm a little hazy on landmarks, but I think we'll see Chevry's church before we spot the house."

It was a peaceful road, lined with cornfields, and patches of oak and maple woodlands. Later in the day the level farmland would become oppressively hot, but now it was pleasant, with a faint breeze ruffling the tall grass in the meadows. Black-and-white cows ambled along the fencerow, watching them solemnly. After an early-morning breakfast in Danville, Edith and Elizabeth had set off for the country. In the trunk of the car, Elizabeth had stashed her notes and references on the Morgan case and the Todhunter historical records so that after the expedition she could drive to the UVA library for research without losing any more time.

For the first few miles Edith had entertained the driver by reading aloud the autopsy report on Chevry Morgan—with perhaps more enthusiasm than was strictly warranted. She then switched to the photocopy of Donna Jean Morgan's account of the last day of Chevry's life. By the time she finished her oral interpretation of that document, they were turning off the main road, and she had to shift roles, from talking book to navigator.

"I don't know what you expect to find out here," Edith remarked. "Not that I mind a nice ride in the country. Do you think the police will have overlooked a clue?"

"There's little chance of that," said Elizabeth.

"I'm sure they were thorough, but there may have been something they overlooked. Something that didn't register to their senses as evidence. Remember, they went in with a strong belief that Chevry had been poisoned by his wife."

"Like what, for instance?"

"I haven't the faintest idea," said Elizabeth. "I only hope we find it."

After a few more miles Edith spotted the correct road sign, and minutes later they pulled up in the gravel parking lot of the little country church. Elizabeth stopped the car and got out to look at the scene of Chevry Morgan's revelations. "So this is it," she murmured.

"This is it."

Elizabeth shook her head at the shabby old building, and then walked past it to the cemetery beyond. The gravestones were worn granite slabs, with an occasional lamb or cross scattered among the rectangles. All the graves were well tended, even those whose inscriptions were faint, their death dates in the 1800s. Here and there a plastic arrangement was propped against a stone. Near the stone wall that marked the cemetery's outer boundary lay a cluster of graves, each marked with a cinderblock-sized headstone. The death dates ranged from 1862 to 1865, and the birth dates were barely twenty years earlier. Each name was followed by the initials C.S.A. These were the Confederate dead, resting in peace under a spreading oak tree that had seen them born and then outlived them by more than a century.

Chevry Morgan's grave was out in the sunlight, heaped with sprays of red and white carnations, and a few bedraggled bunches of roses from parishioners' gardens. There was no headstone yet. The newly dug grave would be left to settle for several months before a permanent marker was installed. Elizabeth wondered who would choose the monument, and what it might say. Would Tanya Faith put down a modern bronze marker, or would the faithful take up a collection for a marble angel to mark the resting place of their controversial prophet? Elizabeth couldn't imagine any marker commissioned by Donna Jean for her errant husband.

"That's an interesting inscription," said Edith, who had been trailing after Elizabeth, reading the older inscriptions. " 'Behold I shew you a mystery.' "

Elizabeth nodded. "It's a Bible verse, but I've never seen it written on a tombstone before. Whose grave is it?"

Edith knelt down to read the fading letters. It was an old tombstone, weathered and chocked with weeds. "Lucy something Tod-something ..."

"Lucy Todhunter! Let me see!" Elizabeth rubbed the dirt from the inscription. "It is Lucy Todhunter. Donna Jean's deadly ancestor. I remember now. In Everett Yancey's manu-script, he mentions that epitaph. I don't remember him saying where she was buried, though. So here she is. Maybe *she* did it."

"I'm still plumbing for divine intervention," said Edith. "This wasn't her house, was it?"

"No," said Elizabeth. "I think her place was closer to Danville. It was badly damaged by fire in the Thirties, and they tore it down. That would have been spooky, though, would-n't it? If she had lived in the house where her great-grandson-in-law was murdered?"

"It would have made an interesting defense for your brother," said Edith. "He could have had Donna Jean plead *demonic possession*."

"Bill is unconventional enough as it is. I just hope we can help him prove her innocence."

A few yards from the cemetery wall stood the house that the preacher had been fixing up for his child bride. They stepped over the low stone wall and started for the back steps. "Did you remember to clear this visit with the widow?" asked Elizabeth.

Edith reached in her purse and pulled out a modern key. "Does that answer your question?"

"Yes, but it still leaves me with about five hundred other questions. How did Lucy Todhunter kill the major? And how did Donna Jean kill Chevry? Or if she didn't, who did?" She shivered as she looked up at the decaying structure nestling in a thicket of weeds. "Maybe it's the house."

"Edgar Allan Poe was from Virginia, but he never got this far west," said Edith. "Let's see what you can find out from the inside. It's hot enough out here to melt polyester."

Moments later they were inside a narrow, old-fashioned kitchen. The imitation parquet linoleum looked new, and the cabinets had been freshly painted, but the lightbulb still hung from a bare socket in the center of the room, and the walls were an unappetizing shade of green, streaked with grease and decades of accumulated dust.

"If I had to live here, I'd drink the poison willingly," Edith remarked.

"It has potential," said Elizabeth, glancing

approvingly at the high ceilings and the oak wainscoting. She tore a paper towel from a roll on the drain board and wiped the sweat from her forehead. "Want some water?" she asked Edith. "There's probably a glass around somewhere."

Edith shook her head. "I'll go check out the rest of the estate."

Elizabeth found a dusty jelly glass, rinsed it out in rusty tap water, and refilled it when the water ran clear. "They need a water filter," she muttered, making a face, but because she was thirsty, she drank it. "Well, I suppose no one needs a water filter here anymore. Tanya Faith will go home to Mommy and Daddy and finish high school. Maybe someday she'll realize how lucky she was that it worked out this way."

She joined Edith for a tour of the rest of the house. The old place had been built at least a century earlier as a simple wooden farmhouse, with two large rooms on either side of the modest entrance hall, where a straight staircase led upstairs to four bedrooms, one of which had been subdivided with wallboard to form an upstairs bath. Each bedroom was resplendent with multicolored deep-pile shag carpeting in iridescent colors, clashing almost audibly with the peeling floral wallpaper from decades past.

"Maybe it *was* the house," muttered Edith, after they had contemplated the riot of color in stunned silence.

"Maybe it would have looked better after he'd painted the walls," said Elizabeth, who was loath to criticize the decorating taste of the recently departed. "Anyhow, I expect he got a good discount on the carpeting, since he was in the business. Let's look around for anything that seems out of the ordinary."

Edith pointed to the pink-and-purple heather shag monstrosity that seemed to be exhaling dust motes before them. "That qualifies."

"I mean, bottles in medicine cabinets, or loose floorboards, or—"

"Secret passages?"

"Oh, sure. Or an empty mummy case, with a sign that says *Back in half an hour*. Any little thing, Edith."

The house's tin roof made the upstairs rooms almost shimmer with heat from the morning sun, but they searched diligently for more than an hour, finding nothing more interesting than a few empty beer bottles tucked in an otherwise empty closet. The bathroom medicine cabinet consisted of two tin shelves behind a paint-spattered mirror. Apart from an accumulation of dirt and two rusty razor blades, it, too, was empty.

Downstairs, they checked the pantry, the parlor, and the dining room, without success. No floorboards were loose. No mantelpieces swung open. No walls concealed hidden rooms. The house was as simple and shabby as it had appeared, offering no clues about the death of the man who had tried to restore it.

Elizabeth and Edith searched the kitchen together, opening every drawer, searching the cupboards, and peering under the sink, much to the mutual horror of Edith and a field mouse in residence. Elizabeth, now on her third glass of tap water, had to keep taking deep breaths to keep from laughing, but Edith was not amused.

It was nearly nine-thirty when Elizabeth, dirt-smudged and shining with sweat, agreed to call it quits. "I know we stayed longer than we intended, and I have to get you back," she told Edith. "Either the crime-scene investigators found everything, or else there was nothing to find."

"At least we tried," said Edith, hurrying to the back door before Elizabeth could change her mind. "Maybe the poison was in the food, after all."

"Apparently, it wasn't. But it certainly isn't here. Maybe someone came to see Chevry Morgan, and brought him something—a poisoned beer, for example."

"Maybe." Edith didn't bother to sound convinced. "Let's head back to town now. Bill's due back today from his Florida expedition, and I need to get to the office."

Elizabeth nodded. "I have some research to do in the UVA medical library." She looked back at the shabby kitchen with its new linoleum shining in an otherwise depressing hovel of grime. "I keep feeling that I've missed something."

Bill MacPherson had returned from Florida on the red-eye flight, and despite his disheveled appearance and lack of sleep, he had formulated a theory about his new civil-rights case, and he was determined to discuss his legal strategy with his law partner. A. P. Hill received these confidences with grave courtesy, but with a notable lack of enthusiasm.

"Bill," she said. "Never mind about the mating habits of your mother's friends. You have a criminal case to worry about. One of your real clients has been charged with the murder of her husband. I had to do the bail hearing for you."

"Good grief!" said Bill, momentarily distracted. "Poor Donna Jean. I was afraid it might come to that. In domestic cases, the spouse is usually the best bet. Did you get her out?"

"No. I argued that she was harmless, and that she really had no place to run to, but the judge took the view that poisoning people ought to be discouraged, and he set bail at five hundred thousand dollars. So, technically, I suppose she could get out, but of course she can't afford it. I told her you'd go and see her today."

"Of course I will," murmured Bill, running a hand through his already rumpled hair.

"You might want to shave and change clothes first. Otherwise, they might keep you on a charge of vagrancy."

"Yes, fine, but let me tell you about this other idea I had, Powell. I've been thinking about it all the way back on the plane, and I really think I'm onto something."

"Are you still raving about dolphins?"

Bill nodded eagerly. "You should have seen him, Powell! He could understand everything anybody said to him."

A. P. Hill wished that she could say the

same about Bill, but she merely nodded for him to go on, resigned to the fact that she would have to hear him out before they could proceed with more serious matters.

"The marine-park people were very helpful, and they all said they'd testify as character witnesses. We'll need character witnesses. It turns out that dolphins often try to initiate sex with their trainers, so you can't exactly call him an unwilling animal victim. Isn't that interesting?"

A. P. Hill pictured a local district attorney of her acquaintance prosecuting a dolphin rape case, but she forbore to comment on the matter. "Go on," she said.

"There's a precedent for this, you know," said Bill, pausing dramatically and peering down at her with what he hoped was a look of great shrewdness.

"Oh, no, Bill ..."

"Oh, yes, Powell! The Dred Scott decision! Remember? In the 1850s, a runaway slave—"

"He wasn't a runaway. His master went north to an unorganized territory in which slavery was banned, and he took Dred Scott along with him."

"Okay. I'll admit I haven't read up on it, but I dimly remember hearing about it in class once. Here's my point: When Scott and his master returned to Missouri, Dred Scott sued for his freedom, claiming that he had been freed by being taken to a free territory. And then you argue all the bits about what constitutes *personhood*. You know, Dred Scott couldn't be denied his rights because he was different from what the courts then thought of as a citizen. And I'll argue that Porky is a thinking, feeling sentient being, whose rights cannot be denied just because he is different. There! Is that a landmark case or what?"

"Aside from the fact that your argument is probably suicidally politically incorrect, because I doubt that Supreme Court Justice Clarence Thomas—to name just one black jurist—is going to enjoy the comparison—aside from that, I do see one glitch in your argument." A. P. Hill leaned back in her swivel chair and propped her feet up on the desk. The pose usually meant trouble for the other person present.

"Glitch?" said Bill. "What glitch?"

"Dred Scott lost the case. The U.S. Supreme Court, under Chief Justice Taney, ruled that black people were not citizens, and therefore could not sue. Which is exactly what you're going to hear if you try to pursue this dolphin business. Your finny friend cannot sue for his rights, because he hasn't *got* any rights."

"Okay, Powell. Maybe I haven't researched this quite well enough yet, and I admit that the Dred Scott case is a setback in my thinking, but don't forget that blacks were granted citizenship in the—um—thirteenth amendment."

"Fourteenth. The thirteenth amendment abolished slavery." She swung her chair round to the bookcase and took down a large, well-worn volume. "Here's what you are thinking of: *'All persons born or naturalized in the United States, and subject to the jurisdiction thereof, are citizens of the United States, and of the State wherein they reside. No State shall make or enforce any law which shall abridge the privileges or*

202

immunities of citizens of the United States; *nor shall any state deprive any person of life, liberty, or property without due process of law, nor deny to any person within its jurisdiction the equal protection of the laws.*' " She closed the book and looked up at her partner. "Fourteenth amendment."

She had expected Bill to be chagrined by this declaration, but he still looked as eager as before. "That's all it says, isn't it?" he asked, grinning.

"That's all," Powell replied. "I should think it was quite enough."

"No, it's great!" Bill insisted. "It says 'all persons... are citizens,' and so on."

"Yes. So?"

"So what is the legal definition of a *person*?" A. P. Hill had opened her mouth to explain the obvious to him, but Bill waved her into silence. "That's where we insert our argument. *What is a person?* Is a person just a vocalizing primate, or does it mean any sentient being who happens to be here? Citizens don't have to speak English. They don't have to be able to walk, or even talk. And the fifteenth amendment guarantees equal rights for all persons regardless of race, color, or previous condition of servitude. I remember *that* one."

"It's bound to be on the books somewhere," muttered a badly flustered A. P. Hill. "Somewhere it's got to say that a person is a human being, a member of the species Homo sapiens."

"Doesn't matter!" said Bill. "The definition got expanded *twice* before: once to include black men, and once to include women. Maybe this is an idea whose time has come."

"Bill, this isn't something that should be tackled by a small law firm in Danville. Surely the ACLU with all their resources ought to be the ones to handle this." And to appear on *Oprah* and *Geraldo*, she finished silently.

For a moment Bill hesitated before his enthusiasm carried him away again. "I took the case," he said. "And I'll see it through."

"Bill—"

"Unless it gets horribly expensive and time-consuming, and *then* I might turn it over to them."

"Fair enough," said A. P. Hill. "Now let's talk about your *other* client. The one who's in jail for first-degree murder."

Elizabeth MacPherson wondered if the air-conditioning in the medical library was malfunctioning. Either that, or she was coming down with something. One minute she would be bathed with sweat, and the next she'd feel chilled to the bone. Her joints ached, too, now that she thought about it. That might be the result of all that tramping around through the cemetery and the Morgan house that morning, but a summer flu seemed the more logical alternative, because her stomach felt queasy, too.

These symptoms had come on slowly as the afternoon progressed, but Elizabeth fought against them. If she had not driven so far to use the library in Charlottesville, she would have given up at the first sign of queasiness, postponing her search for another day, but as it was, quitting now would mean that she would have to make another five-hour round-trip drive at a later date. That seemed such a waste of time and gasoline that she did her best to ignore the symptoms of an oncoming flu. She resolved to concentrate on the search instead of her abdominal cramps.

My illness does set the tone for the research, she thought, trying to tough it out.

Elizabeth was reading up on arsenic in the library's medical texts. To be thorough she had skimmed the section on the history of the use of arsenic as a method for murder in the Middle Ages, when it had been the toxic substance of choice among villains. In those days arsenic was popular for three reasons: (1) it was easy to obtain; pharmacies sold it for rat poison, flypapers, and weed killers; (2) its symptoms could be mistaken for those produced by natural causes; and (3) it was easily dissolved in food or drink, yet it could not be detected by taste. When used as a poison, arsenic was usually in a white powder form: arsenic trioxide (As_2O_3). In the days of the Borgias, arsenic might have passed for natural gastric distress, but in later years a tox screen (if the medical examiner thought to request one) would turn up arsenic in a corpse's vital organs. Nevertheless, each year a significant number of traditionalists continued to use it. Chevry Morgan's liver had been full of it.

The text went on to say that arsenic poisoning had once been so popular among the homicidally inclined that laws were passed prohibiting the manufacturers of embalming fluid from using arsenic in their products. Very sensible of them, thought Elizabeth. It would certainly bugger the autopsy results. During the embalming process the fluid-fixative

205

replaces blood and permeates the viscera; if the embalming fluid contained arsenic, it would be difficult to tell whether the poison had been introduced into the body after death—or before. At least defense attorneys would have seized upon the point to argue a reasonable doubt, and scores of murderers might have got away with their crimes.

Elizabeth had just begun to wonder when the arsenic-free embalming law had been passed, and what they used in the stuff now, when a wrenching abdominal cramp sent her tottering toward the rest room. Typical, she thought as the walls spun around her. The room was full of medical students, and not one of them noticed that I was ill.

She spent twenty minutes in the ladies' room, throwing up and trying to regain control of her body. Many paper towels later, she emerged, pale and shaky, but determined not to give in to a summer virus, or, she was beginning to suspect, food poisoning. "The eggs on the breakfast buffet," she muttered to herself as she sat down again in front of the pile of books. But now that she had vomited, she was probably over the worst of it.

Because Elizabeth wasn't sure how much longer she could hold out against infirmity, she decided to skim through the rest of the introductory material. "Arsenic as medicine," she whispered, stabbing a forefinger at the wavering lines of type. In the nineteenth century arsenic preparations were often used as additives to patent medicines. A topical preparation of arsenic was recommended as a cosmetic for women, because it whitened the skin, and some upper-class gentlemen took arsenic as a tonic, believing that it was an aid to virility. It was known to have been prescribed by physicians as a treatment for malaria and other protracted illnesses in that era; however the book cautioned, once a person became an arsenic-eater, whether from personal vanity or doctor's orders, he became addicted to the substance, and his body developed an increased tolerance for higher dosages. An attempt to cease taking the drug would produce violent stomach pains and the agonies associated with any poison victim. Elizabeth was trying to see through her headache to copy down a most interesting footnote, quoting from an 1885 edition of *Chambers Journal of Popular Literature, Science, and Art,* when the page blurred and began to waver, and the last thing she remembered was a spinning thought about Lucy Todhunter's method of murder.

Her head hit the wooden study table with a crash, and several medical students actually looked up from their reading.

A. P. Hill was pacing the floor as usual. "I hope your sister comes up with something useful in the Morgan case," she told her partner, "because you'll never get Donna Jean out on bail, and I won't have much time to help you with the case."

"Why not?" said Bill. A. P. Hill loved murder cases, so her announcement surprised him. He decided not to be offended that she had assumed he'd *need* assistance from her; she was probably right.

"I've decided not to use any more delaying

tactics on the Royden trial." Powell's face took on that greenish tint that usually accompanied the thought of Eleanor Royden, and she reached for the bottle of pink antacid.

"I thought you said that defense lawyers ought to delay trials as long as possible so that people will forget the victims and the gory details of the crime. You said there was less emotion involved in a trial if you could stall for a year or so."

"That's generally true, Bill, but not this time. Not when the defendant is Eleanor Royden, the Clown Queen of Crime. If I don't get this trial over with soon, everyone on the planet will have heard of her. She's giving interviews left and right, firing off sound bites that I cannot possibly explain away in court. If this goes on much longer, we'll have to get jurors from Saturn to get a fair trial."

"How does she feel about the change of pacing?"

A. P. Hill got herself a glass of water—the chaser for her dose of pink antacid. "Eleanor? She's all for it. She thinks this will get her out of jail sooner."

"I suppose it could," said Bill, who was always willing to look for the pony after he stepped in the fertilizer.

"Yes, but it could also get her out of jail and into prison. Every time I have a meeting with Eleanor Royden, I come out feeling like there's a volcano under my ribs. I can tell her what to wear, and how to fix her hair, but I can't muzzle her! One snappy remark in court, one smirk at the wrong time—and she's had it. I'm not in control of this case. I'm not even sure she'll *wear* what I tell her. For all I know, she could turn up in court in a silver lamé pantsuit."

Bill had never seen his partner so agitated. The problem with trying to offer her consolation was that Powell was absolutely correct in her assessment of the situation. Powell made it her business to be absolutely correct most of the time, but at the moment she wasn't enjoying it. "Well, partner, you know I'll help you in any way I can," he said.

A. P. Hill was still working out a tactful response to Bill's offer when the phone rang. He snatched up the receiver. "MacPherson and Hill... Oh, hello, Mother."

A. P. Hill tuned out the subsequent conversation while she focused on her own misery, and on the fine points of Eleanor's case. Suddenly she heard Bill say, "She's *what*?" And then, "Where is she? Right. As soon as I can." When he hung up the phone, it took him two tries to replace the receiver.

"What is it, Bill?"

"It's Elizabeth," said Bill, with disbelief still lingering in his voice. "She's in the hospital in Charlottesville." He glanced toward the receptionist area. "Edith! My sister is in intensive care. What did you two do this morning before she left for UVA?"

"We had breakfast at Shoney's at six, and then we drove out in the country and looked at Chevry Morgan's love nest," said Edith. "What do you mean, she's in intensive care? What's the matter with her?"

"You didn't see Donna Jean Morgan at the house?"

"No. Neither wife was there."

"You didn't stop by her place for coffee—?"

"Bill." A. P. Hill put her hand on his arm. "Donna Jean is in jail. Remember?"

Bill blinked. "Oh, right. I was forgetting. It's just that the doctors seem to think that Elizabeth has been poisoned. Mother's on her way up there."

"Poisoned," said A. P. Hill, sounding more intrigued than distressed. "I wonder how it was done."

"I have to go now." Bill pulled his car keys out of his pocket and started for the door.

A. P. Hill grabbed her purse and followed him out. "Bill, wait! I think I'd better drive."

"Give me a second to turn the answering machine on and lock the door!" Edith called after them. To herself she muttered, "Hope I don't come down with it, too."

They put arsenic in his meat
And stared aghast to watch him eat;
They poured strychnine in his cup
And shook to see him drink it up;
They shook, they stared as white's their
   shirt:
Them it was their poison hurt.
—I tell the tale that I heard told.
Mithridates, he died old.
                    —A. E. HOUSMAN
                    A Shropshire Lad

CHAPTER 11

Elizabeth MacPherson opened her eyes a fraction of an inch, just enough to discern anxious faces peering down at her. She squeezed them shut again.

"I think she's regaining consciousness," someone whispered. It sounded like Bill's voice.

Elizabeth lay there, silently debating the merits of waking up or not, and whether any action on her part would result in an urgent need of a bedpan. She heard more murmuring, and the word *nurse* was repeated three or four times, at which point she decided that she might as well rejoin the living, because they were only going to poke and prod her until she did.

The light hurt her eyes, and her head still felt like it was in a winepress. "I had a strange

211

dream," she said faintly. "And *you* were in it. And you. And *you*."

"Do you think she's delirious?" The voice was definitely that of A. P. Hill, as clinical as ever.

"I think she's being a smart-ass," Bill replied, with relief winning out over annoyance. "She's quoting lines from *The Wizard of Oz* at us."

A. P. Hill did not think that such behavior was inconsistent with delirium, but since everyone else seemed relieved and amused, she allowed herself a judicious smile. "I'll go out and tell Edith and Ms. Casey that she's coming around," she said.

Margaret MacPherson nodded. "Thank you, Powell." She leaned over her daughter's bedside. "Elizabeth! Do start making sense, please. We want to know what happened to you."

Elizabeth looked thoughtful. "I was having a conversation with Cameron, I think," she said. "He asked if I were angry with him for living so recklessly, taking off in that small boat, and all. I said I wasn't, and I hugged him, and he said—oh, my head!" She closed her eyes again. "Can they give me something for this headache?"

Margaret MacPherson and her son exchanged worried glances. "A nurse should be here soon, dear," she told Elizabeth. "They're going to want to know what happened to make you so ill. And now you come awake babbling about Cameron. Oh, Elizabeth! You didn't do this to yourself, did you?"

"I didn't think of it," whispered Elizabeth. "Isn't that odd? All these weeks of grieving about Cameron, and it never once occurred to me. And now, of course, he has absolutely forbidden it, so that's that." She attempted to sit up in bed, and thought better of it as her joints began to ache. "What *is* the matter with me?"

"Apparently, you were poisoned," said Bill, sitting down again. He scooted the chair close to Elizabeth's bedside. "But we can't figure out how it was done, or by whom. Edith is especially concerned, of course."

Elizabeth managed a grin. "I expect she is! We shared the same breakfast buffet. It's not food poisoning, then?"

"Arsenic, they think. They're running the tox screen again to make sure."

"Arsenic," said Elizabeth. "That is interesting. I was reading about arsenic when I started to become ill. I was in the medical library."

"Hypochondria?" murmured her mother. "Some sort of sympathetic illness?"

"Oh, Mother, really!" said the patient. "You've been eating too much tofu! Of course it isn't psychosomatic. Every muscle in my body will testify to that. I really was poisoned."

"When? How?" asked Bill. "Did you see Donna Jean? No, I keep forgetting. She's in jail. Did she ever give you anything to eat or drink?"

"No, of course not. If Edith isn't sick, we can rule out breakfast, so it had to be something in that house. Dust? Can we ask Edith?"

Edith, wrested away from the March edition of *Field and Stream* in the waiting room, tried to reconstruct the events of the morning. "We walked through the cemetery," she said, frowning with the effort of remembering. "You found Lucy Todhunter's grave. I don't suppose she zapped you, though, after all this time. You didn't chew on her flowers, or anything. Then you looked at some Civil War graves, and we climbed the wall and went in the house. We searched the kitchen, and the pantry. There wasn't any food lying about, though."

"No," said Elizabeth. "Even if there had been, do you think I would have risked eating it? In a house where a man died of poisoning?" She began to cough. "Bill, could you pour me some water, please?"

Edith's shouting made her head hurt even worse, and it attracted the attention of the nurse, thus suspending all conversation for several minutes while the visitors were ushered back out into the hall, and Elizabeth's vital signs were verified and duly recorded on her chart. Even after the thermometer had been removed from her mouth, Elizabeth was unusually quiet. She was thinking about her afternoon's research and about the one substance that she and Edith had not shared that morning: the drinking water from the Morgan kitchen.

Tanya Faith Reinhardt-Morgan had accepted a ride to the mall with two girls she knew from school. She had to get out of her parents' house, and she didn't have much of anywhere else to go. The two girls who invited her were disappointed that she refused to talk about her recent bereavement, which, after all, had been their sole reason for asking her along. As soon as they reached the escalator, they had wandered off to look at cosmetics, an indulgence prohibited by Tanya Faith's funda-mentalist sect (polygamy, yes; lipstick, no).

For lack of anything else to do, and lack of any money to do it with, she wandered into the video-and-pinball arcade to watch the teenage joystick pilots in action. As far as Tanya Faith knew, the Lord had not prohibited Pac-Man, or any of his ilk. She thought that the Lord might have done so, if He'd known about them, but as nothing on the subject had been handed down as yet, she decided to take advantage of the theological loophole and hang around, checking out the guys. As a token of her widowhood, she was wearing a black, below-the-knee-length summer dress with halter straps and a fitted waist. Tanya Faith looked quite fetching in black. She wished she could have worn lipstick, but the Lord was dead set against that, so she got around the restriction with regular and liberal applications of shiny, fruit-flavored (and tinted) lip balm—for medicinal purposes, of course.

"Hello, Tanya Faith. Want to try this?"

"Wh-what?" She was startled out of her reverie by a slender young man with dark hair and rather dazzling blue eyes. He looked familiar. Then she placed him: history class, the row by the window. She saw that he was offering her a brass coin.

"It's a token," he said patiently. "You've been standing there for the longest time, just watching, so I thought you might enjoy playing a game."

"Oh." She shook her head and blushed a little. "I wouldn't have any idea how to go about it."

"I could show you. It isn't hard." He looked embarrassed. "Unless you think you shouldn't because of what happened. Maybe it wouldn't be seemly to have any fun. You know, out of respect and all."

"You mean Chevry?"

The boy nodded. His dark hair had a sort of lilt in the front, and his eyes looked even bluer up close. His name was Mike Gibbs—she remembered hearing him called on in class. He wasn't one of the advanced-placement show-offs, but he wasn't a dweeb, either. "Yeah, I guess the whole school knows about it by now," he was saying. "It was in the paper, your picture and everything. Tough break, after all you went through with him. But I guess you're lucky that old lady didn't kill you, too."

"Donna Jean? Oh, she's mostly talk." Tanya Faith was scornful of her rival. "And she's going to jail anyhow."

"So you're back with your folks now?"

"Uh-huh." She was looking at the flashing lights on the video game. On the side of the machine, there was a picture of a dark-haired young man with a sword, facing a dragon. "Do you think I could try that one?" she asked Mike.

"If you're sure it's okay," he said.

"Oh, Chevry would want me to be happy," she said quickly. "And I know the Lord wants me to go on with my life." Tanya Faith's greatest legacy from her late husband was the ability to determine that God's will always coincided with her own inclinations.

Elizabeth had summoned everybody back to her bedside with that feeble air of authority

216

assumed by many of the infirm. "I have jobs for all of you," she announced. "Bill, I need you to drive back out to the Morgan house and get a sample of the tap water from the kitchen."

"Couldn't we phone the sheriff and ask him—"

"Do it, Bill!" Elizabeth was in no mood for debating with attorneys, particularly those who were her blood relatives. "And, Edith, I hope my purse and my belongings made it to the hospital along with me."

"There're some things in that metal locker," Margaret MacPherson offered. "I know your clothes are there."

"Good. Edith, see if my notebook is in there. I was copying down some information from a periodical called *Chambers*. If you can't find it, you'll need to go to the medical library and start over for me."

Edith looked at Bill and A. P. Hill. "Are we calling this overtime?"

"Send me an invoice," snapped Elizabeth. "It can't be higher than my hospital bill, and I want some answers."

"I was kidding!" said Edith cheerfully. "I don't charge for playing detective. Just for typing and shorthand." She opened the metal locker and began to rummage.

"Powell, you're interested in history. Do you know Everett Yancey?"

"I think we've met," said A. P. Hill. "He's a local historian, though, not a reenactor. Why?"

"I was reading something interesting about arsenic. An article on the history of arsenic said that laws had to be passed prohibiting the

217

use of arsenic in embalming fluids, because its presence could skew the results of an autopsy in murder cases. So, I started wondering when *did* they use arsenic in the embalming process?"

"Is that all you wanted to know?" said A. P. Hill. "I can tell you that. It was during the Civil War."

"Why?" asked Bill, who was trying to think of some nefarious way for the armies to use embalming fluid as a secret weapon. Nothing occurred to him, though: dead was dead.

"Because they had a lot of bodies to contend with, and they were trying to find something that worked better as a preservative," she replied. "Back in the eighteenth century, the recipe for corpse stuffing would have worked just as well on a rump roast: sage, thyme, rosemary. Undertakers just crammed a lot of sweet-smelling herbs into the deceased to keep him from stinking up the funeral. But the body decomposed at the normal, untreated rate, so burial had to take place quite soon after death."

"Which is why a few unembalmed people in comas occasionally got interred," murmured Elizabeth. "No chance of that, these days."

"Right," said A. P. Hill. "The preservative factor became an issue during the War Between the States, because soldiers were being killed hundreds of miles from home, and often their families wanted the bodies returned for burial in the local cemetery."

"I wouldn't want to be on a train with a stack of parsley-scented corpses," muttered Bill. "Anyhow, I thought they buried soldiers right on the battlefield."

"Some of them were," said A. P. Hill. "But some bodies were sent home for burial."

"Officers," said Edith, who had found the notebook and was heading out into the hall to read it.

"That's true enough," A. P. Hill conceded. "Stonewall Jackson is buried in the cemetery in Lexington, a few blocks from his home. And Jeb Stuart is buried in Richmond. They both died of wounds, though, instead of on the field of battle. That might have made a difference, too. Anyhow, in an attempt to preserve the soldiers' corpses long enough to get them home for burial, they started using stronger chemicals, including arsenic, in the embalming process."

"Bill," said Elizabeth. "It's a long way to Danville. Hadn't you better get going?"

"In a minute," he said. "If you're going to explain what all this is leading up to, I want to hear the rest of it."

"Isn't it obvious?" asked Elizabeth. "They put heavy- metal poisons into some of the soldiers' corpses and sent them home to be buried in local graveyards."

Bill blinked uncomprehendingly. "So?"

"In wooden coffins. Right, Powell?"

"Most of the time, yes. Why?"

"Edith and I saw some Civil War graves in that cemetery adjacent to the old house. I'll bet some of them died a long way from Danville. A day's ride would have been far enough away to warrant preservatives, though, especially in the summer."

A. P. Hill looked at her partner. "Get going,

219

Bill!" she said. "We need to get that water sample tested to clear Mrs. Morgan!"

"Will somebody please tell me—"

"Bill, the bodies were packed with poison, and buried in wooden coffins one hundred and thirty years ago. The coffins have long since rotted away, and the bodies have decomposed. Where did the arsenic go?"

He shrugged. "Into the soil, I guess."

Elizabeth nodded. "And into the *groundwater*. The well to the house must be on the side where the cemetery is located. Fortunately the concentrations of arsenic in the well water are not large enough to be fatal in a single dose, but arsenic is a cumulative poison. I drank three glasses of contaminated water, and I became seriously ill."

"I believe your condition is listed as *fair*, dear," said Margaret MacPherson.

Her friend Casey said, "Oh, Margaret, don't be little her symptoms. If you can't dramatize your own poisoning when can you enjoy ill health?"

"Thank you," said Elizabeth. She reached for a glass of water from the bedside table, looked at it for a long moment, and set it back down untouched. "As I was saying, I drank less than a pint of the water, altogether. Chevry Morgan must have been drinking it for weeks in the evening while he worked to refurbish the old house."

Bill nodded. "Donna Jean mentioned that he had been complaining of aches and pains. She thought it was a virus. She said that Tanya Faith had been affected, too."

"Tanya Faith sometimes went to the house with Chevry to keep him company while he worked. But Donna Jean never did. She never ingested any poisoned water. Chevry, who worked there almost every night, drank the most. The concentration levels might have varied, too. Anyhow, sooner or later it killed him."

"Donna Jean Morgan really is innocent," Bill said wonderingly.

"Oh, honestly, Bill, I don't know how you lawyers sleep at night," snapped his sister. "Yes, she does happen to be innocent. I think we can chalk up Chevry Morgan's death to the Confederacy's score: a belated casualty of the Late Unpleasantness."

"I prefer to call it divine intervention," said Edith from the doorway. She was holding Elizabeth's notebook and smiling.

"So Donna Jean didn't use her great-grandmother's recipe for husband poisoning?" asked Bill, trying to assimilate this new information.

"It wouldn't have worked on Chevry," said Edith, grinning. "Old Lucy Todhunter killed her husband with a plain old doughnut."

"I thought so," said Elizabeth.

Eleanor Royden was alone in her cell. She knew that later—if she ended up in the barracks of women's prison—she might actually long for such isolation, but just now she was finding it difficult. Solitude had never been one of Eleanor's favorite things. She liked parties, witty dinner companions, and the sound of friendly laughter. She and Jeb had given some wonderful parties in Chambord Oaks. Everyone had said that no one could match her for delightful dinners and a stimulating mix of people. Jeb had taken that for granted, of course. He thought that sit-down dinners for sixteen simply *happened* while he was in circuit court. He'll find out differently when he tries to entertain with the bimbo, she thought.

And then she remembered: Jeb was dead.

For an instant she wished he weren't dead, because he would know which lawyer to recommend to take her case. (He would not have chosen A. P. Hill. Eleanor could almost hear him accusing her of making a sentimental choice at the risk of losing her case. But what choice did she have, when all of the lawyers he would have suggested were cronies of his who thought she deserved the death penalty?)

And he would figure out some sort of image to project to the public; Jeb was very good about managing his clients' publicity. She wondered what he would think of her new celebrity: her photo in the *Washington Post*, an interview in *Vanity Fair*, and even a mention in Jay Leno's opening monologue. None of this publicity had been *favorable*—she had to admit that—but at least she was famous. Her name was even on T-shirts.

It was quite a change from being the anonymous wife of a local power broker. Now she was somebody in her own right.

But Jeb was still dead. He would never know how important she had become; how cleverly she used her wit and charm to dazzle the press. He would never respect this new Eleanor, because he was dead. He wasn't going to come to his senses, and give up Staci the sex toy. He wasn't going to miss Eleanor, or ask her forgiveness.

In fact, if any consciousness of Jeb Royden survived anywhere, it was probably furious with her. Jeb Royden was actually dead. Eleanor thought it was amazing that someone as confident and powerful as Jeb Royden could actually be killed by a bullet smaller than a tube of lipstick. Such a big, loud, arrogant man, with his law degree, his Armani suits, and his friends in high places—and little, middle-aged Eleanor of the cheap apartment and the dead-end life had snuffed out all that magnificence with a thimbleful of cylindrical metal. Perhaps if she had been able to believe in his mortality, she wouldn't have had to shoot him.

Actually, she hadn't meant to obliterate Jeb Royden altogether. She had wanted to destroy the new Jeb—the pompous status seeker who had no compassion for anyone less powerful than himself. But somehow she thought that when she had killed that monster, the old Jeb would arise out of the ashes, so that she could be reunited with her husband and best friend: the smart, fun-loving overachiever who had dazzled her all those years ago. Wasn't that how it went in the fairy tales? You shoot the beast, and the prince emerges unscathed from the riddled corpse of the enchanted ogre. Only this time, when the ogre died, the prince went with him.

Eleanor Royden was beginning to suspect

that no matter how pretty and charming and victimized she was, a happy ending would not be forthcoming.

Elizabeth was beginning to like the sensation of lying back on pillows while one's troops scurried hither and yon, doing one's bidding. This sense of power coupled with a complete absence of effort was proving to be very pleasant. Unfortunately, the attending physician had stopped by with test results and an evening examination, and he had pronounced her fit enough to leave the hospital in the morning. The quantity of arsenic in her system was relatively small, and she had reached the emergency room in time enough to receive treatment that kept her condition from getting worse. The doctor warned that she might have some joint pains and perhaps a few headaches or dizzy spells until the effects of the poison had completely left her system.

The members of the law firm had used the doctor's visit as their excuse to leave, and they made their farewells, promising further news of the case as things developed. Edith swore to keep the doughnut explanation to herself, since it had no direct bearing on the case of Chevry and Donna Jean Morgan, and Elizabeth assured them that she would explain it all to them as soon as she saw them again.

The room was quiet; the lights were dimmed; and Elizabeth was now alone with her mother, who was determined to sit by the bedside of her ailing offspring.

"You didn't give me a task, dear," she reminded the patient.

"I saved a hard one for you, Mother," said Elizabeth solemnly.

"Really? And what is that?"

"Don't you think someone should notify Daddy that I'm in the hospital?"

"Oh, my, your father. I'd forgotten all about him."

"So it seems," Elizabeth remarked, with a glance toward the closed door. "Would you like Casey to come in? We shouldn't leave her alone in the hall."

"Yes, of course." Margaret MacPherson hesitated. "You know, dear, when we heard that you were seriously ill—dying, for all I knew—I resolved to tell you something, if I ever got the chance. And now that you're going to be fine, it all seems silly, but after all I did promise your guardian angel, or whoever listens to mothers' prayers."

"In your case, I should imagine it's Saint Jude, Mother."

"I'll just go and get Casey."

Elizabeth tried not to imagine what new culture shocks awaited her with the coming revelation. Surely, no one was using the hospital visit to price sex-change operations, were they? Before she had time to raise her blood pressure significantly, Margaret and Casey appeared, and sat down in the two metal chairs by the bed. "All right," she said wearily. "I'm under sedation anyhow. What is it?"

Margaret and Casey looked at each other. "It will all come out anyway when Virgil resigns," said Casey, shrugging.

"True. All right. Elizabeth, I don't necessarily want you broadcasting this about. In fact, don't even tell Bill unless you think you absolutely must, but Casey—"

"Call me Phyllis," said the small dark-haired woman, smiling faintly.

Margaret MacPherson nodded. "Oh, of course. *Phyllis*. Sorry. It has become a habit. Anyhow, Elizabeth, Phyllis and I are roommates."

"Yes, you live together. I know. I came to your housewarming party. So?"

"You don't understand," said her mother. "Phyllis and I are *roommates*."

"Not lovers," said Phyllis Casey helpfully.

Elizabeth's eyes widened, and her jaw dropped. "You lied?" she whispered. "You lied about your sexual orientation? About this whole political lesbian business! You lied? Why would you do such a thing?"

She was prepared to go on for several more minutes in the same vein, but Phyllis Casey interrupted her. "Actually, Margaret did it as a favor to me. Please don't be cross with her. She was being extremely kind."

" 'A little more than kin; a little less than kind,' " snapped Elizabeth. She only wished her cousin Geoffrey had been present to hear her riposte. Geoffrey, an amateur actor with an inclination toward Shakespeare, regarded barding as his chief form of recreation. Elizabeth admired his displays of erudition, but she rarely managed to find an opportunity to use one of the few phrases she knew. "What do you mean, doing you a favor?" she asked Phyllis Casey.

"Phyllis is an English professor at the local

college. She has taught there for years, and because she has always been conservative and diligent, the rest of the faculty has taken her for granted. Lately, the department has become increasingly radical. First it was deconstruction, then it was multiculturalism—"

"They ditched Chaucer and Melville in favor of Comanche war chants and readings from the *Bhagavad-Gita*," said Phyllis Casey, scowling.

"I see," said Elizabeth. "And you were upset over this?"

"Disgusted is more like it," Phyllis replied. "But what really enraged me was the notion that one had to be a radical to get any attention. Nobody cared about good teaching, or decent scholarship anymore. It was all show business. Who can be the most militant; who can make the most shocking assertions regarding conventional texts."

Margaret MacPherson nodded. "I think what finally sent Phyllis over the edge was the course on the Brontës. The young professor who taught it called it Incest and Literature."

Phyllis sighed helplessly. "It did upset me. He said some very nasty things about Emily and Branwell, without a scrap of evidence. Why, the *National Enquirer* has more credibility than that young swine."

"Then the department started assigning all the upper-level lit classes to the flamboyant types, while poor Phyllis was left to teach freshman comp and all the other scutwork courses. She was getting ready to quit, but I

227

told her that two can play at that game. 'You fight back,' I said. Didn't I, Phyllis?"

The English professor nodded, looking a little embarrassed. "It really did seem to be the only course of action," she murmured. "So logical."

Elizabeth gasped. "You told them you were a lesbian?"

"Yes. I announced it at the next department meeting. And I said that as a militant feminist lesbian I objected to having courses about women writers taught by a member of the white male patriarchy who are our oppressors."

"She meant the clown who taught Incest and Literature."

"Yes. I did a good bit of reading to get the terminology right. My colleagues were stunned, I must say. They just stared at me, open-mouthed, like the bowl of goldfishes in Goldsmith's poem. So before anyone could recover I told them that I wanted to teach a lit course called Man-Free: the Creative Spirit of the Unencumbered Woman."

"Let me guess," said Elizabeth. "Jane Austen, Emily Brontë, Emily Dickinson—"

"Precisely." Phyllis Casey beamed with satisfaction. "All the authors I had been teaching all along. As soon as I announced that I was a lesbian feminist, they gave me back all my old courses. They've all been quite deferential to me ever since."

"How did you two pull off this scam?"

"It was quite easy, dear," said Elizabeth's mother. "Phyllis and I had already arranged to be roommates, because sharing the house seemed like such a safe and economical measure.

But people are rather contemptuous of middle-aged women who are simply housemates, so we decided to spice up the act a little."

"People believed you?" asked Elizabeth, still incredulous.

"*You* believed us, dear. I find that most people will believe anything that scandalizes them. And we never resorted to public displays of affection, or even to sharing a bedroom. People simply took our word for it. People seemed so eager to be tolerant and accepting of us that it never occurred to them to wonder if we were conning them. We were amazed ourselves at how easy it was."

"It's a pity we have to give the game away," said Phyllis.

"Why? What happened?"

"Virgil Agnew and I are engaged." Phyllis Casey smiled at Elizabeth's look of astonishment. "You may remember him from the party. He is the professor of theatre and dance who was introduced to you as our token heterosexual."

"Oh yes," said Elizabeth. "He claimed to be in therapy for it."

"He was. His psychiatrist pronounced him incurable, though, so he gave up trying to be like everyone else, and we started seeing each other. Last week Virgil proposed to me, and I accepted him." She sighed. "I suppose I'll lose my lit courses again."

"You're jilting my mother for a guy named Virgil?" Elizabeth demanded. "No, wait. I think I'm relieved. I think."

Margaret MacPherson and Phyllis Casey laughed.

"Really, Elizabeth, I'm delighted for both of them," her mother assured her. "I think Phyllis and I were growing tired of the nouvelle cuisine crowd anyway. It will be quite a relief to close the show."

"I had just gotten used to the idea of you two," Elizabeth grumbled. "In fact I was rather pleased at having a mother who was in the forefront of modern feminist thought. You certainly weren't the dull, conventional station-wagon driver I thought I knew."

"I never was such a person," said Margaret MacPherson. "Perhaps no one is. But for years we play these roles of unchanging reliability so that our children will have a secure and happy childhood. But perhaps you've had that long enough, and I can set about finding me again."

A new thought occurred to Elizabeth. "Mother! Did you ever tell Daddy about you and Casey?"

Margaret MacPherson smiled. "Oh, yes, dear. That was the one bit of selfishness in my otherwise charitable gesture."

"How did he react?"

"He now maintains that he became interested in another woman only because *I* had become interested in another woman. He blames Phyllis for wrecking the marriage, even though I hadn't met her at the time, and his psyche seems to have taken an awful beating over the idea of losing his wife to a lesbian. I believe he's seeing a therapist. Which reminds me, Elizabeth, how are things going between you and Dr. Freya?"

"Oh, all right, I suppose," said Elizabeth.

"I try to keep her entertained for my hourly sessions."

"But, Elizabeth, you're supposed to be trying to feel better."

"No, Mother. I am trying not to feel at all."

In the darkness the water in the holding tank looked black, and the only sound was the soft slur of someone ceaselessly swimming. Miri Malone approached the edge of the pool cautiously, because no one knew that she was there, not even Rich Edmonds, who had been so supportive in her relationship with Porky. Rich was a wonderful friend, but tonight's visit was too private to be shared with him.

Miri paused at the water's edge, listening. It was nearly midnight, and there was a gentle wind, blowing cool night air in her face and raising chill bumps on her arms. It was a bit cool to be out in just a swimsuit, but wearing it had been force of habit. She really shouldn't have bothered. All was quiet. No one was working late in the marine park offices, and no guards were nearby, although, since she knew them all, she was sure she could have talked her way out of any difficulty that arose.

Miri dipped one foot in the cold water and felt a shiver run up her spine. When the water was cold, it was best to plunge in quickly, without thinking about it too much beforehand. Perhaps that also applied to the other thing she intended to do tonight. She pulled down the straps on her bathing suit and eased it down her hips, wriggling out of it and tossing it aside.

231

That was better. Now she could feel the breeze all over. She swung down the metal ladder and into the water, calling out softly, "Porky! It's me."

A moment later a dark form glided up against her in the chilled water, butting the small of her back with his blunt nose. Miri turned and nuzzled the dolphin. "Hello, Porky," she murmured. "How about a moonlight swim?"

She pushed away from him, playfully splashing his face as she plowed past. Porky, still wearing an enigmatic smile, waited a sporting minute, and then plunged after her, past her, and then in circles around her.

For several minutes they splashed and swam together, and the only sounds were Miri's giggles and the rush of the water as their bodies churned. The Sea Park lights made patterns on the dark water, but Miri was careful not to swim into the patches of light. Finally she swam close to Porky, and determined that he had reached the proper stage of excitement.

"Are you ready?" Miri whispered, pressing her wet face close to the dolphin's smile. "Shall we do it?"

She rippled the water with her hands and then turned over on her back, floating, her pale body shining against the blackness beneath her. "C'mon," she said softly, and then she made the clicking sounds that are dolphin speech.

Porky clicked back, bobbed a few times, and then swam on top of her. Miri held on, thinking that perhaps they should have discussed the precise acrobatics involved in such a union. She started to disengage herself, in order to be better prepared, but Porky showed no signs of stopping.

"Wait!" said Miri, before a slosh of salt water silenced her. If she could just get to the side of the pool perhaps, and position herself against the ladder. But Porky's masculine sensibilities were signaling full speed ahead, and he used his flippers to anchor her to him as he drifted downward toward the twenty-foot depths in the center of the pool. Dolphins mate underwater.

Miri Malone's last thought as she drifted into the chilling dark was that she had been right about men, but wrong to think that a change of species would make any difference.

CHAPTER 12

Bill MacPherson was celebrating his client's release from jail and his sister's release from the hospital by treating the client, the sister, and the firm to a celebratory lunch at Ashley's Buffet, a restaurant much favored by Bill for its all-you-can-eat policy, which catered to both his appetite and his income.

Elizabeth, still wobbly from her close encounter with the exculpatory evidence, was limiting her food to Jell-O and ice cream, for fear of causing a new bout of stomach cramps in her recently poisoned system.

A. P. Hill sat hunched over a plain salad, still brooding about the impending murder trial of her own client, but Edith, whose appetite was never affected by the troubles of others, was tucking into her second plateful of roast beef and mashed potatoes, with assorted vegetables piled around them for variety. "This is what I call a party," she remarked, between mouthfuls.

Donna Jean Morgan chewed on a piece of fried chicken with mournful satisfaction. "This sure does beat the food they serve down at the jail."

"That's all over now," Bill assured her. "You've tasted your last meal from the county jail. All we needed was the analysis of the well water, which came back from the lab yesterday. It contained arsenic. Elizabeth was right."

"Of course I was," she said.

"Once I took the water sample in to the district attorney, along with several affidavits explaining how arsenic from embalmed bodies in the church cemetery had contaminated the well water at the old house, he realized that their case against you was weak, to say the least. He even acknowledged that there was a chance that you could be innocent."

A. P. Hill smiled. "They never actually admit that anyone is not guilty. District attorneys can't afford to trust humanity. It would be bad for business."

"They grumbled a bit," Bill agreed, "but I pointed out that the county budget could be put to better use than staging pointless trials against innocent widows, in the face of overwhelming technical evidence. In the end they conceded the point, and the judge expedited the paperwork, and here you are."

"It'll be in the newspaper, won't it?" asked Donna Jean. "I want the congregation and my neighbors to know I didn't kill Chevry."

"I called them myself," said Bill. "They may want to interview you. Channel thirteen might come over from Lynchburg, if you want a press conference."

"I'll talk to them," said Donna Jean.

"You're not going to move away, then?" asked A. P. Hill, who had thought that the local notoriety might be too great, even for one proven innocent.

"No," said Donna Jean. "I don't know anywhere but here. Besides, Chevry didn't leave all that much money. Reckon I'll give some of it to Tanya Faith."

"You are not required to by law," said Bill. He blushed. "I mean, I could look it up, but—"

"No, I want to give her some," his client replied. "I think she ought to go off to college. Maybe Chevry owed her that. Maybe she'll get smart enough not to fall for some man's line of talk if she gets educated."

"Speaking of Tanya Faith," said Edith. "There's bound to be some unpleasant questions if you do hold a press conference. Are you sure you don't want to skip the publicity?"

Donna Jean Morgan shook her head. "I welcome the chance to clear my name, and my great-grandmother's, too."

An awkward silence followed her remark. Bill and Elizabeth looked at each other. Finally Edith declared, "You might as well tell her. She's got a right to know, being a descendant and all."

235

"A right to know what?"

"The whole truth and nothing but the truth," Edith sang out.

"Hush, Edith!" said Elizabeth. "Bill, I think I'd better tell her, since I'm the one who figured it out. Mrs. Morgan, you don't want to mention your great-grandmother at the press conference. What they're trying to tell you is that your great-grandmother, Lucy Todhunter, was guilty of murder. Technically, that is."

"Technically? What do you mean?" Donna Jean Morgan wished these legal types would learn plain speaking. "Either she killed somebody or she didn't."

"Yes," said Elizabeth, who was wavering between sympathy for the murderess's descendant and excitement over her discovery. "She did kill her husband, Philip Todhunter, but perhaps it's just as well that she was acquitted, because the court would have had an awfully difficult time proving that Lucy had murdered her husband with a beignet. That's a pastry covered with powdered sugar."

"Oh, that old doughnut," said Donna Jean. "I thought they tested a bit of the one she gave Great-Granddaddy Philip, and that they hadn't found any trace of poison on it."

"That's true, Mrs. Morgan," said Elizabeth. "The beignet contained no arsenic, which is why Philip Todhunter died. He had trusted Lucy to bring him his arsenic, and instead she brought him powdered sugar, and so he died."

"But there was arsenic in his system."

"Of course there was. Philip Todhunter was an arsenic eater." Elizabeth had looked forward to this explanatory lecture during her own painful recovery from accidental poisoning, and now she was savoring the delicious triumph of having solved a mystery that had confounded researchers for more than a century. She had mentally rehearsed this summation of the case, and she intended to give it in full.

"He took arsenic himself, habitually, just as a drug addict might take heroin or cocaine."

"Why would anyone take arsenic?" asked Bill.

"It was considered a stimulant," Elizabeth told him. "It was supposed to give one energy, and—probably more important to someone with a young bride—it was supposed to increase a man's sexual prowess."

"Oh," said Bill. The four other occupants of the table, all female, were watching him with interest, so he directed his attention to the salad with rather more intensity than perhaps it deserved.

"It was not an uncommon addiction among nineteenth-century gentlemen," said Elizabeth.

"It figures," said Edith.

"The problem with taking arsenic is that it *is* addictive, and it does enable the body to withstand larger and larger doses, so that an addict can ingest an amount of poison that would kill an ordinary person, but according to the article in *Chambers*, there is one fatal flaw in the habit of arsenic eating: *you can never quit.*"

"Why not?" asked A. P. Hill. "Can't you just taper off, until your body is no longer physically dependent?"

"Apparently, withdrawal is so horribly painful, that few if any addicts ever succeeded in quitting. The article was adamant about one thing, though: you can't quit cold turkey, because if you do, the last dose you took acts as a poison on your system, just as it would affect the system of anyone who ingested a large dose of arsenic."

"The last dose kills you," mused Bill.

"Exactly. So the arsenic eater has to take his dose of arsenic every day in order to stay alive. He also has to take it in solid form, by the way."

"I thought poisoners usually slipped arsenic into someone's drink," said A. P. Hill.

"Yes, but that's how you administer arsenic when you *want* someone to die." Elizabeth shivered. "That's why I got so sick from drinking the tainted water at the old house. Apparently, arsenic in a liquid solution goes to the kidneys and other vital organs, and can cause a rapid, painful death." She touched her abdomen gingerly. "I can testify to the painful part."

"Arsenic eaters take their daily dose in solid form, then?" Bill held up a sugar packet between his thumb and forefinger, looked down at his iced tea, and tossed the packet down unopened.

"Yes. And they take care not to drink anything for a couple of hours after ingestion so that the arsenic isn't carried to the kidneys in solution. Arsenic addicts take their drug in white powdered form." She picked up Bill's discarded sugar packet and smiled. "It looks a lot like sugar."

"The beignet!" A. P. Hill had been listening to the evidence, and now she could see where the chain of reasoning led.

"Exactly! According to the testimony from Lucy Todhunter's trial, Philip Todhunter was in the habit of eating a beignet for breakfast every morning. His wife, Lucy, always brought it to him, and the pastry was always covered with powdered sugar."

"She brought him arsenic?" said Bill, whose appetite for dessert was rapidly disappearing.

"Yes—he insisted on it. He was an arsenic addict, so the arsenic beignet would not kill him. On the contrary, it kept him alive. They both knew that he had to have his daily dose of arsenic to survive."

A. P. Hill looked thoughtful. "In that case it isn't attempted murder to give someone arsenic."

"Oh, no," Elizabeth agreed. "It was medicinal. The attempted murder occurred—and succeeded—on the day that Lucy Todhunter brought her husband a beignet covered with powdered sugar."

"Which he thought was arsenic."

"Of course he did! Perhaps he had been trying to stop his addiction. I don't know. The guests testified that he had been ill for nearly two days, and that he had eaten nothing. Obviously, he had given up trying to do without his required dose of arsenic when he accepted the beignet. Lucy, whom he had trusted for all those months to bring him his daily measure of poison, gave him the sugared pastry, and he ate it, thinking that his pains would soon cease once the drug stabilized his system, but instead the pains got worse, and he said to her, 'Why did you do it?' Meaning, I think, why did you bring me sugar instead of arsenic."

"Why *did* she do it?" asked Edith. "I know you lawyers don't set any store by motives, but the rest of us like to think that the world makes sense."

"Let's leave that point for a moment," said A. P. Hill. "I'm interested in proof. Elizabeth, how did you know that Philip Todhunter was an arsenic eater to begin with? Have you any proof?"

"Yes. I first suspected that he might be an arsenic eater when I heard descriptions of him as a hypochondriac. His doctors described him as pale, with a clear waxy complexion. That description tallies with the addiction. Also, I knew that he had been in pain from injuries he'd suffered during the war, and I thought that some physician might have prescribed a tonic with arsenic as part of his treatment then. Arsenic was often used in patent medicines in those days. He could have built up a slight tolerance from taking an arsenic-laced tonic, and then later he might have drifted into a full-fledged addiction, eating pure arsenic."

"Speculation," said A. P. Hill.

"I haven't finished, Powell. Remember that the doctors tested the uneaten part of the beignet *and* Philip Todhunter's stomach contents for arsenic, and they found none. But during the autopsy, hair and tissue samples from Todhunter's body tested positive for arsenic. He had arsenic in his system, but not in his stomach, and not from the pastry he ate on the day of his death. So, where did the residual arsenic come from? I realized that he had to have been taking it on a long-term basis."

"Maybe Lucy was administering it to him on a long-term basis," A. P. Hill pointed out.

"No. Otherwise, he would have been exhibiting the symptoms of poisoning long before that final illness. If the major were being poisoned without his knowledge, he would have had a history of gastric attacks, vomiting, lethargy, and all the other symptoms of systematic poisoning. But there's no evidence of that. His last illness was sudden, violent, and unprecedented. The only theory that fits the facts is the one I gave you: Todhunter, an addicted arsenic eater, was killed because his wife withheld his supply of the drug, thereby triggering an attack that stressed his system so severely that his heart gave out."

"You still haven't told us why she did it," said Edith.

"I know," said Elizabeth. "If you think it's difficult to solve crimes after a century has passed, you should try coming up with motives."

"Don't you have any idea?" asked Edith.

"Not really. I know there was some talk of his selling her farm, but that seems hardly sufficient."

"Motives don't have to be sufficient," said A. P. Hill. "People have been killed for the most trivial of reasons. Last July, a man in Vinton was convicted of manslaughter for killing his buddy over a *tomato*. That's why the law doesn't require good motives, only good evidence."

"So she got away with murder, why ever she did it," said Bill cheerfully. "It happens, we all know that. And she probably lived to a ripe old age on her husband's money."

"She died less than a year later," Donna Jean

Morgan replied, perhaps resenting any implicit comparison. "In childbirth."

"Oh," said Bill. "Sorry. I didn't know."

"Lucy Todhunter was probably resigned to that eventuality," said Elizabeth. "She had nearly died twice before with miscarriages. She'd had to go away for quite a while to the spa at White Sulphur Springs to recover her health. You'd have thought she'd stop trying to conceive."

Edith grumbled, "Some men won't take no for an answer."

"Yes," said Elizabeth. "That's true. They demand an heir. And apparently Major Todhunter was one of those brutal bastards, because he kept getting her pregnant as soon as she could walk again. Ugh. Poor Lucy."

A. P. Hill looked thoughtful. "I think I'd like to have defended Lucy Todhunter," she said quietly.

"But I told you, I'm sure she was guilty."

The lawyer nodded. "I know she was. I would have entered a plea of self-defense."

The next morning the triumph of saving one client had faded, and despite a slight hangover from overcelebrating, Bill was concentrating on his obligations to the other client: Miri Malone.

"Maybe I should represent the dolphin," he said to A. P. Hill, who was trying to drink her tea in peace.

"I have a murder trial coming up, Bill," she said in her most discouraging tones.

"Yes, but you're not working on it at the moment, Powell, so why don't you just listen

242

to some of my ideas for this civil-rights case?"

In the outer office the telephone rang, but Edith got it on first ring, and the partners relaxed again and resumed their conversation.

"All right." A. P. Hill sighed. "I suppose I'd better hear it before you go public with it. Go on—you were thinking of representing the dolphin. Why?"

"Because we're not trying to transfer ownership from the Sea Park to Miri. We're trying to prove that Porky is a person, and that no one should own him. Therefore, he needs his own attorney."

"Have you ever tried billing a dolphin?"

"I see what you mean, but after all, Powell, money isn't the first consideration. This could be a landmark case in animal rights."

"You might consider becoming a vegetarian," his partner advised. "The question is bound to come up in press conferences if you're defending the civil rights of a dolphin."

Bill frowned. "I'm not defending *cows*," he said.

"Leave that aside for now, then. So, you're planning to argue about the legal definition of the word *person*?"

"Right. And I thought I'd bring in some expert witnesses to testify to Porky's intelligence and his ability to communicate. My argument is that *sentient* beings should be considered persons, even if they're not our species. After all, if we ever have to deal with any extraterrestrial races, this question will come up."

"I don't think bringing up the possibility of flying saucers will strengthen your case, Bill."

243

"Okay, maybe not. Anyhow, what do you think of my argument?"

"It's interesting," said A. P. Hill. "I can't say that I can envision a local judge going along with it, but stranger things have happened."

Edith appeared in the doorway. "I've got bad news," she said. "Do y'all want to finish your breakfast drinks before I deliver it?"

"No," said Bill, gulping the last ounces of lukewarm cocoa. "We can take it."

"One of your clients is dead."

After a moment of uncomprehending silence, A. P. Hill said, "It's Eleanor Royden, isn't it? I was afraid she might try to kill herself when she fully realized what she had done."

"No, it's not Eleanor," said Edith cheerfully. "She's probably busy right now answering all the proposals of marriage that she's been getting in the mail. No, the deceased is one of Bill's clients. Miri Malone. That's why I interrupted you. I don't think you'll need all that dolphin defense strategy."

"Miri is dead?" said Bill. "How? What happened?"

"She drowned at the Sea Park in Florida."

"She drowned. But that's impossible! She worked with sea mammals. She was a professional."

Edith handed him a message slip bearing Rich Edmonds's name and telephone number and a scribbled message. "You can call him back if you want to. He told me that Miri Malone's nude body had been found in the dolphin tank, and that the coroner's office is calling it an accident."

"What does Rich think?" Bill squinted at

Edith's hastily written message. "What does *conj-vs* mean?"

"He agrees that her death was an accident," said Edith. "But he has a better idea of what happened than the coroner does. He thinks Miri was in Porky's tank on a conjugal visit, and that she ran out of air before they'd finished."

A. P. Hill shook her head. "Only you, Bill." She sighed.

"That's terrible," said Bill. "Miri was a very nice person. A little strange, I'll admit, but maybe she was a pioneer in animal rights. Which reminds me—what's going to happen to Porky?"

"Apparently, nothing," said Edith, whose cheerfulness was untouched by the tragedy. "According to Rich Edmonds nobody seems very concerned about the dolphin as a threat to human life. He's as friendly as ever. He did all his shows yesterday, and his appetite is good. The park put a female dolphin in with him to cheer him up, and it seems to be working."

"That does it!" said Powell. "I'm having tuna fish for lunch."

"I wonder if I should go on with the lawsuit," said Bill.

"You can't very well petition for a marriage when the bride is dead," Edith pointed out. "Unless you're *really* going to expand the concept of civil rights."

"No, no," said Bill. "I meant the case about whether or not Porky is a person. I was mapping out an argument to free him—"

"I think you'd better drop the entire matter, Bill," said A. P. Hill. "In the best interests of the dolphin."

"Why?"

"Think about it. Do you really want to prove that Porky is a person after he's been involved in the death of Miri Malone? As an animal he has no rights or responsibilities, and he can't be held liable for his actions. But what if you make the court rule that he is a person, and then they charge him with murder?" She shrugged. "I can't believe we're having this conversation."

"Fish jails," murmured Edith. "That would be expensive."

"You're right," said Bill. "Miri wouldn't want Porky to suffer for her death. Maybe we should just leave things as they are."

"Had Miss Malone paid you?" asked A. P. Hill.

"Not yet. I hadn't billed her."

"In that case, partner, the matter is closed."

Several months later A. P. Hill had her day in court with Eleanor Royden. Powell had tried to balance her instinctive defense attorney's delaying tactics against the need for a speedy trial to minimize the damage done by Eleanor's relentless press conferences. "I'd rather defend O. J. Simpson," she said in a moment of desperation. She hadn't meant it, though. She was only tired, and exasperated, and above all frightened that her best wouldn't be good enough to save Eleanor Royden.

The trial lasted the better part of a week—neither side had the funds or the patience for a lengthier battle. Eleanor was vilified by the prosecution as a bloodthirsty shrew who murdered her victims out of spite. A. P. Hill retaliated by presenting the Roydens as a selfish, shallow couple who delighted in tormenting Jeb's ex-wife. Witnesses described the same incidents from opposite points of view: *he* was a monster; *she* was a monster. It all depended on whom the witness identified with, or, in the cases of some of the middle-aged women, it depended on whom the witness was afraid to be identified with. Some affluent wives apparently thought that Eleanor should be belled and cowled like a leper. She was dangerous: she threatened the well-being of all of them. A few courageous souls (most of whom were divorced) hailed Eleanor as a terrible prophet of feminism, who could single-handedly stem the tide of trophy wives and midlife-crisis divorces, but most people treated the case as a bad joke—nothing that need have any bearing on their lives.

Now all the hours of testimony, the psychiatric evaluations, and the media circus surrounding the trial had wound down to one focal point: a spotlight on A. P. Hill for the defense. She looked more pale and waiflike than ever in her navy-blue suit and sensible low-heeled pumps; her hair chopped into a straight bob covering her ears; and her lip gloss smeared on in haste, after she had finished throwing up in the courthouse ladies' room. She looked as insubstantial as a pond reflection beside her client. Eleanor Royden's newly tinted blonde hair shone like a helmet in an upswept coiffure, and her black silk dress reminded no one of bereavement. Perhaps its solemnity was marred by its low neckline and the diamond necklace at her throat. Eleanor's makeup was vivid, and reapplied at short intervals, in case a photographer should be aiming at her with a telephoto lens. She had watched the entire proceedings with bright-eyed interest, and a cheery briskness that suggested that this was someone else's trial. Perhaps it was A. P. Hill's. She was growing thinner by the day as the circles under her eyes deepened.

Eleanor sometimes smiled at the jurors, or nodded in sympathetic agreement with the judge's ruling, but A. P. Hill remained impassive, as if her life, not Eleanor's, depended on the verdict. Now she tottered to the front of the courtroom to begin her summation. The jurors were watching her, expressionless, while Eleanor gave her a grinning thumbs-up sign that almost sent her back to the ladies' room.

A. P. Hill took a deep breath and began. "I'm here to defend Eleanor Royden, not necessarily to praise her. I hope that Jeb and Eleanor Royden do not become the symbolic middle-class couple of the Nineties, because as a nation we deserve better role models than these two shallow, selfish, alienated creatures. But I do think they should have stayed together—because they deserved each other.

"The prosecution has gone to great pains to show you how heartless Eleanor Royden was to have shot her husband and his new wife while they slept, and of course I can't stand up here and say that anybody, any victim, deserves to die, but ..." She paused here, and shook her head. "I'd have to say that Jeb and Staci came close.

"The legal community here in Roanoke knew Jeb Royden as a capable attorney, a good friend, and a community leader. They all told you what a nice guy he was—and so he was—among his equals. But there was another side to Jeb Royden that his colleagues, his fellow officers of the court, never saw: Jeb the bully; Jeb the adolescent, addicted to self-gratification; Jeb the domestic tyrant, whose arrogance knew no bounds.

"Jeb Royden made a lot of money. He thought that made him important—certainly more important than fluffy blonde Eleanor, whose very food and clothing came from his bounty. He thought he was entitled to have his own way in all things because he was the one who mattered. Eleanor didn't matter. She was just another one of Jeb Royden's possessions, as bought and paid for as his sports car. And as replaceable.

"For much of their lives, Eleanor Royden had acquiesced in her husband's delusions of grandeur. She let him have his own way. Sometimes that's the easiest way to keep peace with a tyrant, but in the end it costs you, because tyrants feed on people who let them have their own way all the time. They take it for granted.

"Imagine Jeb's surprise when he wanted a new toy, and insignificant old Eleanor said no. He had the palatial house in Chambord Oaks, and the midlife sports car, and all the money he needed, and now he wanted the trophy: a new young wife—the hormonal equivalent of a face-lift, I guess. And Eleanor said no.

"How dared she? Wasn't he the rich and important attorney? Didn't he deserve the best of everything? He could certainly afford it. Eleanor had tried to thwart the mighty Jeb Royden, and he thought she deserved to be punished for it.

"His indifference toward an aging and no-longer-beautiful wife turned to hatred for an enemy. He began to use his legal skills, his power and influence, as weapons to turn his divorce into a chess game. He would make Eleanor suffer for her presumption. The tragedy is that he began to enjoy tormenting her.

"Jeb Royden forgot that it is dangerous to torment the weak. They have nothing to lose." A. P. Hill noticed a movement in the back of the crowded courtroom. She saw her partner slip into the last row of seats. A. P. Hill felt ridiculously glad to see him. He had driven all the way up from Danville just to give her moral support. No one could help her now, but she was grateful to see someone who was on her side. She couldn't smile at Bill now; she would thank him later.

A. P. Hill turned away and picked up where she had left off: "You've been told in detail all the things that were done to punish Eleanor Royden for the sin of not going away quietly. She was arrested for trespassing; the furniture she had chosen for their home was given away so that she should have none of it; she was ridiculed in front of her former friends, and made to live in poverty by a man with a high-six-figure income, while he continued to live in his usual splendor. And through it all Jeb and Staci Royden laughed at Eleanor. They made fun of her. You saw a check he wrote her, on which he put: *for upkeep of cow.* That *cow* was Jeb Royden's wife of twenty years, the woman he had promised to love for better or for worse.

"Then there was Staci Royden, Jeb's little Giselle. Eleanor had a host of other names for her replacement. Can you blame her? Staci Royden knew that her prospective suitor was married from the moment she met him. She didn't particularly care. Jeb was rich, and Staci was young and beautiful. And Eleanor didn't matter.

"Our society seems to say that to people, through our advertising, our television shows, the attitudes of public figures—they all say: 'Rich people, young people, pretty people matter. The rest of you don't.'

"Eleanor Royden thought that she mattered. Perhaps a wiser woman would have been content to wait for Staci to grow old and learn the unhappy truth about youth and beauty not lasting forever, but I think Eleanor's pain was too great for wisdom. She isn't much given to introspection, anyhow. She is shallow. Could anyone who wasn't shallow have loved Jeb Royden? I don't think so.

"Eleanor is not without pride, though. And there was a limit to her endurance. Jeb and Staci taunted Eleanor for a couple of years, and finally she decided that it had to end. You know what she did then. She took her pistol, and she went to Jeb's fine mansion, and she put an end to the torment. You believe that she shot Jeb and Staci. I believe it. But you know who doesn't believe it, not really, deep down?"

A. P. Hill pointed to her client, who was no

longer smiling. "*She* doesn't believe it! Eleanor Royden cannot comprehend what she has done, because it is still incredible to her that someone as almighty as Jeb could be stopped by a nickel's worth of lead. She still talks about him in the present tense, ladies and gentlemen. Now, you may think that it is insane to shoot someone, and then refuse to believe that they are dead. It certainly suggests that no intent to kill was there.

"Jeb and Staci made sport of Eleanor—and you know which sport it was? Bearbaiting. It's an old, barbaric custom that we've done away with as far as bears are concerned; sometimes our next of kin are less fortunate. The way it worked: people chained a bear to a wooden stake, and they let dogs loose to attack it, forcing the bear to fight back. Usually the bear was hurt or killed, but often it managed to dispatch some of the attacking dogs before it died. That's what the Royden case reminds me of, ladies and gentlemen. A poor trapped creature who could not defend herself against a rich and powerful ex-spouse was baited and teased and ridiculed until she snapped. And she fought back.

"Don't use this tale as a parable of divorce. Most people are not Jeb and Staci and Eleanor. But this one time, two cruel and brutal people underestimated the rage of their victim, and she struck back, with fatal results. Whether they drove her insane, or whether she was acting in self-defense from the emotional abuse, the fact remains: Eleanor Royden did not commit murder in cold blood, and she should not be made to suffer further. The bear is still tied to the stake, but it has managed to defeat the dogs. Can we not call a halt to the sport now, and let her go in peace?"

The rest of the trial was something of a blur to A. P. Hill, who tended to develop stage fright after a performance rather than before. Dimly, she heard the prosecution's argument, and she made herself watch the jury as they filed out to begin their deliberations. Then she went back to the ladies' room, and was sick.

Eleanor Royden was returned to the cell to await the verdict, and A. P. Hill hung around the courthouse, pacing and wishing she smoked, for as long as she could stand it. Finally, Bill MacPherson lured her back to the Marriott with take-out hamburgers, after first securing promises from everywhere that they would be notified the moment any word came from the jury room. "We're only five miles away," he told her. "You could get there in less than ten minutes if you drove like a madwoman. Which you would."

"I keep wondering if there was something else I should have said," A. P. Hill said. She had kicked off her sensible shoes and was sitting curled up in an easy chair, watching hamburger grease congeal on the waxed paper in front of her. It was past seven o'clock now, and outside the light was fading, but A. P. Hill neither noticed nor cared.

"You gave a good speech," said Bill. "Maybe better than your client deserved. I'm not sure I approve of sympathy for people who execute those who annoy them."

A. P. Hill nodded. "You wonder how married people can become such strangers. I can't imagine hating anyone enough to want them dead. But, then, I wouldn't choose someone like Jeb Royden for a husband, either."

"No?" said Bill between french fries. "I thought you liked brilliant, powerful people."

His partner considered it. "I admire people like that, yes. They might be wearing on a daily basis, though." She thought about all the bright high achievers she had known in law school. Some of them were even more ruthless than she was, and in partnership together they might have become fast-track legal piranhas, but instead she had chosen—proposed it herself, actually—to practice law in a small Virginia town with good old Bill MacPherson. He would probably never argue a case before the Supreme Court, but he brought her hamburgers and sat with her while she sweated out a verdict. A. P. Hill decided that she had made the right choice—at least for now.

"I can't imagine you ever being a battered woman," Bill was saying.

A. P. Hill looked appraisingly at her law partner. "No," she said. "I don't suppose I will be."

They had finished eating, and Bill was reading the room-service menu in hopes of persuading Powell to join him for coffee and dessert when the phone rang. She sprang past him and snatched up the receiver. "Yes? They're coming in? Of course. Give me ten minutes."

Bill stood up. "Do you want me to come with you?"

"No. I have to do this alone."

He could see that it would be useless to argue with her. "You'll come back, won't you?"

She almost smiled. "It's my room, Bill."

"Well... I hope it goes well. Good luck, partner."

"I'll need it," said A. P. Hill, closing the door gently behind her.

Bill decided that pacing the floor waiting for Powell to return would be a waste of energy. She was doing enough worrying on her own. He had never seen her so emotional. Privately, he thought that it was lucky the case was ending, regardless of the verdict, because A. P. Hill's nerves wouldn't stand much more of the Eleanor Royden circus. She must have lost ten pounds at least, and she didn't have them to spare. He glanced at the half a hamburger Powell had left uneaten. Things had to get back to normal soon. Bill resolved to pour the bottles of pink medicine down the sink as soon as he got back to the office by way of celebrating the end of the ordeal.

Meanwhile, he called room service and settled back on the king-size bed to play remote-control roulette while he waited. He caught the last half of a *Star Trek* rerun, and was flipping desultorily back and forth between CNN, the Home Shopping Network, and *Unsolved Mysteries*, when he heard a soft tapping at the door. "Powell?" he called out.

"Yes." The answering voice was quiet, but that didn't tell him much. He couldn't picture his partner whooping it up because she had won a case. Powell took everything calmly.

He flung open the door, waiting for his

cue. She just stood there for a moment, looking dazed and tired, and then she flopped facedown on the bed, beating the counterpane with clenched fists.

She wasn't crying, though, a fact for which Bill was thankful. He might be able to cope with rage; but grief made him sweat. He hovered over her, wondering if a hug would be in order, but deciding against it. "Tell me," he said.

He heard her take a deep breath. "Guilty," she said without looking up.

"I figured that. But how bad is it?"

A long silence. More deep breaths. Finally A. P. Hill sat up. "First degree. They decided that the crime was premeditated because Eleanor took the gun with her."

"I thought she always kept it in her purse. Which is illegal, of course, but—"

"I'll appeal. I don't think it will do much good, since every silverback in the court system is a friend of Jeb, but I will try." She smiled bitterly. "At least they stipulated that she not receive the death penalty. Wasn't that big of them?"

"It's one less thing for you to worry about," said Bill.

The cold smile again. "Sure, no problem! Eleanor Royden could stay in prison until she's seventy-five, that's all. Good old Jeb wins again."

Bill said quietly, "Jeb Royden is dead, Powell."

"He still wins. He wanted Eleanor to suffer and, by God, she will. It was over for him in an instant, but not for Eleanor. She will suffer at leisure."

"How did she take the verdict?"

"She had that tight little smile that Southern women put on, no matter what. I don't think the truth has sunk in yet for her. She's clinging to the notion that an appeal will save her, but I doubt that it will. I have to get a trial transcript, and start looking for loopholes—"

"Not now, Powell," said Bill. "I thought whichever way the case turned out, you might need fortifying. So I ordered you something from room service." He went to the bathroom, and brought back a plastic ice bucket and a fifth of Jim Beam.

A. P. Hill picked up two glasses from the dresser and held them out. "I'll take it straight," she said.

"Same here." Bill poured two ounces of whiskey into each tumbler. "To a truce," he said, raising his glass, "in the battle of the sexes."

MacPherson & Hill
Attorneys-at-Law

Danville, Virginia

(I bought them some new stationery. Engraved. Elizabeth.)

Dear Cameron,

This will be the last letter, the last time I put pain onto paper so that I can look at it, instead of packing it away, so that I can go on.

I think it's time I gave up, because pretending that you are coming back isn't going to help either of us. You have gone on to wherever it is you're going. So must I. This is my decision, finally, and not a course of action that Dr. Freya has urged upon me. She said once that I would know when it was time to really begin to grieve, and she was right.

I am grieving, but I also realize that at least it is a clean wound. There are other fates that might have been harder to endure.

Some things are worse than losing someone you love. Consider the Roydens, whose youthful romance soured to domestic skirmishing and finally to remorseless murder. Or even my own parents who called it quits out of mutual boredom. At least we were spared those fates.

They don't even seem to realize what they've lost. Eleanor Royden, whose case is being appealed, is giving cheery interviews from prison to the likes of Geraldo. She seems to have forgotten that her husband Jeb was ever a person; to her he has become a legal problem. And Mother is still trying to find herself. She has gone from white-water rafting to being an intellectual sophisticate, and I see signs of restlessness that indicate she may be moving on soon to something else—God knows what. I don't even like to speculate.

At least I escaped their fates. They both seem to be searching for something they wouldn't recognize even if they found it. At least I know what I've lost.

There's a line from A. E. Housman that keeps running through my mind: "Smart lad to slip betimes away ..." Were we fortunate after all? Perhaps in a way we were spared not a greater pain but a more protracted one. I wouldn't have wanted our love to die by inches over the long trickle of years, as so many romances do. At least I can think back over our time together without anger or regret. I don't have to seal off a part of my life as if it had been a bad investment. Eleanor Royden does that. So does Mother.

So, Cameron, goodbye and thank you for being kind and loving and never dull. Thank you for leaving me with happy memories instead of bitterness.

I don't know where I'm going from here, but a part of you will go with me. I will always remember you, and so we will always be together. Isn't it funny? Death doesn't really part people; it's life that does that.

Cameron—goodbye—for now.

Love always,
Elizabeth

If you have enjoyed reading this large print book and you would like more information on how to order a Wheeler Large Print Book, please write to:

 Wheeler Publishing, Inc.
P.O. Box 531
Accord, MA 02018-0531